ROAD A D0232630

The ambushers were hunkered high in the rocks, lining up their rifle sights on the men in blue uniforms and the Concord that was picking up speed to close the distance on the gravelly road.

"A cavalry escort," Little Reddy muttered to Kid Wall. "And that coach ain't bouncin' any too much, so it must be packin' a lot of gold."

The night air was as still as it got in the Dakota hills. The iron wheels of the Concord made grating sounds as it came over the bigger rocks embedded in the road, and the heads of the escorting soldiers bobbed either way as their anxious eyes searched for any movement. And then the death-dealing guns of the road agents opened up, rifles spouting out flame from every angle.

Inside the coach the pair of armed guards began firing back, and one of them yelled at the driver, "For God's sake, Hardy, get us out of here!"

ZEBRA'S HEADING WEST!

with GILES, LEGG, PARKINSON, LAKE, KAMMEN, and MANNING

KANSAS TRAIL   (3517, $3.50/$4.50)
by Hascal Giles

After the Civil War ruined his life, Bennett Kell threw in his lot with a gang of thievin' guntoughs who rode the Texas-Kansas border. But there was one thing he couldn't steal—fact was, Ada McKittridge had stolen his heart.

GUNFIGHT IN MESCALITO   (3601, $3.50/$4.50)
by John Legg

Jubal Crockett was a young man with a bright future—until that Mescalito jury found him guilty of murder and sentenced him to hang. Jubal'd been railroaded good and the only writ of habeus corpus was a stolen key to the jailhouse door and a fast horse!

DRIFTER'S LUCK   (3396, $3.95/$4.95)
by Dan Parkinson

Byron Stillwell was a drifter who never went lookin' for trouble, but trouble always had a way of findin' him. Like the time he set that little fire up near Kansas to head off a rogue herd owned by a cattle baron named Dawes. Now Dawes figures Stillwell owes him something . . . at the least, his life.

MOUNTAIN MAN'S VENGEANCE   (3619, $3.50/$4.50)
by Robert Lake

The high, rugged mountain made John Henry Trapp happy. But then a pack of gunsels thundered across his land, burned his hut, and murdered his squaw woman. Trapp hit the vengeance trail and ended up in jail. Now he's back and how that mountain has changed!

BIG HORN HELLRIDERS   (3449, $3.50/$4.50)
by Robert Kammen

Wyoming was a tough land and toughness was required to tame it. Reporter Jim Haskins knew the Wyoming tinderbox was about to explode but he didn't know he was about to be thrown smack-dab in the middle of one of the bloodiest range wars ever.

TEXAS BLOOD KILL   (3577, $3.50/$4.50)
by Jason Manning

Ol' Ma Foley and her band of outlaw sons were cold killers and most folks in Shelby County, Texas knew it. But Federal Marshal Jim Gantry was no local lawman and he had his guns cocked and ready when he rode into town with one of the Foley boys as his prisoner.

Available wherever paperbacks are sold, or order direct from the Publisher. Send cover price plus 50¢ per copy for mailing and handling to Zebra Books, Dept. 3772, 475 Park Avenue South, New York, N.Y. 10016. Residents of New York and Tennessee must include sales tax. DO NOT SEND CASH. For a free Zebra/ Pinnacle catalog please write to the above address.

ROBERT KAMMEN
BLOODY DAKOTA
SUMMER

ZEBRA BOOKS
KENSINGTON PUBLISHING CORP.

ZEBRA BOOKS

are published by

Kensington Publishing Corp.
475 Park Avenue South
New York, NY 10016

First printing: June, 1992

Printed in the United States of America

One

Far north of the Holy Road in the land of the Teton Lakota an army scout took a last look at Fort Reno back-
grounded by the Big Horns before spurring his dun-colored
bronc down through brush choking an arroyo. The moccasin tracks he followed were so fresh it seemed to Moss Hollabaugh he could still see dust spurting out from them as
the Indian hurried along. And just as fresh were the deeper
imprints made by three horsemen. Shod hoofs meant white
men; not soldiers stationed at Fort Reno but others.

By now he was at least five miles out, he had come across
a dead Indian pony sometime back; just one bullet from a
Henry rifle had done the job. The few markings on the dead
horse told it plain to Hollabaugh, that it had been ridden by
an Oglala Sioux. Probably one of Crazy Horse's braves.
Generally the Oglala stayed clear of Fort Reno. But then the
trouble had started.

Two weeks ago, Wednesday, the commandant at Fort
Reno had called in all of his scouts. There was Moss Hollabaugh and Portugee Phillips, and Crow scouts crowding
into the orderly room as the man temporarily in charge of
Fort Reno, Major Frank Cranston, strode out of his adjoining office. He'd been here less than a month, and before
that had been no further west than army headquarters at
Omaha. And to cover up what he didn't know about the In-

dian problem out here, which was considerable, Major Cranston covered his backside by spouting a lot of army regulations at the scouts and soldiers under his command. Hollabaugh realized that the major didn't know a friendly Indian, some of whom liked to camp out around the fort, from one on the warpath or an Oglala from a Cheyenne.

"Within the last month," the major said caustically to open the meeting, "several Indians have been killed. From what I've learned these killings were done by the Sioux."

The Crow scouts exchanged veiled glances while Moss Hollabaugh, standing by one of the open windows, grimaced his disappointment at the ignorance of this officer. What it boiled down to was that these killings had been done by some miners wanting to get at gold they believed could be found up in the Big Horns. They'd gotten together to organize a secret society called the Big Horners. By keeping the Indians stirred up they were hoping the army would send in more troops and take out the Teton Lakota and Cheyenne.

This had been a peaceful summer so far, with the Sioux keeping to their ancestral hunting grounds and honoring another treaty forced upon them by the U.S. army. Occasionally small raiding parties would strike at those heading up to the Montana gold fields along the Bozeman Trail. Before this there had been the Wagon Box fight and the Fetterman massacre and other battles such as the fight on Crazy Woman Creek which saw the Oglala Sioux led by Crazy Horse coming out victorious. As a result of these battles few dared to venture up the Bozeman Trail.

Then came the Carrington Expedition of '66 which brought about the establishment of Fort Reno and Fort McKinney, up at Buffalo. The order to construct these forts had come directly from Washington City and the office of the President, and the reasons behind this at least to Moss Hollabaugh were as plain as the trail he was following now.

Gold!

The tracks of four horsemen and those made by the flee-ing Indian came out of the arroyo, where Moss Hollabaugh reined up the dun and surveyed the lay of the land ahead. As his squinting grey eyes quartered the horizon in search of any movement, his mind was still on that meeting held back at Fort Reno. Major Cranston had laid the blame for the killings at the doorstep of the Sioux. He ordered his scouts out to bring in some of these killers, along with stating he would request that more troops be dispatched out here. Gold, was all that it came down to, mused Moss with a bit-ter sigh. Hell, everyone, and that probably included the Crow scouts, knew that after four years of fighting the Civil War the United States Treasury was on the verge of bank-ruptcy, needed gold to get rid of a great national debt. Which meant clear access to the Montana gold fields.

"Why didn't the major come right out and say it?" groused Moss, a lean man of around 6'1" and just entering his thirties. "These plains Indian have to be gotten rid of . . . and all the peace treaties in the world aren't gonna change that."

Moss Hollabaugh's eyes flared open when he heard the distant barking of a rifle; a Henry he knew from the sound of it. To the southeast about a couple of miles, and from rugged country this side of the Pumpkin Buttes, a landmark guiding travelers along the Bozeman Trail. He rode on, the black mane and tail of the dun just a shade blacker than Moss's full head of shaggy hair. A ways back an old pair of cowboy boots he favored wore out, and he'd purchased cav-alry boots from the sutler at Fort Reno. But in his role as an army scout he disdained wearing spurs, since the chinking noise they made could give him away in a tight spot. He wore his boots under dark brown corduroy pants, and a cot-ton shirt and light brown leather coat also clung to his wiry frame. The hat was one Moss had worn back in Oregon, a place he'd left in search of a future.

The Hollabaughs had been one of hundreds heading west

to come through the sand hills of Nebraska and to hook onto the Oregon Trail. From the sand hills they struck along the North Platte River, part of what the Teton Lakota called their Holy Road, to leave the river once it meandered past Fort Casper. They came onto the famous trail which would eventually carry them through Utah and so into the Oregon Territory. Upon the death of Moss's father an older brother had taken over the family ranch. Not wanting to be just another hired hand, Moss Hollabaugh had struck out into Montana to savor what that place was all about. Then he headed back into Wyoming to work for a time as a cowhand. Now to Moss's surprise he was scouting for the army. A far more dangerous job, he'd discovered.

Bouncing against Moss's right hipbone was a .44-40 Colt's. The Winchester rifle in the plain leather scabbard was chambered to take the same caliber bullet. With either weapon he could hold his own; he had once used the rifle to down an elk at something over four hundred yards. As for gunfighting, there'd been the time up in Montana when he'd caught a man cheating at cards and he let a slug from his Colt's rip into the other's gunhand. He'd let it go at that, heading out shortly afterwards to get a gander at that Hardin town. And southward from there into Wyoming.

He could no longer see the distant and vague peaks of the Big Horns appearing as a low cloud bank to the northwest. For Moss Hollabaugh's route of travel had taken him into a grassy valley not all that big but thick with prairie grass and sagebrush and rimmed by buttes. The dun he'd purchased just before giving up cowboying had a gentle gait and was a stayer. But even one broke to the saddle would shy away when it scented blood, and Moss had to call out, "Easy now," as it broke away from the tracks cutting toward a treeline and what proved to be a creek beyond. Gazing down as he rode, Moss picked out drops of fresh blood spilling into the moccasin tracks left by the Indian. What Moss was about to say never came out as the erratic booming of rifles sounded just ahead.

He unsheathed his own Winchester and used his knees to guide the dun down to the creek and to splash across as he worked the lever. Ahead on a crumbly ledge protected by boulders he could make out three of those who'd been chasing the Indian. Closing in to about a hundred yards, he could see their derisive grins. What they had in mind was cold-blooded murder. Then he sighted another horseman just dropping out of his saddle, to wave up at his companions and shout, "That damned Injun is down . . . an' tryin' to crawl into some brush."

"Then do it, Miller, kill the bastard."

"I intend doin' just that."

The man, who Moss Hollabaugh reckoned was one of those stirring up all this Indian trouble, started to sight in on his prey. But Moss's rifle sounded first. The .44-40 slug from Hollabaugh's rifle tore into the man and spilled him over the creek bank where he went splashing into the brackish waters. Anger slitting his eyes, Moss pivoted and fired up at the others scrambling out of sight. He kept on levering the Winchester and peppering the ledge with leaden slugs until he heard the pounding of horses pulling out. Whereupon he reined in to have a look down at the creek. The man he'd hit was flopped down at the water's edge clutching at a shoulder wound. In plunging into the creek he'd lost both rifle and six-gun, and through gritted teeth he rained a few curses at the man who'd shot him coming down through a cut in the muddy bank.

"Hey . . . you're that army scout . . . Hollabaugh. Dammit, we almost had that murderin' Indian . . ."

"Seems to me," returned Moss, "you're pinning the wrong tag on that Indian."

"Damn, Hollabaugh, he was one of those doin' the killin' up at Fort Reno."

"That shoulder wound won't keep you from findin' your horse and humping it out of here."

Struggling to his feet, the wounded man waded out to retrieve his hat bobbing on the surface. From here he watched as Moss Hollabaugh rode along the water's edge and then swung around a bend in the creek. Wading out, and with a bitter contempt twisting up his face, Spade DeLong knew they should have kept better watch to their backtrail, after they'd sighted one of those Indians living by the fort sneaking out to have a powwow with that Oglala Sioux.

"Probably to tell that damned Oglala we're the ones been doing these killings." And trailing after, DeLong had managed to kill one of them; the marksmanship of his companions not as accurate. "Go on, Hollabaugh, you damned Injun lover . . . as all you're gonna find is another dead Injun." Despite his pain, Spade DeLong spat derisively to the south as he came up the creek bank to get a glimpse of his horse grazing a short distance away. As far as he was concerned Moss Hollabaugh was marked for death if he ventured back to Fort Reno. "I'll even take the bastard's scalp and leave his corpse for them scavengin' Injun dogs."

Hollabaugh found the Oglala draped over a log that was being pushed along by the sluggish current. He brought the dun out into the creek and reached down to grasp a broken shard of branch to use to guide the log and its human occupant toward the bank. Swinging down, Moss laid a wary hand on the Oglala's bare shoulder as he gazed with some concern at the wound to the lower back.

"Probably won't survive that," he said with some concern. He moved his hand from the shoulder to place his fingers on a neck vein; its steady throbbing against his fingers brought a grimace of relief.

The Oglala by his estimation wasn't all that heavy, and with little effort Moss lifted him up and carried him over to the shading cottonwoods. It was here he saw the other wound, at the left side and not as serious. "Don't know your name . . . but if it was those Crow scouts instead of me you'd be dead and scalped by now. Can't pack him back to

Reno either. Get a fire going and then figure this out."

The wind had started to buffet in from the southwest by the time Moss had fashioned a lean-to snugged under trees. A fire going, and the Oglala stretched out on his bed gear, Moss got out his old blackened coffee pot and filled it with creek water before hanging it over the flames. This wasn't the first time he'd treated bullet wounds, so he had little difficulty in treating the side wound as the rifle bullet had passed on through. But with a lot of concern he surveyed the lower back wound.

"Bullet's still lodged in there. Could be bleeding internally. Which means gettin' him to a doctor."

There was one at Fort Reno. And this was where the men who'd been chasing this Oglala would head. Or they might be waiting someplace between here and Fort Reno hoping to ambush him. Nope, he'd have to go south. Someone he'd developed a friendship with was the post surgeon at Fort Casper, Major Lute Olhman. Just maybe Olhman would remove that bullet as a lot of doctors out here wouldn't come within five miles of a Teton Lakota. Couldn't blame them as too many wagon trains had been wiped out by these Indians. Moss wondered seriously why he was so anxious to keep this Oglala alive just so's he can go on the wartrail again. He took in the breechcloth and fringed leggings and the dark savage features of the Indian where he lay with his upper body wrapped up in Moss's leather coat. The wind tugged at the lone eagle's feather stuck in the hairlock, and he said more to the wind than himself, "Guess it's 'cause he's wrongly accused of murder."

And there was every possibility, Moss realized, that charges could be brought against him as well, even though he had only tried to wing one of those after the Oglala. 'Cause at a range of less'n a hundred yards he could have split that ambusher's skull open with a single round from his Winchester.

"Hoka . . . hey!"

He swung his eyes to the Oglala struggling to sit up. The glittering almond eyes were unfocused, and then Moss bent down to lay a restraining hand on the heaving chest of the Indian, and to speak in broken Sioux.

"They are gone . . . the men who tried to kill you. We are alone."

"You . . . I know you . . ."

"Yes, I scout for the army; name's Hollabaugh."

Pain lines creasing his forehead, the Oglala closed his eyes for a moment, and his breathing was shallow and that of a man sapped of his strength. "Holla . . ." He fell back into unconsciousness again.

Grimacing away his worry, Moss rose to put more wood on the fire. From here he took in the western sky and the lowering sun. Much as he hated to do so, the only way he could save the Oglala was to cut down to Fort Casper as soon as he'd made a travois. The plains had seen the last of the sun when the crude travois made by Moss was hooked up over the withers of the dun and tied to the horn of his saddle. He'd used what rope there was on hand to tie his camp gear to the two support poles and also used some evergreen branches, and the Oglala lay on this as Moss took to the saddle.

He was south of the Powder River crossing of the Bozeman Trail, knew that from here on all he would encounter was more prairie and ground rushing upward toward rimrock forming buttes. He held the dun to a plodding walk, and even so the travois jarred into holes hidden by the night. Once in a while the wounded Oglala would sing out in his native tongue; a mindless delirium.

The vague trail he followed was used by both the army and settlers. He'd used it more'n once, could pick out by moonlight rock formations he had laid eyes on before. Then he was coming over a long grade composed of sparse prairie grass and cacti and small rocks to find off to his right in a draw what appeared to be a deserted log cabin. How far had

12

he traveled? He must be about six or seven miles out as to the south lay the dark hump of Casper Mountain. The sky appeared to be lightening, and with this in mind Moss veered in the direction of the cabin. Every so often he'd swing down to check on the man he was trying to save.

"This bumpy ride is playing hell with that back wound. That cabin . . . get him in there . . . then bust my butt riding to the fort to fetch Doc Olhman," he told the lonely night sky.

One of the sentries on duty at the main gate shouted to the other soldier that he'd just spotted a rider splashing his horse across the North Platte; both men brought their rifles to the ready. In the uncertain light of dawning, and with mist cloaking along river, it could be most anybody, a white man or even an Indian raiding party.

"What do you think?"

"Could be a drunken officer sneaking back?"

"There he be." The soldier's finger tightened on the trigger just as Moss Hollabaugh called out that he was an army scout, and with some reluctance the soldier set his rifle aside and opened the gate to have Hollabaugh nod as he rode past.

Crossing the parade ground, Moss headed toward the houses on officer's row, swung down to leave his dun tied to a picket fence. More than once he'd set on the front porch he was stepping onto now, with his insistent knock bringing a muttered oath from within before the door swung open.

"Moss?"

"Sorry to roust you, Doc Olhman. But I've got me a wounded Oglala out there."

"Come in," he said quickly. "Word came down late this afternoon from Fort Reno about you. That you've got yourself into a pack of trouble."

"Seems it didn't take long for those white scum to blame

13

me as I shot one of them." Sketchily he filled in the details of what had happened. "So they've wrongly accused this Indian of what they've been doing, just to cover their murderin' tracks, Doc. But who'd take the word of an Oglala."

"Seems you did, Moss. Yes, as you said, bringing him here could be risky. Just hope we get there in time."

"Then you'll come?"

"Can't do otherwise. Though I might get court-martialed same's they want to do to you."

"All they can do, Doc, is give me my walking papers."

"Enough jabbering, Moss. Go saddle me a horse as I throw on some clothes. Then we'll stop at my place of business to throw what I'll need into my medical bag. An Oglala? One riding with Crazy Horse?"

"And still alive if we hurry."

The sight of the man who'd just arrived heading out through the main gates with the post surgeon brought one of the sentries heading to rouse the officer-of-the-day. By this time Moss Hollabaugh and Major Lute Olhman were across the North Platte and striking northward. Moss resented the fact that the commanding officer at Fort Reno hadn't waited until he could get back and tell his side of what had happened. Instead a telegram had been fired off to Fort Casper with words condemning him. Going back to Reno could see him thrown into the post stockade or worse.

Hollabaugh set these thoughts aside as he pointed out the scattering of pines and beyond that the log cabin where he'd left the Oglala. At a gallop they came around some large boulders, only to pull up their horses with a sudden abruptness that almost spilled Major Olhman out of his saddle.

The sun was fully up to reveal the hollow where the cabin lay and the Teton Lakota sitting their war ponies in stoic silence, with others closing the circle behind Moss and Olhman. Beyond the creek blackbirds were lifting out of rushes and above this in the spaces between the cottonwoods the sky was a blood red. It was just as it had been on another day some months back when units out of Fort Reno had run into a Sioux raiding party, with blood being spilled on both sides and the enmity between whites and the Teton Lakota deepening. This morning the only blood that would be gushing out would be theirs, Moss realized, as his eyes centered on the one they called the strange man of the Oglalas, Crazy Horse.

Now he knew the stories were true that the great war chief of the Oglalas possessed light blue eyes, and light brown hair hanging loosely down to his waist. A powder-blackened scar at the corner of his nose made his skin appear even lighter. But the features were that of an Oglala. Astride the war pony, Crazy Horse seemed to be more slender than the other chiefs crowding alongside. Unlike their split-horn buffalo bonnets with full tails or eagle feather bonnets, only a single feather adorned Crazy Horse's hair. His dress was plain, he wore no war paint as most of the others and a rifle was cradled before him on his lap. At his back was a bow and quiver.

The other chiefs carried coup sticks to which scalp locks had been attached, and an assortment of rifles either bought from gun peddlers or captured in battle. The braves, around forty in number, carried lances and war clubs. Although most of the horses had no markings, a few warriors astride white horses had painted coup marks and other symbols on their rippling hides, as well as hoofprints symbolizing successful horse raids.

The eerie silence was getting to Moss. Even the birds seemed to have pulled away, and there was no wind to speak of. A flicking glance showed him the Oglalas seated motionless on their war ponies. They had yet to point any of the weapons they carried at the two white men, but Moss knew that a quiet nod from Crazy Horse would shatter the stillness. His horse snorting brought a nervous blinking to Moss's eyes.

Crazy Horse brought up his rifle to point the barrel

northerly, "Your trail was plain, Hollabaugh . . ."

"You know of me?"

"Of you, and all who scout out of Fort Reno." Anger flared for a moment in Crazy Horse's eyes, to soften as he added, "You risked much to save one of my people."

"Seemed the right thing to do," said Moss. "Put him in that cabin. Then rode down to fetch Doc Olhman here. As there's a bullet that needs to be taken out. But guess for that it'll have to be up to you, Crazy Horse."

Nodding, Crazy Horse said, "Many of my people have died before because bullets were still lodged in them. Is your medicine strong, soldier medicine man?"

In a calm voice Olhman replied, "Been doing this a long time, pulling out bullets. I figure though, Chief, time's a-wasting if we want to save your brave."

"He is Red Wolf, an Oglala as I am. I saw his wounds." He speared a quick glance at Moss. "Though you tended to Red Wolf's wounds, the pallor of death has come upon him."

"Then we must hurry."

One of the chiefs spoke gutturally in Sioux, the gist of which Moss Hollabaugh took to be an attempt to overrule the wishes of Crazy Horse.

"We will build a council fire," responded Crazy Horse. "But what we say around a council fire, Lean Elk, does not change things—only the soldier medicine man has the magic to take out the bullet which is killing Red Wolf. So be it."

The Oglala bestirred their war ponies to allow passage for the hated white men toward the log cabin wreathed in morning shadows spilling down from screening trees. "First thing," said Olhman as he swung down, "is to start a fire in there, an' I'll need water."

"Doc, you know if that Oglala doesn't make it—"

"We might not ride out of here. Got that part figured out, Moss." Hefting his medical bag, he pushed into the cabin to

16

throw over his shoulder, "Part of being a doctor, I guess."

"That Crazy Horse is something," said Moss as he watched Olhman examining the wound to the back of the Oglala. "Would be a general in our army."

Running a hand through his bristly salt and pepper hair, Olhman said, "He's weakening. Lost a lot of blood. Even if I get that slug out he might not make it. But, as I said out there, Moss, time's a-wasting."

The fire started by Moss in the stone fireplace drove the chill and some of the encroaching shadows out of the small cabin but not enough to the satisfaction of the man about to operate on the Oglala. Moss out to confer with Crazy Horse, who ordered some of his warriors into the cabin. They became torchbearers, the flaming torches they held high revealing the veiled hatred in their dark almond eyes. Moss tore up a spare shirt he carried in a saddlebag to be used afterwards as a bandage. Doctor Lute Olhman had ordered that the Oglala be placed on the only table, with his stomach pressing into the worn planking of the table and his legs extending beyond it to be supported by a couple of chairs. Olhman had brought along a bottle of corn whiskey, to use to sterilize as best he could the open wound, and now to steady his nerves as he shaped a wry grin for Moss Hollabaugh.

"Appears to be in there damned deep. But this Red Wolf isn't all that old and tough as rawhide. So, here goes."

All the while from outside there had been the insistent and ominous beating of Indian drums, and closer, the chanting of one of Crazy Horse's medicine men as he shuffled about outside the log cabin in one of his dances. Aware of this as Doc Olhman brought one of his instruments probing into the mouth of the wound, Moss took stock of their present situation. He could have let those white men have their way with the Oglala, but he'd realized later as he headed southward toward Fort Casper that there'd been no other choice for him. Someone had to take a stand against those wanting to kill for personal gain. Inwardly there came this silent prayer, Took a stand for what I believed was right, Lord—hope you consider that.

Moments after the hated soldier medicine man had sewn up the back wound some Indians came crowding into the cabin. An Oglala medicine man under the watchful eyes of Chief Lean Elk cut the bandage away from the wound. He held in his gnarled old hands a poultice made from the leaves of an adder's tongue herb-plant. Lifting up his arms, the medicine man chanted prayers to the Spirit Who Rules The Universe, turning as he did so that blessings would come from the four corners of the earth. Finished with this ritual, he laid the poultice over the wound and tied it there with a bandage he'd brought along. Now Moss Hollabaugh and Major Lute Olhman were brought out of the cabin.

The other chiefs were clustered around a council fire near the creek. The sun was cleaving an early afternoon sky and the birds that had settled back amongst the trees would flutter up at times. The point of a lance nudged into Hollabaugh's shoulder, the Oglala holding it gesturing toward a shading cottonwood. Olhman had been unarmed, and the Sioux had confiscated Moss's weapons, but just upcreek their horses were tethered to willows. He stood there as Doc Olhman hunkered down to place his back against the tree, and he said quietly, "Did what I could, Moss."

"I know," he replied. "If that Oglala pulls through this that medicine man will take all of the credit. He'll be the first one to want our scalps if it goes the other way." At another campfire Moss took in some braves putting on war paint. An Oglala had a nasty habit of packing along a buckskin paint pouch and maybe an eagle bone whistle or a medicine bag. Armed with this and a rifle the Oglala had proved to be a formidable foe.

And there was Crazy Horse. More than once his cavalry

tactics had proved superior to those employed by the U.S. Army. But a lot of troopers had died before army generals had learned to accept the strange genius of this Oglala chief. The word from friendly Indians hanging around Fort Reno was of Crazy Horse being a man of compassion, which Moss was counting on.

"You know, Moss, they saw us leaving Fort Casper."

"They could send out a patrol, Doc, as men of your trade are few and far between out here. An' they'd send a helluva lot more troopers if they knew of Crazy Horse being here."

"What about you, Moss, if we get out of this?"

"Army justice can be damned harsh at times. It'll be my word against other white men. To tell you the truth, Doc, this job of scouting was wearing on me. Go back to Fort Reno? They've got me earmarked as an Indian lover, but it was my choice, I reckon."

Some time passed before several braves returned to the encampment, one of them having a mule deer draped over his horse. Quickly fires were built up, and soon the pleasant aroma of frying venison came to the captives of the Oglala. As the day wore on both were denied access to the log cabin. Their guard was changed, and shortly after this Moss could make out Crazy Horse coming their way through late afternoon shadows.

Striding over to them, Crazy Horse said, "Red Wolf still lives."

"Suppose I could look in on him?"

"Yes, since your medicine is powerful." A quiet word from Crazy Horse dismissed their guards, and he fell into step with Hollabaugh and Olhman. "Many words were spoken at our council fire . . . and we smoked many pipes." Then they were entering the cabin to face the wrathful eyes of an Oglala medicine man. A gesture from Crazy Horse brought Doc Olhman over to the wounded Oglala now stretched out on the floor near the fireplace and covered with an Indian blanket, which Olhman lifted aside.

19

With his black bag in hand, Olhman crouched down to examine the wound, and then the pulsebeat of Red Wolf. He said without looking, "Seems to be breathing easier." He spread the blanket over the Oglala and then rose to shape a smile for Crazy Horse. "That poultice will help to draw out any poisons, so I guess between us, me and your medicine man, we helped save Red Wolf."

The Oglala digested these words as his eyes held to those of Olhman's. "You have done well, soldier medicine man. There were some at the council fire who spoke against you . . . and you, Hollabaugh. But this is the word of Crazy Horse. Go with the thanks of this Teton Lakota."

"That sets right with me," said Moss as he thrust out his hand to have Crazy Horse grasp it. "Perhaps we'll meet again some day . . ."

"That shall come to pass," Crazy Horse said firmly.

They wasted little time in reclaiming their horses, where Moss found his rifle still in the scabbard and his gunbelt hooked over the saddle horn. With some apprehension they passed through the camp of the Oglalas and in short order found themselves out on open prairie and heading southerly. Steady riding could bring them to Fort Casper around nightfall, but Major Lute Olhman advised the man who rode alongside him to do otherwise.

"Heading back could see you facing a firing squad, Moss. I could add my testimony of what happened, but just being an army doctor doesn't carry that much weight. And they sure in tarnation won't believe we met up with Crazy Horse and lived to tell about it."

"The strange man of the Oglala they call him. And for me, Doc, going back could do away with any future plans. And they can always hire another scout. Oregon—don't cotton to heading that way for now. You'll make it okay from here on in?"

"Yonder's Casper Mountain."

"Then I'll take my leave, Major Olhman."

Reining up, Olhman watched as army scout Moss Hollabaugh set a southeasterly course into the lengthening
shadows of day. "There goes a man of firm convictions."
Then, the parting words of Crazy Horse came to mind, as
to him and Moss Hollabaugh running into one another
again.

"Just got this feeling that'll happen," murmured Olhman
as his last glimpse was of Moss Hollabaugh cantering his
bronc over a hillock, before he set his horse in motion toward beckoning Casper Mountain.

Two

The road to the goldfields in the Black Hills coursed straight as the barrel of a Winchester up through Nebraska. It actually started down at Sidney on the Union Pacific line, where prospective goldseekers sought passage by horseback or buggy or one of the stagecoaches run by the Western Stage Company. But upon leaving Sidney they were at the mercy of road agents.

In the scant five months of Moss Hollabaugh's sojourn into Nebraska there'd been a lot of killings, and these outlaws didn't just limit themselves to stagecoaches. They took to robbing lone travelers, ranches, stage stations, wagon trains and rural stores, and once in a while a train. The same held true over in territorial Wyoming where another stageline ran from Cheyenne to Deadwood. Both routes were around two hundred or more miles on desolate and unguarded trails.

But at least down here in Nebraska there were no Indian attacks as the Teton Lakota confined their raids to the western fringes of the Black Hills. Had it been over two years since that encounter with the Oglala chief Crazy Horse? What Moss saw in the chipped mirror hanging from the log wall of the Butte Creek stage station was the image of a man tired of riding shotgun for the Western Stage Company. There were more lines crowfooting away from his grey eyes, and traces of grey hair were cropping out along his temples and along the sideburns. His cheekbones were cupped in more, with the windburned skin stretched across his angular face. In his mid-thirties, Moss looked and felt a lot older.

The first job he'd landed after vacating territorial Wyoming was one being offered in a Denver newspaper. To secure gainful employment he told of being a scout for the army but up in Montana. So he became a field operative for the Pinkerton Agency, his first jobs down in Arizona and western Colorado. He found he enjoyed that kind of life until the day a missive arrived from the home office at Denver telling Moss Hollabaugh he was let go. His past, he'd reckoned at the time, had caught up with him. And perhaps the chief reason the army hadn't sent someone out to clap him in irons was because a lot of soldiers were deserting to try their hand at panning for gold in the Black Hills.

"Just like going fishing," he mused, and with a sidewise glance at driver Johnny Slaughter coming up, "you don't catch all the fish in a stream."

"They're long overdue, Moss."

Here they were, midway between the gold fields of the Black Hills and Sidney, loaded down with passengers and a strongbox filled with gold bullion. The southern route ran along the eastern fringes of the hills, and it was up there they'd shot their way out of one ambush and narrowly avoided another. Coming up from Sidney to escort them the rest of the way should be at least four guards, now long overdue as they'd pulled in here around noon and now the sun was spiking the sky westerly. He shared Slaughter's worry. But along with this were their six passengers, a woman, a Negro with big soulful eyes and four men packing a lot of gold dust. These were miners heading out with their spoils, garbed in rumpled clothing and armed with pistols. Back up the line when those road agents had appeared, in his fear one of the miners had blazed away narrowly missing one of his fellow passengers but adding more bullet holes to those already decorating the stagecoach. Now here at this stage station it was the complaining of these men which was rasping at Moss's nerves.

"What do you think, Johnny?"

"Make a go for it?" A slat-faced man some five years older than Moss and back a time a muleskinner, Johnny Slaughter scooped a dipperful of warm water out of the drinking bucket and regarded the implement of his trade, a Concord stagecoach. Painted a dull yellow, the high China seat to the rear was laden down with luggage as was the flat top, and when they got underway by unspoken agreement the Negro would take to the roof seat behind where Johnny Slaughter and Moss would be riding. Harnessed and in their traces were the wheel horses and the swing team and the pair of leaders, the larger wheel horses in the back. A lot of bottle flys were picking at the horses as was a wind picking up sand and clouding the air around the buildings. Both of them were casting anxious eyes along the southern reaches of the trail as Slaughter muttered, "Might's well head out as the accommodations at this station are pretty bare."

Moss grimaced in agreement as he hung on a wall peg the old towel he'd just used to dry his face. Meals served by the stage stations were a dull routine of hardtack, beans, coffee, and pork. When overnighting the passengers slept on hard bunks. The big Concord coaches were mounted on leather thorough braces causing them to swing in most every direction like a ship bucking a rough sea. Because of this, some passengers became ill and had to lay over at a stage station. The going fare from Sidney to the Black Hills was high, fifty dollars—another reason for the passengers to complain to the driver or Moss Hollabaugh.

"If we don't break down, Johnny, we should pull into the Snake Creek station around about sundown."

Moss reached for his Henry, a rifle he'd taken to using.

All bronzed metal from muzzle to stock, the tubular magazine under the barrel held fifteen rimfire shells. It had a longer range than most rifles and heavier hitting power. More than once the Henry had been the difference when road agents had appeared. He made a beeline for the stagecoach as Johnny Slaughter poked his head into the stage station to announce they were leaving. Clambering onto the front seat, Moss had a friendly nod for the Negro stretched out on the other seat built a little higher on the roof of the coach. Curiosity held Moss's eyes to the man. All he'd found out in a quiet conversation was the man's name, Wilbur Robeson.

Robeson was a chocolate-colored man with a pensive smile on a bony face that seemed too large for his thin frame. He wore a floppy black hat, the front brim coming down to shade those soulful eyes. He had on sturdy work shoes and an old grey suit and a shirt with no collar and buttoned at his neck. His hair was black and kinky, and he appeared to be a man in his forties. The smile holding, Robeson said in a rhythmic baritone voice, "Yassuh, Mistah Hollabaugh . . . glad to be pulling out."

"Call me Moss. Could be some trouble ahead."

"Trouble?" The word came out kind of trembly, but not for any danger that might be lurking along the trail, as in the dark brown eyes of Wilbur Robeson came a faraway sparkle. "Every man has his private troubles, Mistah Moss." He wanted to say more, but now he sat up straighter as the other passengers neared the coach.

With the helping arm of driver Johnny Slaughter the woman got into the coach. The name on the passenger list was that of Melba Thurman, and judging from her appearance the wife of a prominent businessman or rancher. But Moss knew different, as the look she'd thrown him back at the Piney stage station bespoke of her with him in a four-poster. Now it seemed she had set her eyes upon another passenger. Melba Thurman was a handsome woman

25

though kind of plump through the hips, and just maybe an opportunist, something that miner should beware of.

Trailing behind to the stagecoach were a pair Moss figured were hardcases. Philby was the name of one miner, a bulky man in a plaid coat and overalls. He couldn't recall the other's name, though it was obvious he was of a like mind frame as the loudmouthed Philby. The pair of them had been drinking, and instead of being mellowed out they'd turned ugly with their words.

"Where the hell are those guards?" Philby threw at Slaughter standing patiently by the open coach door.

"And look, dammit," said the other miner, "Another hour and it'll be too dark to travel."

"I say we wait here until those guards show up."

"Suits me if you two drunks linger on here as we're pulling out," spat out Johnny Slaughter.

"Watch your lip, driver," shot back Philby. " 'Cause for what I paid for a ticket I could buy me a couple of those horses."

Pivoting, Slaughter closed the coach door and swung toward the front wheel, from there to go up to his seat, while with muttered oaths the two reluctant passengers hurried to open the coach door and clamber aboard. Barely had one of them closed the door than a loud *kiyeee* from Johnny Slaughter brought his six horses into a quick walking start away from the stage station.

"Mouthy cayuses," said Slaughter.

"Probably brought some whiskey with them. An' men of that breed don't share their spoils."

"What do you think, Moss?"

"Those guards not showing up? You've heard the rumors as to this stagecoach company calling it quits. That could be it, Johnny, as armed guards don't come all that cheap. But," he checked the lever action on his rifle, "outlaws could have taken them out."

"Some bad spots ahead."

26

"There's the pair of us and four in the coach. And Robeson makes seven." Moss brushed his coat aside and unleathered a six-gun, and easing sideways on the seat, he held it out to the Negro riding the high seat behind him. "You ever fire one of those things, Mr. Robeson?"

"Been a spell since I did, Mistah Moss. Got some licks in during the Civil War. Trouble. My bones tell me it'sa coming. Mistah Moss, suh, if somethin' happens to me. . ." The sudden smile coming from Wilbur Robeson wreathed up his wide cheeks and showed the even rows of teeth, then it seemed as if a cloud shadow was passing across his eyes to have him lapse into silence.

Troubled by this, Moss said softly, "Something you want to talk about, Mr. Robeson?"

Gingerly he placed the revolver in suit pocket as he said hesitantly, "Perhaps there is, Mistah Moss." Then he leaned back to look away.

From westerly came lowering sunlight punching hotly at the big Concord coach being pulled by horses Johnny Slaughter had reined into a canter. Distantly, by Slaughter's estimation about four miles, lay the Piney stage station. In between was a lot of rugged land escarped by a low butte. Ahead of them the trail narrowed before it dipped into an arroyo shielding one of those nameless creeks familiar to this part of the country. A sharp tugging of the reins by Slaughter brought them to a halt about a hundred yards this side of the arroyo and more jagged prairie to either side and flowing out for several miles.

"The only way through here," Johnny Slaughter said worriedly. "So what do you think?"

Producing a field glass that he always carried, Moss Hollabaugh sighted through it what he could see of the main trail. From where he sat on the high front seat the stage station up ahead was hidden by a hillock cutting northeasterly across the trail. These were the discernible things, but what Moss was actually looking for through the field glass were birds lifting away from the brush clogging the arroyo and other low places ideally suited for an ambush. The more he scanned the lay of things ahead, the more uncertainty began to grip his thoughts.

"Quiet as a cemetery after dark, Johnny."

"Except for that bitching coming from our passengers."

"Maybe what you said before, Moss, is what happened, that this stageline can't afford to hire extra guards. As they've damned well lost a lot of money to these damned road agents." Slaughter spat out tobacco juice as he twisted on the seat to squint up at Robeson. "Your bones still tell you something's gonna happen?"

"I've been in some cemeteries after dark where a lot of tomcats been doing a lot of catting about, Mistah Drivah."

A cackling laughter came from Johnny Slaughter. Putting the reins into his right hand, he brought his left to a shirt pocket to lift out a box of snuff, which he passed back to Robeson. "Here, that stuff will take the worry out of your bones."

"Seems peaceful enough," murmured Moss as he lowered the field glass.

"Let's get this thing the hell moving!" came a shout from inside the coach.

"Watch your mouth, Philby," Slaughter shouted back, "as there's a lady aboard." He grumbled out some more words, finally to add, "Should have left them drunks back at our last stop."

"We'll pull out, Johnny, as soon as I have a talk with our passengers." Clambering down, Moss opened the coach door to take in the sullen eyes of their passengers, all but Melba Thurman's fixed to the face of the miner squeezed in beside her.

"What now, shotgun?" groused Philby, a half-filled bottle of whiskey propped in his lap and speaking around the stub of a cigar.

"The Snake Creek station is just ahead, folks. But as those guards didn't show up we'll go in easy. I suggest —"

"Yeah, that we unlimber our armament; reason I brought along this big old Peacemaker."

"Easy with that, Philby. As I was saying, no sense taking any chances."

"And if we do encounter road agents?"

Moss had a quick smile for Philby's drinking companion, a sour-faced man wearing a derby. "Keep up a steady fire as we'll try to make a go for the stage station."

"I'm scared," said Melba Thurman, but her fear of the moment didn't keep the woman from placing a hand high on the miner's inner thigh.

The miner seated next to Melba Thurman slid an arm around her shoulders as Moss closed the door. Back on the seat, he picked up the Henry and said, "You notice anything different on the way down from Butte Creek? Meaning we haven't passed anyone heading up to the gold fields. Too bad there isn't a way around those breaks ahead."

"Sometimes the road gets washed out down by that creek," said Johnny Slaughter, reining the horses into a walk.

With the stagecoach passing down into the arroyo and coming onto the creek, Moss kept scanning the sky, then dropped his gaze to the land on either side, closing in more now and studded with brush and stunted trees, and with prairie birds flitting away. If those sent out from Sidney had been gunned down by outlaws, turkey vultures would be picking away at their bodies by now. Again Moss took in the vast blue dome of sky barren of clouds but for some scavengers fringing hazily to the northwest. All he sighted was a lonely hawk winging away. Then it came to him, and he told Slaughter and Wilbur Robeson hovering behind them of his suspicions.

"Maybe so, Moss," agreed Johnny Slaughter.

"Reason we didn't spot any vultures," Moss finished. On the other hand, maybe they wouldn't find any road agents at the Snake Creek stage station, Moss pondered. They'd worked out a signal with Pops Merced, that if he came out to greet them bareheaded they would come on in. The reason for this was that too many stage stations had been hit, and now Moss braced himself as Slaughter whipped the horses into a canter to bring them through muddy road sucking at the big wheels of the coach. Uptrail they went to follow further undulations of ground until they were heading up that last hillock behind which lay the next stop on their long journey from the Black Hills.

"Pops knows we're behind schedule."

"Should have the fresh horses harnessed up and in the east corral." Cresting the hillock, Slaughter tugged back on the reins to slow down the horses even while taking in the stage station and the other log buildings. They were still out about a quarter of a mile, the trail passing through meadow grass bending in the wind. Backdropping the buildings were screening trees and higher land through which a draw passed. A side window in the main building faced the way they were traveling, with lamplight from within yellowing against the glass panes. Then the station agent, Pops Merced, moved out onto the front porch to hold up a hesitant hand, wearing that old battered felt hat he favored.

"Dammit," swore Johnny Slaughter, "Pops ain't got nary a chance out there. You was right, Moss, about them bastards coming in here. Those guards we was expecting, they must have dumped their bodies in that shed or in the barn. Okay, Moss, got any ideas?"

"Just keep headin' in natural like," Moss said quickly. "Most likely those outlaws will be in the main building, one in the shed, a couple of others in the barn. The only chance we've got to keep Pops from getting killed is to have you angle in between Pops and the porch. Just don't stop when we get there but whip them hosses on toward the barn."

"It'll be hairy at best, Moss, but guess its all we've got. Just hope Pops figures it out." Lifting his hat away, Slaughter waved it at the station agent and at the same time hawked out more tobacco juice, the wind catching the brownish stream of tobacco to fling some of it against the coach.

Without glancing back Moss said, "Mr. Robeson, hold your fire until Pops grabs onto the coach."

As the trail spilled into the barren ground around the buildings, Slaughter angled the Concord toward Pops Merced as if that's where he intended pulling up. Somehow, Merced, a rail-thin man somewhere between fifty and old age, sensed Johnny Slaughter's intentions as he began moving further away from the porch in an ambling gait like a man with no worries on his mind. Only when the leaders began shying away from the overhanging porch did the man driving the Concord lash out with the ends of his reins to startle the horses into a run.

This was a signal for gunfire to begin spitting out of the stage station building. Behind them, without Moss or Slaughter realizing it, was the Negro bracing himself with one hand as he hung over the side of the coach to clutch onto one of Pops Merced's arms and help lift him up. Merced clung there as the big Concord hurtled toward the side wall of the hiproofed barn out of which came the barking of gunfire. Then a leaden slug coming from either the shed or barn struck into Wilbur Robeson, and though flinching from the impact of it, he managed to cling to Merced's arm. Moss and those inside the coach were returning the gunfire as best they could as the coach swept around the side wall of the barn. Slaughter reined up sharply by the double back doors and kicked at the brake lever.

"Get into the barn!" he yelled.

Jumping down, Moss levered a shell into the breech of his Henry, and then he flung one of the doors open and crouched into the barn to draw six-gun fire from a man

31

crouched by the front doors. Moss fired, to have the outlaw slam back into the closed door, hang there for a moment as the slug from his sidearm slapped into the dirt floor. Moss's Henry roared again and the outlaw crumbled onto fresh horse droppings. Now it was Moss Hollabaugh finding the rungs of the wall ladder and easing up into the hayloft while those he'd shared danger with rushed into the barn.

"Get up to those front windows," ordered Slaughter, "as those damned outlaws are heading this way. You"—a finger gnarled and calloused from handling leathery reins stabbed at one of the miners—"keep an eye out the back door as they might try for the coach."

The sight of Moss's Stetson in the floor opening brought the booming of a Winchester, the leaden slug gouging out wood slivers in the wall and studding. "Close," he muttered and ducking below the level of the upper floor. Then he sailed his hat through the floor opening to have that Winchester sound again. As it did, Moss hurtled upward and worked the lever on his Henry to punch out three shots, two missing, the last ripping into the outlaw's crotch, causing him to forget Moss for a second and stab a frantic hand toward his privates—a mistake as Moss slammed two more slugs at the outlaw.

Hurrying past the dying outlaw clutching both at his crotch and musky-smelling hay littering the floor, Moss bellied down and brought the Henry sighting out of a small door. He counted five road agents spreading out and coming in, and when one of them barked out a command, Moss fired at the man and grimaced when he missed. From below came the sporadic sound of the miners using their guns, and there was the familiar sound of Slaughter's .44-40. After a while, as the road agents dropped out of sight, the firing tapered off. Then it came to Moss what Wilbur Robeson had done and of Robeson being wounded.

"Saved Pops is what he did," he murmured respectfully.

Worriedly now he surveyed the way darkness was creeping in amongst the buildings. This barn was a tinderbox, and if he was one of those outlaws, he'd go for burning it down. Scrambling to his feet, Moss found the wall ladder and on the center runway between the stalls Pops Merced tending to the Negro.

"How bad is it, Pops?"

His face creased with pain lines, Robeson said, "Mistah . . . Moss . . ."

Kneeling down, Moss tipped his hat back. "I hear you, Mister Robeson."

Robeson lifted a hand from his chest and tried bringing it into an inner coat pocket, letting it fall limply there. "In my pocket . . . Mistah Moss . . . a letter . . ." That Wilbur Robeson knew he was dying showed in his eyes. "Got some gold . . . in this money belt. Please, Mistah Moss . . . for my family . . ."

"Robeson, you can't pack it in now," pleaded Moss as he reached down and gripped the man's large hand. He ignored the rattling of gunfire starting up again as there was a last tightening of his grip from Wilbur Robeson before he went limp.

"He had more craw than a lot I know."

"Yup, Pops, there was a man." Shrugging out of his coat, Moss placed it over Robeson's upper body. "Pops, check out back. I'll try that loft again."

Once he was back in the loft, Moss found to his surprise that the road agents were scattering away. Then he realized that the rifle he was hearing came not from the barn or the road agents, but distantly. An outlaw tumbled over and another stumbled, compliments of that hidden rifleman. Moss brought up the Henry, but too late as the outlaws were behind the stage station building and probably heading for their horses.

Johnny Slaughter called out, "Hey, Moss, those damned thieves have cut out. Awright, they're gone." These last words were for a couple of the miners still firing their weapons.

When Moss reached the lower floor his first concern was for the passengers, Slaughter reported that by some miracle nobody had been hit. Slaughter added, "Folks, we'll overnight here."

Pops Merced came over carrying a coal oil lantern and he said to Moss, "They was bragging on how they killed those guards. Had the same in mind for me."

"Strange," speculated Moss. "How did these outlaws know about those guards coming up here?"

"Same thing happened a couple of months before you hired on as shotgun. Just two got killed that time."

"Well, I'll go out and take a look around, Pops. Make certain those outlaws cut out of here."

"Damned right they're gone," blustered one of the miners, as with a flourish he holstered his six-gun. "You got any whiskey up at that station of yours, Pops?"

Then Moss Hollabaugh was slipping out into the first remnants of night beginning to cloak the buildings and silhouetting the few trees and the rising land beyond. The wind was buffeting against the open shed door he passed to bring up the Henry as he approached the stage station building. But what caused Moss to work the lever on his rifle was the glimpse of a rider bringing his horse in at a walk on the stagecoach road. Stepping back to keep from being haloed by light pouring out of the open front door, he held there until his eyes widened in recognition. He said around the beginnings of a wary smile, "A man could get himself killed coming in like that, Siringo."

"Could," responded the horseman.

"The army send you after me?"

"Nope," said Charlie Siringo out of Denver and a Pinkerton agent, and now swinging down by the front porch. "Last I saw of those road agents they were hauling ass thataway. Came across a wounded man heading his horse for

34

Sidney who spoke of being a guard for the stagecoach company. That the three with him had gone down in an ambush."

"So, Charlie, what brings you up to these parts?"

"You, Mr. Hollabaugh." He took in Pops Merced carrying the lantern as he shepherded all of the passengers across the barren yard. "There a place we can talk?"

Stabbing Charlie Siringo with a speculating glance, Moss finally nodded in the direction of a side wall, and after Siringo tied up his horse, he followed after Moss going around the corner of the log building. He caught up with Moss waiting under a stunted pine tree.

"Those rumors, Moss, you've been hearing about the Western Stage Company selling out aren't rumors any more."

"Been expecting it."

"Sold to the Cheyenne-Black Hills Stage and Express Company. They've been hit by Indians, and outlaws, too, which is why I'm here. Got a job for you, Moss."

"Must be doing something for you on the sly, Charlie, because if you remember the Pinkertons fired me."

"You don't seem interested—"

"I expect they'll still try to run this stageline. But as for me holding on as a shotgun, maybe I've got some other plans. Which don't include working for you."

"I can understand how you feel, Moss. Remember, we did talk once about what happened to you back when you were scouting out of Fort Reno. Me, I'da done the same. What we have here is pretty much the same story. One of your fellow employees has been tipping off these road agents."

For a moment Moss Hollabaugh was back in Wyoming. With his gun answering the barking of those white men trying to kill one of Crazy Horse's Oglala. And afterwards, the great chief of the Oglala had prophesied them encountering one another again. Here at the Snake Creek stage station had been another mindless killing, that of Wilbur Robeson,

35

a man knowing more sadness than most. He heard himself saying, "Okay, I'll hear you out."

"What you'll have to do is get hired by the Cheyenne-Deadwood stageline, as the same thing is happening up there. There are two owners, one partner running the operation in Cheyenne. But it's the other one you'll be working for, this being Jason Hassrick up in Deadwood. Don't know if there's any connection between what's been happening down here and where you'll be going, Moss. Guess you can find that out."

"Guess I can, Charlie."

"Anything goes wrong the Pinkertons will deny your being one of their operatives. It boils down to only me and Jason Hassrick knowing about you. You still interested?"

"Soon's I get me a saddle hoss I'll head up to Deadwood."

"Take mine. And, Moss, here's a little to tide you over."

"Never asked what I'd be paid for doing this?"

"Same's me, standard operative wages."

"Figured I'd be working for next to nothing." He smiled back at Charlie Siringo. "I'll pull out in the morning. Right now I've got a grave to dig."

Moss Hollabaugh striding away had a silent anger etched on his face. As he'd said before, there was a man, Wilbur Robeson. "Someone killed by others lusting over gold. Gold, a curse to the Indian, the god of the whites. Up in the Black Hills, men working like pack rats to get at it. What a shitty world this is."

Three

The highlight of Orrin Risdale's rather unsavory life had been his encountering Mark Twain on a Mississippi riverboat. This was after the famous author had given up piloting these steamboats on this very same river. At the time Orrin Risdale was traveling upriver, on the run from New Orleans with a lot of stolen money. A bookkeeper, Risdale had emptied out the company safe. His sudden departure left behind a wife and two children. Just useless luggage, he'd thought at the time. Before New Orleans there had been other places where the bookkeeper had committed like crimes. He had sired another child with a common-law wife, left them just as callously. Passing himself off as a plantation owner had allowed him entry to a high stakes poker game in which there'd been some big spenders and the effusive Mark Twain.

Afterwards Orrin Risdale had sought out some of Twain's books, but it was one of the things Twain had spoken of on that steamboat which Risdale uttered now, "Let us be thankful for the fools. But for them the rest of us could not succeed."

Such a man was the manager of the Western Stage Company down at Sidney. It was to Cheyenne that Orrin Risdale had intentions of going, had gotten as far as Sidney to find most of the passengers on the Union Pacific train getting off with the intentions of heading north to the gold fields in the Black Hills. High living and a bad run at cards caused him to take stock of the situation, which brought him off the train. That same day he found out while waiting in line to buy a ticket that the stageline was sorely in need of someone knowing how to tote up figures and handle office chores. After that it was merely a need to introduce himself to the stageline manager, portly Herman Benson.

Part of the money stolen by Orrin Risdale had been used to purchase a new wardrobe. Everyday saw him decked out in an expensive suit with all the accessories as he took particular pains to curry the favor of his new boss. Risdale's daily routine was getting a shave at a local tonsorial shop, and then heading for the stagecoach office with the ends of his mustache waxed so they curled up and reeking of scented lotion. Any dog loafing downwind on the street generally sought an alley. Another part of the crooked bookkeeper's fawning makeup was of his telling others what they wanted to hear. Herman Benson was an unkempt and slovenly man too cheap to buy a suit that fit properly, so it was music to his ears when his new bookkeeper told him that he had a certain elegance of dress and manner; not a fat slob as bantied about by the locals. One day Orrin Risdale was elevated to the role of assistant manager, the next found him aboard a stagecoach and on his way up to Deadwood to take over operations of the end-of-the line office.

While down in Sidney it was Risdale's love of the pasteboards that had found him out playing cards most every night. As he'd grown accustomed to the western way of things in this Nebraska town located on the main line of the Union Pacific Railroad, he took note of some of those who'd just arrived from the Black Hills flashing around a lot of gold nuggets. More than once he shared in drinks on the house compliments of some miner. Another fact tucked away by the bookkeeper was of gold shipments coming in, then to be hustled aboard a train and shipped on to either Cheyenne or to eastern destinations. This provoked in Orrin Risdale the need to get more out of this sudden prosperity than a drink bought by a miner or a weekly wage. The promotion came for Risdale, but before departing for the Black Hills he took into his confidence one of the clerks and hatched a plan that could see both of them coming into a lot of money. Later on a letter from Risdale to manager Benson down in Sidney saw the clerk taking over Risdale's former position as bookkeeper.

Deadwood—Orrin Risdale found it a place as unsavory as he was. On every street corner lingered sharp-eyed men and oftentimes brazen women. Prices were as high as the canyon walls hemming in this squalor of a town, the walls so narrow it seemed a strong-armed man could unleash a gold nugget spanning neighboring rimrocks. And shortly after his arrival, Risdale's clandestine inquiries at a place known to be frequented by road agents—the notorious Green Front—found him holding a meeting with a man known only to him at the time as Little Reddy from Texas.

The results of that meeting brought about a lot of Western Stage Company coaches being hit by road agents. The deal worked out by Risdale was for him to receive a handsome share of monies and gold nuggets plucked from those stagecoaches by his thieving associates. In the span of a few months Orrin Risdale had acquired a lot of money and women more than willing to share one of the bedrooms in that new house of his looking down in red brick splendor at the growing mining town of Deadwood. The only thing Risdale hadn't counted on was all of these robberies causing the stageline to be sold.

"Damn, sold to that Hassrick outfit."

Orrin Risdale was in his cups, standing at the moment at the long bar in the Bella Union, and sunken in cursing self-pity. The news about the stageline being sold had arrived yesterday, marking the end of the best deal he'd ever been involved in. His fear was of the new owners letting him go. New money would be used to keep the stageline in operation as it was the shortest route up to the Black Hills, which meant Orrin Risdale must call upon the new owners. In his ramblings about Deadwood he'd learned that one of the owners lived in Cheyenne, had in fact married the daughter of principal owner Jason Hassrick. Workmen were just putting the finishing touches on Hassrick's pretentious brick mansion located on the southern fringes of the city. Risdale had also heard there were a couple of other daughters. Once he'd glimpsed Jason Hassrick and one of his daughters about to enter the Deadwood Opera House.

"About ready for the grave," he could remember muttering at the time. Jason Hassrick was in his early seventies, and had taken to using a cane to help ease the pain of arthritis affecting his left hipbone. All he could remember about Julie Hassrick was a comely woman with a mass of chestnut hair.

Shoving the half empty bottle of whiskey away, Orrin Risdale decided he needed a change of scenery. But first he pulled out his big pocket watch, the case of which was embossed with gold in the shape of leaves; going on nine o'clock on a bustling Friday night. Usually he would find a poker game. Taking his leave of the saloon, he held outside on the boardwalk, to prudently decide that instead of a session at cards he would head over to the Melodeon.

"Risdale—"

The man he turned to face wore a mustache bigger'n his, and a patient smile on a blocky face, and he had all the earmarks of being a cowhand. In a voice slurred by whiskey Risdale said, "Don't believe we're acquainted?"

"We will be," the stranger replied. "My boss wants to have a word with you."

"And who might that be?"

"One of those owning the Cheyenne to Deadwood stageline."

He said protestingly, "I'm hardly in the condition to get together with Mr. Hassrick."

"It isn't Hassrick you'll be seeing." Cado Greer was big all over, but had a soft way of speaking. One never knew what was on Cado Greer's mind as he never seemed to change expression. He gave his name to the shorter Risdale, and continued, "You want to keep on being employed you'll go with me. Just upstreet, the Cricket Saloon."

"Yes, I will hear what Mr. Payne, I believe, has to say."

He set out along the crowded street with Cado Greer on the outside edge of the boardwalk, and with Risdale puzzling as to the whys of this meeting being held at a saloon. What did he know about Claiborne Payne? Only that Payne had married one of Jason Hassrick's daughters, a marriage that had no doubt caused Hassrick to make Payne an equal partner. There was a flicker of envy. Under the same circumstances he would have gotten hitched if it meant profit, past wives or no. A long time ago Risdale had shed what folks had gotten to calling scruples. Though some would call him a crook, Orrin Risdale considered himself an entrepreneur, a title setting more easily in his mind.

"I didn't know Mr. Payne was a practitioner of fisticuffs."

Cado Greer hung back to allow Risdale passage through the front door of the Cricket Saloon. The main attraction besides the bar girls were the bareknuckle fights, and Risdale was no stranger to this place. The saloon was one big room where smoke hung thick near the raftered ceiling and all the attention was centered on the boxing ring where a couple of pugilists were hammering away at one another. It was a standing room only crowd except for those lucky enough to be seated around tables or on the few benches lining the side walls. When one of the fighters punched his opponent in the mouth, Risdale smiled at a tooth popping out along with a spattering of blood, the bell sounding to sweep the fighters apart.

A prod in the back from Cado Greer brought the manager of the Western Stageline office here at Deadwood pressing through the crowd to one of the tables. Though he got his first look at Claiborne Payne, it was the presence of Harry McGowen seated alongside that brought a feeling of fear. For McGowen was his confederate down at Sidney. What kind of game was this? McGowen, a small, dapper man with thick reddish hair, took off his derby and smiled up at Orrin Risdale. The foxlike smile of McGowen's held as a nod from Claiborne Payne brought the third man seated there up from his chair. Now Payne gestured toward the empty chair, and an unwilling Orrin Risdale sat down to draw the chair closer to the table.

In one way Claiborne Payne was quite handsome, as he had wavy brown hair and unblemished features. He seemed every inch the successful businessman in the western cut suit, the matching light brown hat set at a rakish angle. On each hand folded before him on the table diamond rings glittered. But it seemed to Risdale as if something were missing, even though the smile held on both lips and in Payne's eyes, the pupils of which were tinted a vague yellow color. Once before he'd come across a man with eyes such as this, and had hastily departed the man's presence. Perhaps this was it, though Orrin Risdale felt that part of his uneasiness was finding Harry McGowen up here. He said to McGowen, "Should have let me know you were coming up, Harry. As I've got plenty of room over at my new house."

"I requested Mr. McGowen's presence," spoke up Claiborne Payne. He spun the empty shot glass around to watch it spin against the bottle of whiskey. Then the bell rang and Payne sat back in his chair to enjoy the fight.

Nervously aware of the man who'd been seated at the table and of Cado Greer hovering nearby, Risdale tried watching the fight, but couldn't keep his eyes from flicking to Harry McGowen urging on one of the fighters. There was a surge of the crowd toward the ring as one fighter was hammered down. Caught up now in what was happening, Orrin Risdale half-rose to view the referee trying to restrain the other fighter. In the excited roaring of the crowd he didn't hear the shocked gasp of pain come from Harry McGowen, nor glimpse the sudden withdrawing of a knife held by Claiborne Payne. But when he turned to regain his chair, he barely had time to see McGowen slumped over the table like a man not being able to hold his whiskey.

Then he was rising as was Claiborne Payne, who said through a fixed smile, "Your pal Harry told me all about your little scam."

The next thing Orrin Risdale realized he was being hustled away from the table by Cado Greer and his companion. And when they exited the Cricket Saloon it was through a back door. Risdale had the feeling he would be the next to feel the sting of Claiborne Payne's knife. They went through the litter scattered along the alley, and then passed into a vacant lot occupied by a couple of tents.

He cringed away when Claiborne Payne draped a hand on his shoulder, a shudder of fear beginning to sober him up. To kill a man that way, in the midst of others, bespoke of a steely nerve. Even Payne's easy smile couldn't stop him from shaking. One slip of the tongue and the same would be done to him. McGowen must have spilled the beans to Payne, and if so, why hadn't Payne turned the matter over to the U.S. Marshal's Office?

"Your partner Harry was all set to turn you in to collect that reward money." A gesture from Payne caused Cado Greer to pass over a cigar and to light it, the flaring of the match revealing the pondering set to Payne's yellow eyes, cold and without emotion. "So, with Harry out of the way, I figure you can either throw in with me . . ." He left it there to inhale cigar smoke.

"So what it comes down to is that McGowen had words with you, Mr. Payne."

"Even before this I suspected something of this nature was happening. In a way it helped us acquire the Western Stage company for next to nothing. McGowen was of little consequence. But you, Risdale, have quite a track record . . ."

"Seems you have me, sir."

"What I have, I trust, is your complete loyalty. A man with your unique qualities is a rare find in these parts. You should do a commendable job with our stageline. Meaning, Risdale, that you will be my liaison here in Deadwood. You know Cado." He gestured with his cigar at the other man, a leaned-out hardcase from his appearance. "Ace Taylor; Ace'll hang around to give you a hand."

"I see," murmured Orrin Risdale, and now he ventured this, "I gather this means you have some plans of your own regarding gold shipments."

"See," said Claiborne Payne as a smile deepened a dimple lodged in his left cheek, "didn't I tell you, Cado, about Risdale having a quick mind. We'll work out the details later." He tossed the cigar down to stomp it out with the heel of his boot. "Tomorrow morning, despite the objections of a certain young lady, you'll report for work at our main office here in Deadwood. Ask for Jason Hassrick. If that agrees with you, Risdale?"

"Most certainly it does," he said quickly, his response bringing from Claiborne Payne a cocky grin as Payne and the others broke past one of the tents and toward a crowded street.

Only when Orrin Risdale found himself alone did he realize his shirt was stained with sweat rolling down his armpits, and he took out his handkerchief to dab at his face as he stumbled back into the alley. Before it had simply been a matter of him getting word to Little Reddy from Texas about any gold shipments heading out of here. He had been detached from the actual violence of those robberies and the few killings. What happened to Harry McGowen was ample evidence that Claiborne Payne was a very dangerous man. A sudden gust of night air lashed out at him, and he hugged in closer to a back wall. He choked down an impulse to break out of an alley and seek the warmth of a saloon. He simply couldn't gather his thoughts, held to a shambling walk — a man alone and afraid.

"Think, dammit." His presence stirred up some rats poking around in a barrel, to have him shy away from the barrel and quicken his pace. "Can't leave at least until tomorrow. Got to clean out my savings account. But what about my house?" he vainly reasoned aloud.

On the other hand, most of the gold shipments left here on the Cheyenne to Deadwood stageline. And Cheyenne was where Payne resided. So, if he played his cards right, out of this he could still make a handsome profit. Another puzzling thing . . . why should Claiborne Payne try to bring about the demise of his own stageline? What would Mark Twain have to say about this . . . but, no matter . . . at least Risdale was not in jail or . . . The thought of the sudden demise of Harry McGowen brought him onto a street where Orrin Risdale sought the sanctuary of a saloon.

"Your impression of him?"

Cado Greer said flatly, "A weasel looking for a hole to disappear into."

This provoked from Claiborne Payne chuckling laughter. His smile held for Ace Taylor standing quietly to one side. The three of them and Claiborne Payne's wife, Mandy, had come in just the day before on a stagecoach and would return to Cheyenne later this week, but with Taylor staying behind. In the weeks before it had been Cado and Ace Taylor heading down into Nebraska by order of Payne. Within a matter of days they'd pieced it all together, had Harry McGowen come along to Deadwood with the promise he could still be of some use.

"McGowen," Payne murmured as an afterthought, "was the kind you can't trust. As for Risdale, right now he's running scared. Wondering just what our plans are."

"Having someone like Risdale here in Deadwood will make it a lot easier."

Then Claiborne Payne left the men working for him standing outside a saloon as he proceeded upstreet. His opinion of this mining town was considerably less than that of Jason Hassrick's. Once the gold petered out this town would probably go under. But the amount of gold being shipped out on his stageline told him otherwise. Not only was it being found in Deadwood Gulch, but in a scattering of places that had created such towns as Central City, Lead, Two Bit, Flatiron and others. Gold shipments went out about every other day in special coaches, and aware of this, outlaw gangs infested the Black Hills.

Claiborne Payne wanted more than just to be a conveyor of this gold, and worse of all, a junior partner to Hassrick. Even Hassrick's daughter Julia had a bigger say in things as she assumed more responsibilities in the main

46

office here in Deadwood. Part of his plan to get at a lot of the gold being shipped meant for Orrin Risdale to work in the main office. A couple of their bookkeepers had taken off to pan for gold, but to hire Risdale meant getting Julia's approval.

"A headstrong bitch."

It was back in Dubuque, an Iowa city spread along the Mississippi, that he began courting Mandy Hassrick, to eventually take her hand in marriage. He'd drifted in the summer before after being released from the Illinois State Prison down at Joliet. Like his father before him Claiborne had been a pickpocket and bunco artist, but while in prison his cellmate turned out to be Cado Greer. The rustling activities of Greer had brought him out of Colorado, where he soon ran out of money and decided to rob a bank, only to be captured. Greer was released first, with the promise from Claiborne Payne to head west when he got out. A lack of money had sidetracked him just after he'd found his way into Iowa. Then it was while working at Jason Hassrick's meatpacking plant that he first set eyes upon Mandy and around the same time local newspaper articles telling of her father's interest in the gold fields in the Black Hills.

"How gullible is my lovely Mandy," said Payne as he passed a brick warehouse to leave the street and began laboring up a steep flight of brick steps set into the canyon wall, where Jason Hassrick's spacious brick mansion lay. And not so gullible, he mused, is Julia. A pity he wasn't dealing with the third daughter, Crissy, whose forgetful antics amused everyone.

He passed through a wrought-iron gate set in a brick retaining wall; there was a short expanse of lawn, then he was in the foyer and handing his hat to a colored servant. In the closet were the hats of young beaus coming to call upon Crissy, which he found amusing. "Too bad Julia didn't take up with one of them and stay away from the office," he grumbled. He considered her the loveliest of Jason Hassrick's three daughters, tried to keep from thinking that part of his resentment toward Julia was the fact she simply didn't care for him. He would like nothing more than to take her to bed, and oftentimes had lustful dreams.

Brushing this aside, Claiborne Payne felt that Julia was more like her father than the other daughters. Perhaps it was her father's failing health that had brought Julia to working at the stagecoach office. It was from here that word of gold shipments was leaked out to the Sam Bass gang. Then his contact in Deadwood, one of the bookkeepers, had suddenly up and quit. Now he had Orrin Risdale, someone he knew he could control.

With his share of the stolen gold Payne was buying up ranchland laying northwest of Cheyenne and fringing onto the Laramie Mountains, since beef was needed in the gold mining towns and back east. He'd taken the precaution of registering his brand, the Flying CP, over at Laramie, and neither his wife nor her relatives knew about his becoming a rancher, though he left the details of this up to Cado Greer. It been an easy step from bunco artist and pickpocket to robbery on a grander scale. As for murder, that had occurred once before during a fight with another con artist. The killing of Harry McGowen had been premeditated, to let Risdale and his other associates know he wouldn't brook their disloyalties. And he savored it being done in that saloon, so adroitly nobody detected the sudden gleaming of his knife, and then to walk casually away.

Everyone was in the billiard room, as with some of the other rooms opening onto a covered walkway u-ing around the back of the house. Julia Hassrick stood by the open glass-paned doors holding a glass of wine. The gentle breeze ruffling against her light blue dress carried with it the scent of pine. She had the barest of looks for

48

Claiborne Payne as her hazel eyes flicked back to the conversation being carried on by Crissy and two young men attired in suits and eager smiles. Beyond the billiard table Mandy Payne threw her husband an anxious look, but held to where she sat talking to another of Crissy's suitors.

Trays holding glasses of wine reposed on one of the tables recently imported by Jason Hassrick from France, and a servant hovered behind the table. And taking all of this in from where he sat in a corner chair was Hassrick. At his elbow was a bottle of sour mash whiskey, the cane tucked in his lap, the questioning look for his son-in-law.

"You missed supper."

"Sorry, Jason, I just missed Risdale. But was fortunate enough to run into him at the Bodega."

"Can't see why you want to keep him on."

"We've acquired," he said patiently, "another stageline. In doing so we mustn't overlook the knowledge Orrin Risdale brings with him. He did a commendable job up here."

"Suppose so," came Jason Hassrick's grumpy response. He had on a smoking jacket and slippers on his feet. There were moments when all of his thoughts were on the old life back in Iowa. The meat packing business had seen him acquire a small fortune, but he had no regrets about selling out. For Deadwood and the stageline business were keeping him young, though he considered this damnable arthritis nothing more than a highfalutin word for gout, as this new doctor of his charged accordingly. Man's got money, someone's always after it, he intoned sourly to himself. He considered this husband of Mandy's in about the same light. But he wasn't one to condemn anyone until all the facts were in. "Any of you young sports play pool?"

"Daddy . . . really . . ."

"Now, Crissy," he said, struggling out of the deep-cushioned chair, "what the hell else can an old coot like me do?"

49

"Sir, I have played billiards," one of her suitors said hesitantly.

Carrington, he remembered, the son of a local banker. Julia Hassrick moved over to hover by her father who was limping over to the billiard table. He waved her away as a Negro servant brought Jason Hassrick a pool cue, which he laid on the table. "Name your poison, son."

"Er, sir, I'd be honored to engage you in a game of eight ball . . . ah, sir, and spot you a couple of balls . . ."

"I've got the gout, so's to speak, son, not senility of the mind. You rack 'em and I'll break; I'll take that spot say for five bucks a game."

"Daddy—"

"Splendid, sir."

Under his breath Jason Hassrick uttered, "Kind of stupid but got some spunk."

When the game began, Claiborne Payne requested to talk in private with Julia, and with some reluctance she went out to turn and face a man she felt had married not for love but merely for profit. Whenever Julia appeared in a room, heads turned. The long silky dress concealed slim legs and a figure the envy of most women in Deadwood. She had a springy step and a certain vibrancy which revealed itself in a sudden smile or a quick look flashing out of those hazel eyes. Tonight the flowing chestnut locks were twisted into a single braid of hair spilling over her right shoulder. Her mood had been pensive, but with the arrival of Claiborne Payne a lot of old suspicions had arisen.

"I notice you didn't have time for Mandy."

"But I will," he said lamely, and resentfully. "Look, Julia, despite what you think we're in love. But tonight, what's troubling me is, well, these robberies. I'm in Cheyenne, remember. I have to listen to these bankers when a gold shipment fails to arrive. And to our passengers when they pull in. What . . . what can we do about it?"

Over the rim of her glass, a speculative glimmer appeared in her eyes. All Claiborne had was his position as a junior partner in the stageline. And she resented him saying that only he had to answer for what was happening. People here owned that gold, and from what she had heard since taking a more active role in the running of the stageline, it wasn't just one or two outlaw gangs but seemingly a horde of them terrorizing the Black Hills. Beyond this were the Indian attacks. Perhaps, and she'd voiced this to her father, they should sell out and leave.

"Julia, I've lost good men to the gold fields. And so have you here in Deadwood. It boils down to us needing men like Orrin Risdale. Spoke to him; isn't interested in looking for gold. But he wants to stay here, and if we don't take him on, will look for work elsewhere around town."

"He has some experience, I suppose."

"He's presentable; would be a valuable addition to our company."

"So be it then. You're leaving tomorrow?"

"I owe Mandy some time. Perhaps the day after. And, Julia, thanks. I know we don't get along all that well. And I suppose it's my fault."

Passing her glass to a servant, Julia left the billiard room and headed up the curving staircase to find her bedroom. It was still early, around ten o'clock, but none of Crissy's young men interested her. There were a few men in town, some her age and others a little older, who'd come over to find out more about this Julia Hassrick. At twenty-four, an age when most women were married and had children, a restlessness stirred in Julia. There was Jason to consider, a man as stubborn as she, and starting to show his age. Perhaps she was being overprotective of her father. And if the Cheyenne-Deadwood Stageline Company did go under, they could still survive.

"Come off it, Julia," she murmured to her reflection in a dresser mirror, "you love the stageline as does dad . . ."

Her first view of rawboned Deadwood and the tree-gulched Black Hills had aroused in her a passion to become a part of this rugged life. The stageline had given her an outlet. Though she'd never told her father, to ride shotgun on a bucking Concord was one of her dreams. And there had been one or two men that had aroused an interest, but it had been the stageline and the difficulties of running it which had chased away any thoughts of becoming married.

"As for Claiborne, I just have this feeling about him," she confided to her reflection.

On a recent trip to Cheyenne she had been introduced to Cado Greer and a couple of other hard-eyed men. She added this to the list of things she mistrusted about the man married to her sister. Mostly, she berated herself for knuckling under to what her father had said, that if Mandy loved the man, let it go at that. Everyone had a past, and Julia Hassrick was coming to the conclusion that Claiborne Payne's might produce some surprises.

She lit a cigarillo, one of her secret vices, and strode to a window to take in the lights of Deadwood strung along the high walls of the gulch. This was her town. A sense of expectancy about what tomorrow would bring lifted Julia's spirits, a prophetic thought since tomorrow would see the arrival of Moss Hollabaugh.

Four

Moss Hollabaugh had in fact ridden into Deadwood that afternoon. There had been a moment of hesitation when he'd pulled over to allow passage for a freight wagon. From rimrock he took in the untidy mining town crowding Split-tail Gulch. He was astride a good horse and had some money. So perhaps it was time to cut back to Oregon and see his kin.

"But I've told Charlie Siringo otherwise."

As he'd discussed with Siringo, a job of this nature meant that he might have to operate outside the law. Now that the Western Stage Company had been bought out by this outfit belonging to Jason Hassrick, most of the employees would be kept on. But without question Moss knew that one or more of them had been tipping off these outlaws as to gold shipments. This was something he intended to discuss with Hassrick, who according to Pinkerton operative Siringo was having similar problems. Could it be he'd find a connection? With that possibility in mind, Moss Hollabaugh kneed his bronc onto the downsloping road.

He stood now on the Lee Street stairs looking up at the few large homes making up the posh Forest Hill section of Deadwood. Darkness had settled around Moss, and taking in Jason Hassrick's brick mansion, his eyes went to an upper window brightened from within. He could make out the vague outline of a woman smoking a cigarette. Earlier he had sauntered past the holdings of the Cheyenne-Deadwood Stageline Company. The main building, somewhat barnlike in shape, housed the main offices and where Concords came in to be loaded or in rainy weather to load passengers. In back of this were holding pens for the horses and some sheds and the tack house. A glance into the waiting room showed a few citizens buying tickets or shipping out small parcels, clerks behind the long counters, and a woman of unusual beauty. Perhaps she was the silhouette framed in the upper window.

Moss had come here hoping to have a few private words with Jason Hassrick. The lower, well-lit rooms of the mansion had given him pause, and with a last lingering glance at the upper window he swung around to survey Deadwood's long and crowded main drag. It was a narrow street where buildings huddled against one another, while further out it seemed the whole floor of the gulch was infested with motley buildings and tents.

Before all he did was overnight here, then climbed aboard a Concord the next morning to begin another perilous journey out of the Black Hills. Going out was worse, for as a general rule they would be carrying gold. Down on main street he held to the inner reaches of the boardwalk as a buggy splashed by. A late February thaw had struck into the Black Hills to bring up more fully the underlying stench of a place not having any place to dispose of its sewage. Summers you could hardly stand it down here in the gulch, which Moss supposed was why the locals drank so much. He drank, but sparingly, favoring the biting taste of whiskey. Everyplace he cast his eyes along the street there were saloons and dance halls, a sprinkling of theaters.

Perhaps, Moss debated, he should seek out a hotel room; it had been over a week since he'd slept in any kind of bed. But the incident down at the Snake Creek stage station was still fresh in his mind so that even if he did call it a day he wouldn't be able to sleep. He moved on at an ambling gait. A couple of whores crossing just upstreet spat out their cursing wrath when a horseman loped by splattering them with mud. Their anger followed Moss into the Bella Union, where he bellied up to the bar, with one boot in sawdust, and the other propped up on the brass railing. His request for whiskey caused the flopeared bardog to reach to the back bar for a bottle as Moss dropped some coin on the worn bar top.

On the way over from the batwings he'd taken in Wild Bill Hickok engrossed with others in a poker game, but it wasn't Hickok his eyes sought now but a palefaced man provoking in him a chord of remembrance, as did the other man seated at the table. He'd seen them recently, and not here in Deadwood.

He downed the first two fingers of whiskey in the shot glass, his first in over a week, and refilled the glass. Then he recalled seeing the pair of them hanging around Sidney. Yup, seems to be they were friends of Harry McGowen's. An' the pair of them have got all the earmarks of men looking to get some easy money, he reminded himself.

Hollabaugh took in that the two men were snaking occasional glances toward the gaming tables, and when he chanced to gaze that way his eyes squinted thoughtfully. One of the players at a poker table was Orrin Risdale. Maybe it was just coincidence Risdale being here, he pondered, but the feeling came it was more than that. He turned and caught the bartender's eye.

"You know those two men over there?"

"Don't know the big gent . . . but the other's a two-bit punk named Ace Taylor. Say, you've been in here before?"

"Once or twice."

"Yeah, you ride shotgun for that stagecoach line."

"Not any more as it's been sold."

"Heard that. Name's Smiley Blake."

"Hollabaugh."

"You hear about the killing? Over at the Cricket Saloon. When the boxing matches were going on. Found him there, just slumped at a table. Some gent named McGowen."

Moss straightened up to say, "Would that be Harry McGowen—"

"Yeah, his first name was Harry. Killer used a knife; done it when a fight was going on. Damned nervy to kill someone in a saloon full of witnesses."

"They know who did it?"

"So damned packed in there it could have been most anybody."

As the bartender moved to wait on someone else, Moss Hollabaugh let a grimace play across his face. The killing of Harry McGowen was a case of cold-blooded murder. And he knew it was tied in with the killings and robberies that had been plaguing the Western Stage Company. He stole another glance at Ace Taylor's table, and beyond to Risdale dealing out cards to the other poker players. Once in a while upon their arrival at the stagecoach office he would get a glimpse of Orrin Risdale barking out orders to his clerks as the man disdained coming out to greet the passengers. Or they would see Risdale in some downtown gaming joint, a man aloof from the drivers and men riding shotgun for the same stagecoach company.

Just because a man's got highfalutin notions as to who his friends are doesn't mean he was doing something crooked.

But it was there, as it had been when Moss Hollabaugh was a Pinkerton, an instinct telling him that Orrin Risdale had been more than the manager of the stageline office here in Deadwood. Backing up his feelings were the presence of Ace Taylor and his table companion. And what had he heard not too long ago about Risdale putting up one of those fashionable mansions, and this on a salary not much larger than Moss was drawing as he rode shotgun.

"I'd bet the horse Charlie Siringo loaned me that our Mr. Risdale has a sizable bank account to boot," he predicted.

Moss left the saloon, letting the cooling air of night chase away his simmering anger. What it came down to was that the stageline company was no longer his concern as it had been sold. Perhaps this wouldn't be the case after he'd gotten together with the bossman of the Cheyenne to Deadwood stageline company. He'd keep that promise to Charlie Siringo but reserve for the future a determination to find out the secrets of Orrin Risdale.

"Owe those who got killed that much . . . and maybe a heap more," he told the empty streets.

Every working morning Jason Hassrick would suffer the indignity of having to get into a carriage and be driven to his place of business. Before there'd been the enjoyment of taking the front staircase down to main street where oftentimes he would duck into a cafe and discuss the latest happenings with his fellow businessmen. The cane was another indignity. This morning his driver was Dee Ripley, about the best checker player around and the man in charge of repairing the Concords, and like some, a former gold miner.

"This morning weather will sure raise hell with the roads."

"That it will, Mr. Hassrick. How you feeling this morning?" A light touch of his whip brought the horse onto the narrow pathway running behind the house.

Grumpily he replied, "This new specialist has me rubbing on something called Barker's bone and nerve liniment every damned morning. Just don't come down with arthritis, Dee, as it's a crippler. Did those spare parts come in?"

"Not yet."

"Should have known better than to ship them through the mails. But shipping in anything is a problem because of these damnable road agents."

"Now don't go to fretting about road agents again, Mr. Hassrick. As I hear the army is sending in more soldiers." Dee Ripley knew that under the gruff exterior was a man deeply concerned about his employees, be it a lonely agent out at a stage station or those riding the Concords from here to Cheyenne. Another gauge of Hassrick's character was of his coming out to jaw in the same salty language thrown about by the hired help. Once out by the holding pens the man he worked for and shotgun Wacey Rydell and Shady Glover, one of the drivers, were heating up the air with some choice words when that daughter of Hassrick's came storming out to scatter everyone away. He liked Julia Hassrick, too, but felt she still had a ways to go to compare to her pa.

"More soldiers isn't the answer. Anyway, Dee, they should be out chasing after those Indians of Crazy Horse's."

"That's right, Mr. Hassrick, it's rumored Crazy Horse has been seen in the Black Hills."

"Guess rightfully this place belongs to the Sioux." He reached for his cane as Ripley brought the carriage in close to a back door. Jason Hassrick thought it another indignity locals seeing him struggling to get out of this carriage. He chased away the twinge of pain with a fixed smile when he dismounted, and stood there for a moment after the carriage had rolled away.

Had it been over a month ago that he'd contacted the Pinkerton Agency? Their response had been a letter back to him, detailing the imminent arrival of one of their operatives. Would this be enough, he pondered, at least it would be a start in an attempt to get to the bottom of this baffling mystery. They had removed the passenger seats on some Concords and put in reinforcing holding metal strongboxes. Stronger doors had been put on with armed guards peering out of gun slots, and although army patrols were out on the main stagecoach road, the robberies continued. A couple of times Hassrick had overseen the filling of the strongbox in a Concord with rocks instead of gold bullion, but strangely enough these stagecoaches got through to Cheyenne.

With more and more gold being found in the Black Hills, it had been necessary to hire more employees to handle all of the gold being shipped out. There were over thirty people working for his stageline here in Deadwood, not counting the men riding the stages. There were also the different banks entrusting him with their gold bullion. "A man," he said as he went inside, "can accuse most anybody of selling out to these road agents." The short passageway brought Hassrick into his office.

The front door stood ajar letting him view a few clerks out in the bullpen offices and beyond that the counters where customers were milling about. Doffing his outer coat, Jason Hassrick limped past his desk and pulled open a cabinet door to lift out a bottle of brandy and a tall glass. The worry of all that was happening had been handled a little easier by his partaking of a couple of fingers of the amber liquid. Julia knew the bottle was there, but thus far had refrained from making an issue of it. She'd be in soon, a notion he was coming to grips with.

"Handy to have around . . . but wish she'd find a man," he grumbled. He became aware then of another's presence, felt a tremor of unease when he half-turned to look at the back office door to take in a man shadowed by the dark entryway.

"Sorry to intrude, Mr. Hassrick."

"You generally buy a ticket up front," he said edgily. "Well, spit it out, young man?"

"Charlie Siringo sent me up here."

"The Pinkerton." With an appraising eye for Moss Hollabaugh entering his office, Jason Hassrick limped up to close the front door. Coming back to step around his cluttered desk, he gestured at a chair, and reached over to find a dusty glass in the cabinet door. "I expect you're used to a little dust."

"That . . . and some saddle sores. I'm Moss Hollabaugh. Just a few days ago I rode shotgun for that Western outfit."

"That's interesting as they sold out to me. What did you do before that?" Placing the bottle of brandy and the glasses on his desk, Hassrick sought the padded swivel chair, the cane he let clatter into a nearby wastebasket.

"Scouted for the army . . . and worked for the Pinkertons, too."

"I expect Siringo told you what I'm up against —"

"He did, sir. That only him and you are to know why I'm here."

He passed a glass to Moss. "Even my junior partner won't know about this, Mr. Hollabaugh. Nor have I told Julia; my daughter works here too."

"As Siringo detailed it to me it could be some of your employees tipping these outlaws off to gold shipments going out of here."

"In a nutshell that's it, Hollabaugh. But I won't rule out some of the banks. A man no matter how honest he is can do funny things when he's running his eyes over a lot of gold bars. We ship out damned near two hundred thousand dollars worth at a crack. Got outriders out there, too, accompanying those Concords. Sometimes it's the Indians hitting us. So I pay my hired hands hazardous duty pay, as the army calls it."

The brandy brought a warm glow into Moss's belly, while some of his hesitance at coming in here went away the more he studied the owner of the stageline. He'd decided here was a man of unwavering principle; the eyes told him that and the firm thrust to Jason Harrick's jaw. He took another drink before placing the glass on the desk top. "A man got killed a few days ago, here in Deadwood. Harry McGowen worked for the Western stageline down in Sidney. He could have been let go, sir."

"If this McGowen was brandishing gold here in Deadwood at any of these saloons he was a damned fool. What do you think, Hollabaugh, that he might have been mixed up in other things?"

"Can't rightly say. We were hit damned hard down there, men getting killed, and just maybe I was glad to get out

60

alive. You intend keeping that stageline going?"

"If I don't others will."

"That's a fact as a lot are still hitting up here from the main Union Pacific line. Gold fever is more a curse than anything."

"Getting back to those Indians, the Sioux. I hear rumors that their big chief Crazy Horse has been seen in the Hills. A lot of newspapers tell of how Crazy Horse is playing hell with the cavalry out in Wyoming and further north. A ghost they call him."

"Yes," Moss Hollabaugh said quietly, "he's all of that and more —"

"That mean you've dealt with Crazy Horse before?"

"Back some time ago. Up near Powder River." He let it go at that, as into his mind's eye there appeared a vivid image of the strange man of the Oglala, and Crazy Horse's spoken words of them encountering one another again. Well, here he was in the Black Hills, and it just could come to happen. "Scouting for the army you see a lot of Indians."

"Hollabaugh, you look solid enough to me," he said gruffly. "I'll hire you on to ride shotgun; same's you did before. What I'm thinking is you could find a way to get in good with these road agents . . . whilst I try to get to the bottom of things at the home office. It'll probably be slow going and kind of dangerous, but unless you've got something else to offer . . ."

Moss watched as Hassrick scribbled something on a sheet of paper, which he folded and passed across the desk. Unfolding the paper, Moss glanced at it and said, "Report to Pat Grady. Good enough."

"Any weapons you want just purchase them and bill me, Hollabaugh. I don't know what kind of deal you've got worked out with the Pinkertons, moneywise. Here you'll draw wages same as the others. But commencing this morning I'm setting aside some money for you. If you've got any kin to send it to in case this doesn't work out let me know."

"Didn't expect anything extra, Mr. Hassrick." Moss glanced over his shoulder at the door being pushed inward, and rose when a young woman came striding in.

"Oh, I'm sorry I barged in like this," she apologized.

"Just taking on another shotgun. My daughter, Julia; headstrong like her ma was."

Moss formed a tentative smile as he suddenly discovered there was something about Julia Hassrick that he liked, though those hazel eyes of Julia's contained a probing frostiness. This morning she had on a dark green dress buttoned to the neck and long-sleeved, and even so it revealed her full figure. He felt kind of awkward standing there with both hands hooked around his Stetson, and he stammered, "My pleasure, Miss Julia. I'm—"

"Father, when you're alone." Then she was gone.

Her departure brought from Jason Hassrick a sort of chuckling laughter. Picking up the bottle of brandy, he replaced the cork as he said, "I guess she doesn't cotton to cowboys. Likes her men meek and kind of mousey."

"Your daughter is very pretty."

"Got three of them, Mr. Hollabaugh. Wish there'd been a son. As it is, guess I'm satisfied with the way all of them turned out. And I guess that about concludes our business. Pat Grady will treat you square." With an effort he pushed up from behind the desk and came around it to grasp Moss's hand. "Maybe working together we can get to the bottom of this, son. My daughter had you sort of buffaloed there, Hollabaugh. But pay her no mind."

"Charlie Siringo named some of the outlaw gangs hanging out in the Black Hills. Some of them come in here to gamble. Anyway, Mr. Hassrick, I know how it feels to be done an injustice. That maybe one of your employees has sold you out. I tried helping a man once, an Oglala by the way. I'll keep in touch."

When Moss left it was through the front office door to pass by Julia Hassrick poring over an account book.

Around them other clerks were working and there were a few customers at the front counters. Moss's shadow falling over her desk lifted Julia's eyes.

"Is there something?"

"They didn't have pretty women like you back in Oregon," he smiled. "But frowning like that causes wrinkles I've heard." He slipped away to let Julia's retort die in her throat.

Outside with the front porch shielding him from bright morning sunlight, Moss stared upstreet at a man approaching the stagecoach office. He doubted that Orrin Risdale would recognize him, and it came to Moss that he hadn't told Jason Hassrick his suspicions about the man. But Moss Hollabaugh would have had he known that Risdale had just been hired as a bookkeeper. Then he passed around the front wall to cut back toward the activity around the holding pens and the big sheds where the Concords were stored.

Pat Grady turned out to be a tall, loose-limbed man with ruddy features and a quick smile, and there were a couple of men Moss had run into around town.

"Howdy, Wacey," said Moss. "Guess I'll be riding shotgun same's you. And I believe you're Shady Glover."

"Was when I got up this morning."

To which Wacey Rydell said cheerily, "Yup, recalls his name awright . . . but there's some days he plumb forgets the route to Cheyenne. How you been, Moss? Yeah, heard you boys have been troubled by road agents down thataway, too."

"Moss," cut in ramrod Pat Grady, "is there anything you'll need in the way of guns?"

"Mine'll do nicely, Mr. Grady. Just work me into your schedule, I reckon."

"That'll be on tomorrow's run, Moss. You as shotgun and Gator Gruwell doing the driving."

Moss hung around for a while to engage in further small talk and to work off the uneasy edge he'd picked up on the trail. Ever since leaving Oregon it seemed trouble had been dogging his heels. A less stubborn man would have cleared out of these parts. Charlie Siringo had played a small part in fetching him back up here, and now that he was, there was the sure knowledge in him about his running into Crazy Horse.

Some of those Teton Lakotas were visionaries, he mused silently. There was an off-chance of his running into Crazy Horse out there, and an even slimmer chance that the great chief of the Oglala could tell him where to find those outlaws behind all of these robberies.

At least Crazy Horse will tell me the truth of things . . . as I figure he owes me something . . .

Five

In late February, the Moon of the Dark Red Calves, a Chinook came out of the northwest to bring about snow melt as well as some traders with the white man's newspapers and their stories. From these the Teton Lakota learned that it wasn't only the Indian having to endure this harsh winter. Of greater concern to Crazy Horse were other stories in these newspapers telling that the yellow-haired soldier, Custer, was preparing wagons and soldiers for a spring expedition into the Black Hills.

"Ahh-h, they go to *Pa Sapa!*"

"Yes," another Oglala said angrily, "To *Pa Sapa* . . . into our sacred hills."

Over a week ago Crazy Horse and other Oglala had left the winter encampment on the Little Big Horn to head east into land claimed by the Crow. With the departure of the hunting party the camp had been moved, the signs on the buffalo heads left behind pointing toward the Tongue. The hunting party led by Crazy Horse searched but couldn't find any buffalo, though they scattered a Crow hunting camp. The following day a herd of elk was discovered, with the Oglala killing five bulls before the herd scattered away. Now, on their way back, and with the temperature plummeting, a sense of foreboding began to grip Crazy Horse.

"There . . . the bluffs along the Tongue . . ."

"Below, I see the horse herd."

"But no one comes out to greet us."

Passing through a shallow draw their horses kicked up swirling snow. The wind was stronger, a cold-edged knife of this long winter. They came upon the Tongue to ride anxiously across the narrow expanse of frozen river, and with the camp opening up to the returning hunters. Blue smoke hung along the bluffs below which the tepees were spread out. In the summer dogs would be coming out to yap at them, but the dogs had been killed and eaten and some horses. For a moment Crazy Horse feared the camp had been attacked by the Pawnee or Crow, and then he saw something that chilled his blood. First one woman than another appeared, and still more of his people, their hair loose and cut off, the women with dried blood on their gashed arms and legs.

The dread of what this meant rode with Crazy Horse toward his large tepee, where his wife, Black Shawl, lifted the flap aside and came outside. Following behind were his father, Worm, the aging Oglala bringing out Little Hawk, the only son of Crazy Horse. Worm stepped past the woman and came to place a sorrowful hand on his son's forearm.

"When the traders left us up along the Little Big Horn, my son, they left behind the white man's coughing choke."

Then Crazy Horse knew, and a sob burst out of his throat, and he looked fully at his wife and the tears and the pain twisting up her face, but still he had to ask. "Our . . . daughter . . ."

"Yes, my husband . . . our daughter, They Are Afraid of Her—"

"Why?"

"The white men, my son, are as full of disease as their words. Either can kill the Indian." Worm went on to tell of how Crazy Horse's daughter had passed away shortly before they'd broken camp up at the Little Big Horn, and of the place where they left They Are Afraid of Her.

That night it began snowing again, a halfhearted storm that rode along the river southeasterly. The new snowfall was still coming down to strike at Crazy Horse leaving the encampment before sunup. But this time he was mounted on his finest warhorse and leaving so quietly that not even those guarding the horse herd picked out the lonely rider heading to the north and into the land of the Crow.

The full bitterness of this new tragedy Crazy Horse let enter his heart. Later that night the storm passed away but not the Oglala's deep well of anger. He seemed immune to the cold of this wintry day and of the wind buffeting and shrieking around him. The spotted pony stepped lightly on the prairie dusted with snow. In the afternoon he found the place of trees as described to him by Worm. Amongst the trees on a scaffold lay a small red bundle.

Bitterly he knew there rested his daughter, for on the posts hung the playthings she had loved, a rattle of antelope hoofs, a willow hoop, and a deerskin doll. Just as familiar to Crazy Horse was the beaded design on the cradleboard, which was also woven into her dresses, a design that came from Black Shawl's family.

The sight of these things brought Crazy Horse out of the saddle. He had to lean against the scaffold as the sorrow locked in his heart brought a great weakness to his limbs. He let the tears spill unashamedly.

Although Crazy Horse had returned to his people, he could not cast away thoughts of his daughter. March came, and the warming winds that caused a lot of snow melt, and during this time the strange man of the Oglala sought the solitude offered only by the plains. Every return to the encampment brought more news of not only the soldiers led by Custer striking into the Black Hills but of others going there in search of gold. Gripped by a bitter anger over this, Crazy Horse decided on a rainy day in late March that he would take a look at the Thieves' Road, a route created by Custer on his southward passage into the Black Hills.

On the morning of his departure some of the older chiefs tried to talk Crazy Horse out of going alone, but he would have none of this. Perhaps along the way, he told them, he would build a sweat lodge. Perhaps a vision would come to him as to how to deal with these intruders of the sacred *Pa Sapa*.

"Ahh-h, gold! It brings a craziness to these white men. Remember back when the Black Robe, De Smet, told us to bury the shining stones deep in the earth . . ."

"What about the people of Red Cloud . . ."

"Red Cloud. The treaty he made with the army is no good . . . for they want not only *Pa Sapa* but all of our lands . . ." Crazy Horse sprang lithely onto the back of his war pony. "Already those Mandan Scouts of Custer's have killed Old Stabber and wounded Slow Bull, the son-in-law of Red Cloud. And Black Elk's camp near the Black Hills was attacked by soldiers of Long Hair."

Crazy Horse's moccasins jabbing into the flanks of his spotted pony brought it cantering away from the small gathering of Oglala. What angered him most of all was that Long Hair came into the Black Hills and then left without encountering any resistance from the Teton Lakota. Also of harsh reality to Crazy Horse was that Long Hair's wagons were full of guns and ammunition.

But there will come a time for vengeance, he promised.

He was a ghost rider passing along the northern fringes of the Black Hills. In the midst of a spring snowfall he held under some pine trees to take in a wagon train passing under the high brow of Bear Butte and on the wide trail left by the Custer expedition. It is right to call it Thieves' Road, came Crazy Horse's bitter musing. He counted twenty wagons strung out in a ragged line, and heavily laden so that their iron wheels sank into ground softened with the coming of spring.

And in the sacred reaches of *Pa Sapa* settlements, havens for these thieving gold miners had sprung up. He knew of this, and of the two stagelines, one coming up through the sand hills of Nebraska, the other a knife cutting through the heart of Teton Lakota land until it reached Cheyenne.

How easily it would be to notch an arrow and kill one of these outriders slumped so carelessly in their saddles. For they were cutting past the site of the great Teton council, the thought of it now bringing Crazy Horse back to a more happier time. Through eyes blinking away falling snowflakes he could make out the big double lodge of painted skins just at the base of Bear Butte, this wide verdant plain below the dark-treed heights of *Pa Sapa* filled with the many tribes of the Teton Lakota—Minneconjou, No Bows, Oglala, Brule, Two Kettles, Blackfoot and Hunkpapa—all in the sacred circle. This was when he was young and known among the Oglala as Curly, but he'd embraced his memory with such names as old Four Horns of the Hunkpapa and that of Sitting Bull. And other chiefs, Long Mandan and Man Afraid and Lone Horn and Red Cloud. And wistfully he recalled the presence here also of seven-foot Touch the Clouds; dead now at the hands of the white men.

"What good are memories," hissed Crazy Horse as the last of the wagons vanished into the curtain of falling snow, and the lonely Oglala pressed on.

He did not keep heading for Bear Butte but began angling in toward the beckoning heights. Many of his ancestors were buried here, and scarcely for a moment it came to Crazy Horse that they were calling out to him in the shrilling cacophony of wind-driven snow. Perhaps this was true, he surmised, since their spirits had been disturbed by these white intruders. Many times in the past he'd been a part of hunting parties coming in seeking deer and bear in the hills, and sometimes buffalo called *Pa Sapa* their sanctuary. He knew

69

better than the workings of his mighty war bow the lay of the Black Hills, where there was water, and the box canyons and the many caves where an Oglala could make camp.

On the long and hazardous journey eastward across what the whites now called Wyoming Territory he had thought it all out. He must make war against these white intruders. But not with his rifle as it was a weapon taken from the hands of a white man he'd killed. He would kill silently with his bow and arrows and war club. His venging war path would take him from one end of *Pa Sapa* to the other, so that the terror of these killings would be spoken of with fear by every white man that comes here to look for gold.

My daughter . . . only then shall your spirit rest in peace.

Only after several days spent scouting out the places where the white men were looking for gold did Crazy Horse come to realize how many of these intruders had poured into the Black Hills. Crazy Horse spent that first night just to the southwest of Bear Butte in a cave snugged deep in a ravine. The next day with snow still tumbling out of a vague grey sky, he went boldly along the wagon road which eventually gave him from Rimrock a long look at Deadwood. He'd been surprised at the number of buildings that had sprung up seemingly overnight, and with his bitterness a lump sprang up in his throat. Then he passed on to head deeper into the hills to view other small settlements where chimney smoke bespoiled the holy sky above the hills. The creeks seemed choked with miners braving the chilly waters in search of the shining rocks.

One white man had stolen up onto another panning for gold in a swift-flowing creek, and after plunging a knife into the miner's back, had pawed clumsily and greedily through the dead miner's pocket until a triumphant smile showed as the killer found a small pouch filled with nuggets.

"They even kill one another for the shining rocks," he'd

muttered at the time. "Tomorrow . . . then the terror begins . . ."

Having scouted out deep ravines where the white intruders feared to go, Crazy Horse had picked out some caves high on a bluff screened by pine trees. From here he could see parts of the stagecoach road and there were glimpses of creeks. Quickly the snow was melting away to bring the murmurous sound of water running downslope. The birds of spring had returned to add their harmonious voices to a place loved by the Oglala. He'd chosen his hidden camp wisely as there were several escape routes, but through a bitter smile Crazy Horse knew it was the white thieves who should seek to escape the killing bite of his war club and arrows.

In the morning in an elaborate but short ceremony he put on his war paint. In a broken piece of mirror found in a wagon ravaged by his Oglala braves, Crazy Horse took a final look at his painted countenance. Vermillion paint touched against the powder-blackened scar at the corner of his nose, with the other cheek adorned with a matching red stripe. His mood was as black as the paint covering his forehead and encircling his glowing eyes. When he rose, it was to put out the smokeless campfire. Since it was a warm day Crazy Horse had left his robe in the cave. Mounting the spotted pony, he brought his eyes tracking distantly to a creek where he knew the thieves were searching for the shining metal. Some of them had been bold enough to put up makeshift cabins, curling smoke rising into the early morning sky marking a cabin site.

A good day to die.

Micah Gentry figured that at his age most men were stuck wasting their lives in a rocking chair. But with the recent passing of his wife, Gentry had sold his Indiana holdings and brought his two sons out here to the Black Hills. The

71

claim staked by the Gentrys lay in Blacktail Gulch, and so far it looked promising. Further downstream other miners had staked claims, which set well with the elder Gentry since the rugged hill country hereabouts was a haven for outlaws and roving bands of Indians.

The Gentrys' mining claim ran three hundred feet up and down the creek and from rimrock to rimrock. On it they had put up a crude cabin, and had one horse grazing on short grass in an attached corral. Below a few yards the rocker they'd made to get at the gold was dug into a stretch of gravelly bank, the creek water clear and running around numerous rocks.

The sons of Micah Gentry were in their thirties, one a former drayman, the other, Dake, a ne'er-do-well and not all that ambitious when it came his turn to wade out into the cold creek water and shovel bottom sand into the rocker.

Coming outside for the first time that morning, Micah Gentry adjusted his suspenders while peering upstream. One thing about the hills, he'd found out, there didn't seem to be any mosquitos. But up here it could snow one day, be blazing hot the next. And the thick stands of trees choking the gulches hindered anyone trying for the settlement. He went on gimpy knees down the short pathway to the creek and crouched to scoop up cold water and splash it against his bearded face. Patches of fog clung to the banks and seemed to dance further out on the creek, and higher up on the gulch wall sunlight touched rimrock.

"Gonna be a warm one," he said wearily, as he pushed up and stepped over to take a gander at the rocker box. Just fetching his two sons out here had been done at considerable cost. Eating a lot deeper into his savings was what he'd shelled out over at Custer for grub and mining equipment. Burt had more than pulled his weight where his other son, Dake, seemed to be more interested in sucking on a whiskey bottle than mining for gold. Takes after his ma's kin, Gentry rationalized.

72

He took out a grimy handkerchief and dabbed water from his beard as he took in the first tendrils of chimney smoke and noticed through the open cabin door Burt Gentry putting slab bacon in a frying pan. Beans and bacon and sourdough bread and honey when they had it, staples that would keep a man alive but sure as hell whet his appetite for better fare. Just a little longer, he figured, and there'd be enough to grubstake him through old age.

"Burt," he called out, "roust that lazy brother of yourn . . . and what about some coffee . . ."

"There ain't all that much coffee left, Pa."

"Means another hard ride to Custer. Maybe tomorrow, or the day after. This time we'll leave Dake behind to watch things."

"Dake sure as hell won't like that."

"I don't give a hoot in hell what Dake likes. Just roust him." Snapping irritably at a suspender strap, Micah Gentry turned to head back to the cabin. Then, his eyes flickering in puzzlement, he heard a hissing sound an instant before a feathered arrow pierced into his back. The handkerchief fluttering out of a shocked hand, he stumbled forward, and then dropped to his knees. A hand grasped his hair to pull his head back and choked off Micah Gentry's cry for help; the knife held by the Oglala Crazy Horse darted around to slice across the throat.

Quickly he shoved the dead man away to slip up the gravelly path. He ducked in close to the open door and sheathed his knife. In the other hand Crazy Horse held his bow. But now he reached to his waist for his war club, held there as someone in the cabin spoke.

"Dake, let's move it. It seems every damned mornin' I get stuck with fixin' somethin' to eat."

"Yeah . . . yeah," came a vague response.

Easing forward, Crazy Horse gazed inside to espy one man bent over by a crude stone fireplace where flames crackled around a blackened coffee pot and a black frying pan set

73

on burning chunks of wood. The scent of frying bacon drifted out to him, and from downstream came the haunting cry of a loon. His attention flicked to movement on a lower bunk and the man stretched out there, clad in red flannel underwear, the bare feet hanging over the end of the bunk.

"Well, dammit, Dake, chow's about ready . . ."

The one in the bunk responded by pulling a thin blanket over his face and shoulders, and with this a signal to Crazy Horse to ease on moccasins over the threshold. In two strides he was behind the one by the fireplace. "Yeah, yeah, Pa," muttered Burt Gentry without bothering to look, "coffee's done perking."

The eyes of Crazy Horse blazed with contempt and terrible anger, he brought the war club down with all his strength to have it penetrate deep into the white man's skull. Without bothering to pull the war club out of the man's crushed skull, he sprang toward the double bunks as his left hand sought the knife at his belt.

"Burt?" Dake Gentry flailed the blanket away from his face. The sleep left his disbelieving eyes even as the scream tearing out of his mouth wailed through the open cabin door. "No . . . noooo . . ." Too late he tried reaching to block the arm of the Oglala bringing the knife toward his chest. The blade plunged in, was ripped out by Crazy Horse, who thrust it in again . . . and again.

Then he used his knife to tear away the scalp lock of the man in the red flannel underwear, did likewise to the other dead man. Contemptuously he cast the bloody scalp locks into the fireplace. He would have kept them had they been those of a Crow or Pawnee. Spinning toward the doorway, he held there while looking creekward, took in the flapping wings of a pair of mallards just dropping onto the watery surface, and went back to step over the dead man slumped by the fireplace. The thick slabs of bacon tasted as good as they smelled, and they went down hot and greasy. He used his fingers to scoop out some of the beans heating in an open

74

can, placed them on his tongue only to spit the beans away with a displeased grimace.

Not even the Crow would eat them, he decided.

The rifle Crazy Horse had left back at his camp was an old Henry, and he could scarcely believe his good fortune when he noticed the repeating rifle leaning on the wall by the table. Slipping the bow over his shoulder so that it rested against his back, he went over and picked up the rifle. He liked the way the lever worked, ran an admiring hand along the blue-steeled barrel, grunted out an *hoye* of approval as he spotted the boxes of shells perched on a leather-bound trunk.

He went outside to find the sun just clearing the gulch wall; his long strides carried him past the dead white man and downstream to find his war pony. In the afternoon of that same day he killed another of those seeking the shining stones just outside the settlement of Custer.

Thereafter the days passed quickly for the strange man of the Oglala as he roamed throughout the sacred *Pa Sapa* leaving here and there men killed at his venging hands. And as Crazy Horse had spoken before, the terror of what was happening carried to all of the settlements in the Black Hills. But much to his dismay the white men still kept coming.

"Ey-ee," he cried out plaintively one day, "Nothing seems to stop these thieves from seeking the shining stones. They even kill one another in search of it. And though I kill many of them . . . I still have this anger . . ."

Six

They pulled out of the Chugwater stage station sometime in the afternoon on the northward leg of their run to Deadwood. The trip to Cheyenne a week ago had been un eventful. Along the way driver Gator Gruwell had pointed out possible ambush points to his new seat companion. Though nothing had happened, both Gruwell and Moss Hollabaugh welcomed that first glimpse of Cheyenne spread out on a wide plain.

Clinging to the top of the big Concord were three men anxious to reach the Black Hills and a lot of luggage was tied on top and to the back of the coach. Seven more passengers were packed inside the coach, still the horses had no difficulty in keeping at a fast trot on a wide trail scarred by wheel ruts. Still touching the limits of their vision westward was the Laramie range, purpled by haze and which they lost sight of when the trail passed through low spots. Closer in were red-tinted buttes and deep gorges choked with brush, with gaps of prairie opening up before them.

As Gator Gruwell had mentioned before, the plains banditos held further east along the Black Hills along with the Indians. Moss was vigilantly keeping his eyes peeled to the terrain around them, and he had the Henry propped between his knees. The sun struck at their backs to throw long shadows ahead of their bouncing coach. The wind was there, swirling at times so that dust devils lifted impishly.

"According to what you told me, Gator, a lot more outlaws are showing up out here."

"Moreso than what you had in Nebraska I expect." He'd shucked his coat to show long arms on a lanky frame, the cuffs of his woolen shirt not quite covering knobby wrists. Gruwell had a horsey face, the skin wind-beaten, and one eye kind of gaping because part of the upper lid had been torn away. The brim of his hat which was stained with sweat was pinned up and strands of dark hair came over his forehead. A repeating rifle was wedged behind him in the seat. "Doubt if they'll bother us on the return trip, but then again . . ."

Moss smiled at Gruwell rolling his eyes, and said, "That hog ranch . . . the Six Mile station . . . kind of an unsavory place."

"Attracts all kinds of scum," agreed Gruwell. "Owned by Adolf Cuny, though he's never around much. Too bad we can't skip the place. As there's been some killings there."

The passage of two hours found Gator Gruwell sawing at the reins as he brought his horses onto the final approaches to the Hutton Ranch stage station. They were still a considerable distance from the Black Hills, just a vague streak of black lining the eastern horizon. Here they held up to give the horses a breather, and their passengers time to dismount and walk about.

While Gruwell tended to watering the horses, Moss wandered off to take his ease underneath a cottonwood. The long journey to Cheyenne had brought them through at least twenty stage stations, and had consumed the better part of a week. Once they'd cleared the Black hills it had been all prairie on a stageline road in some places almost a quarter of a mile wide. It was in Cheyenne that he first laid eyes upon Claiborne Payne, the son-in-law of Jason Hassrick. Upon pulling up before the stageline office, Payne had come out with a sprinkling of others. There'd been a woman with

Claiborne Payne who bore a striking resemblance to Julia Hassrick, whom he'd seen so briefly back at Deadwood. Then he recalled this was Mandy, one of Jason Hassrick's daughters. With the departure of their passengers Moss had held to the seat as Gator Gruwell brought the coach around to the barns. Here they'd encountered Cado Greer, who in Moss's opinion hadn't been all that friendly. Some others working amongst the barns and corrals also had the markings of hardcases.

Pondering on this now, Moss got to thinking that perhaps he held everyone working for the stageline under suspicion. There was a lot of gold being shipped out by Jason Hassrick's stageline company, more than enough to tempt even the most honest of men. There was a curse called gold fever that could make a man take a bribe or even think of holding up a stagecoach. Then a man forgot about family or his good name or the future consequences of his actions.

On the westward run out of Deadwood he'd sounded out Gator Gruwell about the other drivers and men hired to help guard gold shipments. Somewhere along the way they'd gotten to talking about Claiborne Payne. Kind of standoffish, Gator had remarked. After getting a glimpse of Payne over at Cheyenne, Moss had deeper misgivings about the man; like when you spotted what you mistook to be a bullsnake sunning itself on a rock only it turned out to be a sidewinder. One of their passengers had been a woman and her husband, she was quite comely with chestnut hair spilling below her bonnet. Despite the presence of his own wife, Claiborne Payne had bold eyes for the other woman. But Payne's being a womanizer didn't hold that he had anything to do with these robberies plaguing the stageline. Moss's conclusion was that it had to be someone working out of the Deadwood office. Or if more than one person was involved, probably someone riding the stagecoaches as shotgun or driver.

Just thinking of Deadwood again after being away for a few days brought a vague picture of Julia Hassrick, and a

78

smile tugged at Moss's lips. On the way out she'd been there, too, sort of clinging to his thoughts. What was there about her? Maybe that sassy air of hers? Whatever the reason, Moss had to admit she'd gotten to him. Women as pretty as Julia and of that caliber were as scarce as a hot meal out here.

Another mystery worth looking into.

Back more than ten miles lay the Eagle Nest stage station. It was back there they'd been told of some Teton Lakota being on the prowl, word of this having been brought to the stage station by a plainsman passing through. The only buildings at Eagle Nest were the small station building and one shed and the corrals; it wasn't a regular overnight stopping place. Gruwell, after getting fresh horses hitched to his Concord, struck out northeasterly.

"Think we should tell our passengers about those hostile Indians?"

"No need to alarm them, Gator." Moss grimaced at the lowering sun piercing in from the west as he glanced at his seat companion. It could be that those hostiles were after bigger prey than a lonely stagecoach. Here the trail narrowed to strike up between rocky ground, the horses laboring along at a walk. On the downslope they picked up into a canter, and Moss gained a closer view of the North Platte River still some distance away.

Up ahead squatting by the river lay a place that Moss was concerned about, the hog ranch owned by Adolf Cuny and one of the stage stations. They'd pull in there to spend the night. On the Cheyenne leg of their journey some of the passengers had been fleeced in a crooked poker game, and then there were the women hanging out at the hog ranch.

"Think those whores will still be at Cuny's?"

Gator Gruwell said under a winking eye, "You got any particular one in mind?"

"Expect they've got a right to make a living. Just thinking on what you said before about them consorting with outlaws."

"Those whores will consort with anyone willing to pay for it. But, yup, Moss, outlaws do drop in at Cuny's."

"As long as it's only to wet their whistles I don't object, Gator. One of them whores you pointed out to me —"

"You mean Pawnee Liz. There's rumors she rode with that Sam Bass bunch, and lately, a gang headed up by Little Reddy from Texas. Now there's a cold-blooded son of a gun. Little Reddy sure likes to use that gun of his. He rode with that Bass gang, too, so I reckon that's how he come to know Pawnee Liz. Despite them cold eyes she's kind of pretty."

"Still think she's involved with Little Reddy?"

"Don't rightly know, Moss. But don't leave your wallet lying around at Cuny's place. Awright" — Gruwell lashed out with the ends of his reins — "mosey up now as there's just them trees between us and suppering."

A string of bad luck began for Spade DeLong when he'd first run into that army scout up near Powder River. At the time DeLong and some other Big Horners had been chasing after an Oglala, only to have the Oglala rescued by the same man he'd seen scarcely two weeks ago.

"Still can't believe that damned Hollabaugh has taken to honest work."

About a half month ago Spade DeLong had been hanging out at Adolf Cuny's hog ranch, down to his last few dollars, and brooding over what to do next. Long before this DeLong and a lot of others had drifted away from the Big Horns since gold up in those mountains was more a rumor than fact. He was just about to head into Colorado when word came that gold had been discovered in the Black Hills. So along with many others DeLong headed up there. But not having any money to stake himself to mining gear, hardcase

Spade DeLong turned to petty crime, and then to holding up miners coming in with gold dust. But being a lone gunman proved to be too dangerous a venture, and his last attempt at holding up a miner found him dodging rifle bullets and an army patrol that had chanced by.

Somehow he made his way out of the Black Hills and southwesterly to Cuny's hog ranch. Over beers he got chummy with one of the bar dogs working in Cuny's big rambling hog ranch. He also took up temporary residence in an abandoned log cabin snugged further west along the North Platte. But it was in the dingy barroom that DeLong spent most of his time. Here there were whores a'plenty and hardcases and a lot more passing along the main stagecoach road. And there was Pawnee Liz, more or less the ramrod of the other girls working at Cuny's.

Pawnee Liz. A cold bitch if ever there was one, he stewed.

Once he'd approached her only to have the comely Pawnee Liz spurn his offer of a few moments in her upstairs bedroom. "Take your pair of silver dollars ugly man," she'd lashed out, "and get yourself a squaw if'n one would have you." Thereafter he'd kept well away from Pawnee Liz, letting his resentment burn inwardly at her and the fact he was as ugly as they come. The nickname Spade fitted handily as he had stringy black hair hanging in a tangled mass to his shoulders and a bulbous nose and dark acned skin. Always there seemed to be a bitter glare in his eyes, which served Spade DeLong well as it kept others at bay.

What had hammered at his thoughts the last couple of weeks was sighting Moss Hollabaugh again. Shot me in the shoulder and left me to die, he mused darkly. An' just why isn't that backshootin' Injun lover serving time in some federal prison? At first there'd been musings of turning Hollabaugh over to the army to collect any reward money. But ever since gold had been discovered in the Black Hills a lot of soldiers had deserted to head up that way. Besides, the army was shorthanded because of this and having one helluva time providing protection for the miners.

One thing about Spade DeLong — he was always sharp-eared to the threads of conversation going on around him at Cuny's. Agilely he could shift through the joshing and grousing to pick up occasionally some guarded words spoken by hardcases sharing a table or lined up at the bar. A glance at DeLong sitting stony-faced and generally by his lonesome would cause no break in the flow of words when these men were planning to hold up a stagecoach or heading into the hills to lift the pokes of miners.

Just last week a couple of men he took to be outlaws had batwinged in to settle down at a table a few feet away from the roulette wheel. Right off, he'd caught the eye message flashed by one of them to Pawnee Liz. When she'd gone over to their table, Spade DeLong had ambled to stand by the roulette wheel to watch the action and to overhear the voice of Pawnee Liz rising in anger. It was then he'd stepped around the roulette wheel and said, "Figured what they'd said about you was true."

"You're trespassing," snapped Pawnee Liz. "Man ugly as you ought to . . ."

"I'll handle it," came the voice of the man seated to the whore's right. His shoulders bunched, but then he held to the chair as Spade DeLong lifted his hand away from the six-gun thonged down at his right hip. "So, Pawnee Liz, you know this gent?"

"All I know is he's been hanging around the last couple of weeks," she said sullenly. Lamplight plucked at careless locks of dark brown hair piled atop her head, and she was big-bosomed and heavy through the hips. The dress was a gaudy red to match the rouge on her high cheekbones and the slash of red dabbed on her downturned lips. Strapped to her inner thigh was a Derringer; contempt clouded her eyes.

"Me, they call me Spade . . . Spade DeLong. An' I eavesdropped a'purpose as I figure I've got me an ace in the hole."

The other man spoke up, somewhat younger than either

of his table companions, and seated himself. He'd removed his hat to reveal a shock of black curly hair, and his sudden smile cut through the air of hostility. "Let's see that ace, Spade DeLong—"

Pawnee Liz said impatiently, "He's just a drunk . . . so why bother—"

"A dead ugly drunk if he only comes up with a deuce instead of that ace. So play your hand, DeLong."

Hastily Spade DeLong said, "Me, I'm on the dodge; an outlaw I figure same's you gents. Hear a lot in here . . . as to how Pawnee Liz, here, knowed some in your business. What you were speakin' of was how to get at some gold shipments."

"What do you think?"

The woman said, "Guess it can't hurt none hearin' him out." She gestured to the only empty chair at the table. "Perch, ugly."

Resentment filmed DeLong's eyes as he went around the table to claim the chair. He said quietly to their eyes boring into his face, "There's this hombre riding shotgun for the stageline who's wanted by the army for desertion. Me, we run into one another back when . . . Hollabaugh's his name . . . was scouting for the army up in Powder River country. Hollabaugh should be coming in on tomorrow's stage heading out of Cheyenne." He sketched with words the rest of that encounter with Moss Hollabaugh.

"Man wanted by the army might not have too many options open to him," said Pawnee Liz, and she revealed the names of the two hardcases.

One of them was named William Bevans, long of face, his eyebrows sidling upwards under a wide forehead, but rather short of chin clefted in the middle. He was dressed sloppily in a worn coat and soiled shirt, and Bevans had a mean mouth out of which came few words. The name of the other hardcase turned out to be James "The Kid" Wall. DeLong barely had time to digest this before he felt the muzzle of a gun nudging at his belly, and its owner saying softly, "Man named Hollabaugh?"

"Yessir, Mr. Wall," he stammered. "Been three years now but it's Hollabaugh. Owe him for winging me in the shoulder."

"What do you think?"

"Outside of his being ugly as sin it just could be we can use what he's told us. DeLong, we ride for Little Reddy from Texas. That is, ever since Sam Bass pulled out of these parts. As for this Moss Hollabaugh, what if he doesn't throw in with us?"

"Then gun him down," suggested Spade DeLong.

"As we just might do to you. So, Bill, what do you think?"

William Bevans shifted on the chair like a man undecided about the whole affair. Though that suspicious glint never left his eyes as he gazed across the table at DeLong, there was an approving nod of his head. "That stageline has hired a lot of guns to protect those gold shipments. Having an inside man won't hurt."

"We have a man up in Deadwood," countered Pawnee Liz.

"Sure, a bookkeeper. Not someone where the lead'll be flying."

"Bill's right," said James Wall. "With this Hollabaugh riding shotgun we've got our ace in the hole."

Spade DeLong said, "I'm handy with a gun. Would like to join your bunch as I'm about down to bedrock when it comes to hard cash."

"That'll have to be up to Little Reddy."

That night and the following day a lot of doubts ran through Spade DeLong's mind, for the table mates of Pawnee Liz had disappeared, while she didn't put in an appearance until late in the afternoon. His noon meal had been the last of a hunk of salt pork, at which time he mulled over thoughts of pulling out. But a man down to pocket change had no choice but to hang in there. Now, as he took in Pawnee Liz entering the barroom behind a couple of other whores, he centered worried thoughts on his ace in the hole, Moss Hollabaugh.

"Just my lousy luck he packed it in at Cheyenne and is long gone." Heaving up from the table, and with one hand lifting what change he had left out of a trouser pocket, he headed for the bar. Only to have Pawnee Liz place a restraining hand on his shoulder.

"They just rode in."

"Yeah?"

At her nod they moved to gaze out the batwings. "Past that shed there's a draw cutting down toward the river. And if I was you, DeLong, I wouldn't expect too much out of this . . ."

"Seems you never liked me."

"I always thought ugly only went skin deep."

"What's that supposed to mean?"

"That I don't trust you. Maybe I told you too much . . . about me and Bevans and Kid Wall."

He cut off the retort that was sliding up his throat as a chilling unease tugged at his mind. It was more Pawnee Liz's eyes than anything else which told him here was a woman capable of most anything, even murder. Waiting down by the river was a man to whom murder was also a pleasurable event.

Swinging away and out of the barroom, Spade DeLong picked his way past a manure pile and horse droppings littering the barren ground lying around buildings weathered into a bony sheen. The stories he'd heard here at Cuny's and back in the Black Hills about this man they called Little Reddy From Texas came to his mind. Chiefly they spoke of the Texan as being hot-tempered and packing a conscienceless gun, for Little Reddy thought nothing of gunning down unarmed men. The reward posters DeLong had seen didn't mention these facts, only that the Texan's real moniker was Robert McKimmie.

"An' a thousand dollars reward money to the man with

gumption enough to go after Little Reddy," DeLong recalled softly.

Coming onto the draw, with the surface of the river glistening beyond, DeLong could see the side wall of an old trapper's cabin and the tethered horses, and the two men watching his noisy passage on the pebble-littered pathway. All that one of them did when he came up was to gesture toward the front porch, and a nervous Spade DeLong moved around the wall and recognized the man seated in the only chair as Little Reddy from Texas. Two other hardcases were on the porch, one sitting on the steps, the other slouched against the log wall.

"Pawnee Liz was right about you."

Spade DeLong just grimaced at what the outlaw leader had just said, and he responded with, "Ugly don't mean nothing to a whore when you're flush." He glanced beyond Little Reddy at William Bevans still leaning against the wall. "I expect Mr. Bevans likes what I told him . . . otherwise you gents wouldn't be here."

Little Reddy flicked cigarette ashes onto the planking. He took more pride in his appearance than those with him, as he had on a boiled white shirt and black cravat under the soft leather coat fringed with a black collar. His features were regular and not unhandsome, and DeLong was betting that the black hair was neatly combed under the low-crowned hat. He couldn't read much of what Little Reddy was thinking behind the wall of passive eyes.

"Well," DeLong said impatiently, "what's it to be?"

"We can always use another inside man," responded Little Reddy. "Just turning Hollabaugh over to the army won't be all that profitable. You busted, DeLong?"

"Could use some money," he said grudgingly.

"Okay, if this works out that could be arranged. Dunc, give him some money for now."

The man seated on the porch steps laid soulful eyes upon Spade DeLong. The checkered coat worn by Duncan Black-

86

burn was buttoned clear to the lapels and threadbare. The face was thin, the brows tapering downwards, and Blackburn was sort of scrawny as if he'd missed a lot of meals. He didn't speak but passed to DeLong a couple of double eagles.

"Spade, is it? We'll head in to Cuny's. But you keep out of sight as there's the off-chance Hollabaugh might recognize you." Little Reddy pushed up from the chair.

"What . . . what if he don't go along with this?"

"Then," Little Reddy said, showing a cold smile, "I expect Dunc will want his money back."

Seven

Anytime a stagecoach he was aboard pulled into a stage station there was a release of tension from Moss Hollabaugh. But coupled with this as the sun took that final plunge to darken the plains was a nagging sense of unease. Maybe this was brought about by some hardcases coming with the whores out of the saloon to eyeball the Concord just pulling up before the station building. Could be that on the Sidney to Deadwood run he'd sighted in on some of those hardeyed men. For these were drifters, going where there was money and easy pickings.

"About time we got here."

Another passenger said, "At least this place has got some action."

Moss had left his Henry up on the seat as he came down to hold by the coach. While Gruwell, after tying up the reins, had crouched back to begin handing down pieces of luggage pointed out by the passengers. Moss took the luggage to pass the assortment of carpetbags and valises on with a tired smile. Afterwards, the stationmaster shepherded everyone toward the main building, which also housed the barroom.

Removing his Stetson, Moss slapped it against his leg to remove some of the traildust as he walked behind the coach rolling toward a nearby barn. He took in the deeper blackness of the hills bearing the same name, which brought to mind the news of an Indian raiding party and the Oglala, Crazy Horse.

"Haven't heard of him being killed by pony soldiers." There was a shift of feelings from the unrest of a moment ago to one of mystical wistfulness. He couldn't count the number of times within the last couple of years that he hadn't read about Crazy Horse and his Oglala in some newspaper. According to a lot of printed accounts the strange man of the Oglala had killed hundreds of settlers. If so, pondered Moss, it would have to have been by omnipresence, the spiritual ability to be everyplace at once. A lot of it was military hogwash and fear hysteria spread by those not knowing an Oglala from a petrified tree. What did the Teton Lakota call those hills — yup, *Pa Sapa*.

"That gold fever I see burning in your eyes?"

He grinned at Gator Gruwell and a hostler uncoupling the horses from their traces. "Just telling myself not to believe everything I read in a newspaper."

"Another thing too, Moss, I seen you eyeballing some of those barflys as we came in . . ."

"Force of habit, Gator. As I recall, come nightfall snakes slither out from under rocks and seek the saloons and cathouses. Speaking of which, I owe you for being so generous back at Cheyenne."

"A sip of whiskey or two will set just right before we tackle the chow served here."

"It be kind of gamey at that."

The hostler said to Gruwell, "I can handle them from here, Gator."

"Okay, Benny, but check the shoes on that lead hoss." He swung away to move with Moss at a slow shambling walk toward Cuny's hog ranch and the other buildings spread around like smaller trees paying court to an old mossy oak. Twilight was still hanging in with its paling light as if reluctant to die away. There was no wind, which set well with the pair of them. Stopping under a high window pouring out light, Gruwell bent to the task of washing up, and afterwards to toss away the dirty water in the wash basin. Then Moss had a go of removing some trail dust.

"You mentioned Red Canyon," Moss said as he reached for the hanging towel.

"A place where them Oglala like to hang out. Sometimes an army patrol comes in to clear out these hostiles . . . but mostly its hair-raisin' time cuttin' through the canyon. That Oglala you told me about, Crazy Horse, its rumored he's the one lifting a lot of hair and killing over in the hills."

"To all Oglala it's a sacred place. Which justifies these killings in the eyes of Crazy Horse." He let Gruwell go ahead into the main building, to find most of the passengers in the barroom, and with some of the whores trying to cage drinks.

At the bar, Gruwell said quietly, "Don't see that Pawnee Liz."

"Maybe she headed out."

"Wouldn't surprise me none. Place is crowded." He curved a hand around the stein of beer and raised it to salute Moss before blowing some foam away. "Obliged."

Nodding, Moss Hollabaugh took a look around the smoky room, large and raftered, just a lonely poker game going on but most of the other back tables occupied. The clunk of glass on the bar swung his eyes to a bartender setting down two shot glasses, which caused Moss to fork a couple of silver dollars out of his pocket. They emptied the shot glasses, at which Gruwell beckoned for a refill.

"There's still a little trail dust stuck in my throat. See anybody you know?"

Moss said, "Could be someone back there with his picture adorning a wanted poster."

"Expect there is."

"Driver, you, Gruwell," said one of the passengers as he shouldered up. He was one of the two passengers who'd made the trip from Cheyenne on the China seat at the back of the coach, a roly-poly man whose face seemed all muttonchop whiskers and grimace. It seemed that everytime the Concord struck into a pothole muttonchops let out a whine of protest to about drown out the clip-clopping of the horses on the barren trail. Beer spilled from the glass he was holding in a pudgy hand to splatter onto Gruwell's scuffed boots and down upon sawdust.

Vexation wrinkled up Gruwell's forehead. "What is it this time?"

"I paid the same rate as those seated inside your coach. So from here on that's where I expect to ride."

A smile showing, Moss picked up his beer stein and slipped away from the bar. One of the whores crooked her arm into his on Moss's way over to the roulette wheel, and he said, "I'm about flat busted."

"But you're one handsome gent."

"Beat it, hussy," came a voice to Moss's side, "as I want private words with Mr. Hollabaugh."

As the whore turned her attention to someone else, Moss turned to face the man, and remarked, "You're awful damned rude, mister."

William Bevans, a member of Little Reddy's gang of road agents, forced his lips into a grimace of a smile. "She's no lady . . . and you once scouted for the cavalry up around Powder River . . ."

"You must have me mixed up with someone else."

"Cut the crap, Hollabaugh. We know all about you . . . so maybe you'd better come back to our table and get better acquainted with the rest of my friends."

Sooner or later, Moss realized, he would run into someone remembering him from those Wyoming days. If all this man confronting him wanted was to palaver than it was plain to Moss the main issue here wasn't that reward placed on him by the U.S. Army. For all this man and his friends had to do was set an ambush, and then dead or alive he'd be delivered to the nearest army post. "Your face doesn't ring any bells, mister. But to clear this up I'll hear you out. Nope, you first."

91

He followed behind Bevans to a back table, and past other tables where steely-eyed men threw him suspicious glances. Only one man sat at that back table, and pushed up from the chair to shape a friendly smile as he held out his hand.

"Name's Robert McKimmie."

"Now you look familiar," Moss said boldly as he ignored the outstretched hand.

"Yup, you've got gumption, Hollabaugh. As the wanteds plastered about these parts call me Little Reddy from Texas. And you're the reason I'm here."

Moss took a cautious look at the nearby tables before easing gingerly upon a chair. "Well, McKimmie, spell it out."

"From what I hear you left a lot of enemies back there . . . back at Fort Reno. I expect you remember Spade DeLong?"

"Can't say that I do."

"He remembers you, alright," smiled Little Reddy, "as the man who plugged him in the shoulder just to keep some damned Oglala alive."

"So that was DeLong." Raising his glass, Moss sipped at the warm beer. Over the rim he quickly scanned nearby faces of those seated at the tables in an attempt to spot DeLong, recalling only that the man was swarthy of face and closing on six feet. But DeLong had to be here. A lucky break for him, as this could gain him entry into the outlaw fiefdom. "Thinking back, DeLong didn't have lily white hands either."

Grinning, Little Reddy said, "But Spade DeLong ain't wanted by the army. You could help us in some business ventures we're thinkin' of getting into."

"What choice does he have?"

Little Reddy had a quick smile for Bevans scowling across the table at Moss Hollabaugh. "Easy, Bill. As we don't want to violate Mr. Hollabaugh's constitutional rights. What we need, Hollabaugh, is for you to keep on riding shotgun. We've got other connections up at Deadwood."

"Who'll tip me off about gold shipments."

"That's about it. Only with you riding shotgun it'll be a lot easier getting at that gold."

Moss shrugged and smiled back at Little Reddy. "Riding up on that Concord seat leaves a man with plenty of worries as he's awful exposed. A butterfly has a longer lifespan, I reckon. So for now, I guess I ride on to Deadwood—"

"Guess you will."

"I don't expect you'll tell me just who these people are up there . . . at Deadwood . . ."

"Later, maybe, if this works out." Little Reddy extended his hand, which Moss grasped, and the outlaw added quietly, "You'll get a share of what gold we get out of this."

"Seems to me you rode with that Sam Bass outfit?"

"Did, Hollabaugh. But the law hereabouts seemed to have singled Bass out for special attention. Last I heard Sam Bass pulled out. By the way, you want to renew friendships with Spade DeLong?"

Moss rose and said, "Not especially."

"DeLong sure enough wants a piece of your hide though. Which could happen if you pull out of this deal."

"I'm in," Moss said crisply, and he allowed anger to flicker in his eyes. "There were about five of them trying to take out one lonely Oglala as I recall. So I don't reckon someone as cowardly as DeLong would be willing to face down a man. Adios, partners."

The stage stations fell behind, Rawhide Butte and Running Water and the one at Alkali Springs. Beyond here the road came under the scrutiny of hills studded with pines and red-streaked buttes, places which Moss Hollabaugh held under long scrutiny. Grass fringed up into the shadowy recesses of the hills and in the low and wide spaces between there were prairie flowers and taller grass. Redwinged blackbirds and meadowlarks seemed unconcerned by their passing but the horses loping along sent a woodchuck scurrying back into its burrow. The wind was just a whispery interlude barely ruffling a man's hair.

They came in to Cheyenne River Crossing stage station under an early afternoon sun. Ever since leaving Six Mile stage station it had been mostly small talk shared by Moss and the man handling the reins, and just a mite of tension between them. He knew that Gator Gruwell had seen him in conversation with those hardcases back at Cuney's hog ranch. And he could understand Gator's suspicions, as he'd just been hired on to ride shotgun. Out here a man didn't extend the hand of friendship too easily.

"Gator," he said, "I'm not gonna say those hardcases mistook me for someone else. Fact is, one of them knew me when I scouted for the army out of Fort Reno."

"That Little Reddy," Gruwell snapped, "is not your average hardcase. He's killed for a fact . . . held up some stages, too . . ."

"When we pull into Deadwood I'll tell the sheriff about this. It was the other one, Bevans, wanting to sound me out."

"About working with them," groused Gruwell as he reined up to throw down the reins to one of the men waiting to unhitch their horses from the Concord.

"Something like that. Guess back at Fort Reno I enjoyed hanging out at bars too much — got in a few fights. Like that gambling action, too. Which is where I ran into Bevans. Mostly he remembers me from my cleaning him out in a poker game. So, back at Cuny's, he must have figured I'd like a chance at some bigger paydays again."

"That, Moss, relieves my mind some. What we get paid on these runs won't see a man through tougher times . . . but at least it's honest work." Then he called out for everyone to dismount and head into the station. "Last meal you'll get until we hit Deadwood."

Trees hemmed in the stage station on the South Fork of the Cheyenne River, mostly cottonwood, and with a lot of screening underbrush. Behind were scattered hills but easterly rose a barricade of more hills and greater danger from road agents. While the next place on the trail they would head into was notorious Red Canyon. Moss, with this on his mind, came down to seek a shading cottonwood. He stood there as Gruwell accompanied the men leading away the six-span team of horses. Off to Moss's right stood the main building, made of raw boards nailed to wooden studdings and whitewashed.

That story he'd told Gruwell would have to do for the moment. For weighing what he'd been through down in Nebraska where there seemed to be no law to take a stand against those outlaw gangs, he could live with telling a few white lies. By throwing in with Little Reddy from Texas it meant he would be ridin' the high lines, a place trod only by owlhooters. Most outlaws had a past plumb full of black holes. Some got into the robbing life 'cause it was their nature, a lot of them got into it because they'd been unjustly accused of some crime. Then, like a cloud shadow passing by, Moss caught movement out of the corner of his eye. He glanced leftward expecting it was one of the passengers or working men, and had to suck in his stomach some when he took in an Oglala bedecked in war paint. Habit brought his right hand hipward, a sudden jab in the back freezing that motion and his scattering thoughts.

"You . . . Hollabaugh," the Oglala he was staring at muttered in broken English, "you come."

A couple of more jabs in his back from what Moss surmised to be a lance got his mind working again as well as his legs. He swung around to get a look at the Oglala holding the lance and merged into the screening brush were more Indians. Scarcely a sound was made as they brought Moss deeper into the underbrush that a mongrel lazing by the buildings barely stirred its tail. During the hike, the shadows of Moss's thoughts parted to spout out the name . . . Crazy Horse. This took away some of the uncertainty pounding at his temples.

Now at a trot they forced Moss westward along the grassy riverbank. Trees surrounded them, and birds flitted away at their passage. Suddenly they were spilling down a grassy knoll, and Moss set eyes again upon the strange man of the Oglala.

Crazy Horse broke off the conversation he was having with three other war chiefs. Lounging about the campsite were about thirty more Teton Lakota. They seemed almost indifferent to the white man being brought into their midst, but Moss could see the bitter hatred encased in every eye as he got closer. At a walk he came up to Crazy Horse, sensing there was something different about his appearance. Thinner and eyes a lot sadder, he mused.

"No harm will come to you," said Crazy Horse, whose casual gesture dismissed the others. He turned, to have Moss walk alongside down to the water's edge. Tree shadows made eerie patterns on the unrippled surface of the mud-colored water, and with the trees a shield against a quartering wind.

"The words you spoke were true."

"Yes, Hollabaugh . . . as I know many things . . . many things of mystery . . ." His long hair hung freely over bony shoulders. He folded his arms across his chest, a pensive gesture; Crazy Horse hadn't yet dabbed on war paint. "Why did you come back to the land of the Teton Lakota?" Crazy Horse demanded.

"I expect for the same reasons you're here."

"You seek the shining stones also?"

"Gold," Moss said glumly, "sometimes proves out to be a curse."

By way of agreement Crazy Horse said, "Ahh-h, it is so."

"I've heard stories about you," Moss questioned, "coming alone into the Black Hills. Seems you've scared off a lot of folks."

"Perhaps it was there," he said evasively. "But too many have come to *Pa Sapa* . . . so very many. That is why I and my people shall leave here for a while. We go north, to the Little Bighorn. Many are already there, Sitting Bull and his Hunkpapa, the others tribes of the Teton Lakota . . . and other Indian Nations. Your pony soldiers know of this."

"Means you're going to war," Moss murmured.

"I could have killed you, Hollabaugh." He turned and swung sad eyes upon Moss, and forced a smile. "When you went south on the white man's wagon. But I held the flight of my arrow. How does one kill a friend?"

"Glad you recognized me, Crazy Horse. What happens now?"

Following the trail of Moss's eyes to the other Oglala, Crazy Horse said, "No, no harm will come to you . . . or those with you. Perhaps this will happen another day. Soon it will be the time of the Moon-of-Making-Fat." His voice broke away, his eyes taking in distant places beyond the river. It seemed at that moment as if the inner presence of the Oglala chief had also departed, but then, with a lazy smile gracing his face, his turning brought both of them up the riverbank.

Everyone had mounted their horses except for the Oglala holding the reins of Crazy Horse's war pony. Claiming the reins, the strange man of the Oglala, this Crazy Horse, held out his right hand in the white man's way.

"This time my dreams tell me we depart forever. You go now, Hollabaugh. Tell your people that before the time of the Moon-of-Making-Fat is over blood will be spilled in the valley of the Rosebud. Tell everyone betraying the sanctuary of *Pa Sapa* to beware. So, *hou cola,* you go."

"Take care, my friend," said Moss as he drew his hand away to wheel about and began striding up the grassy knoll. He didn't expect anything to happen and resisted the urge to steal a backward glance. When he did look back upon cresting the knoll, not an Oglala could be seen.

"Hou cola; he called me friend."

He pressed on to work his way through the underbrush.

Upon emerging he drew a scrutinizing look from Gator Gruwell who was just about to climb up on the Concord seat. Moss clambered up too and settled in comfortably as Gruwell brought the horses away from the stage station.

About a mile out and with Red Canyon gaping amongst the hills, Moss said, "Sometimes it pays to lend a helping hand."

He drew a probing glance from Gruwell.

"Just had a powwow with some Oglala."

That bold statement caused driver Gator Gruwell to tug at his hat and sit up straighter. He gummed the wad of chewing tobacco about in his mouth, undecided if the man sharing the responsibility for this stagecoach had been touched by sunstroke or was dead serious. "Yeah?"

"You've heard of Crazy Horse, I expect—"

"The whole danged territory's heard of that killin' Injun! All I know is you was gone about a half hour . . . and Lord knows where?"

"We won't have to worry about Indians when we hit Red Canyon, Gator. As they've pulled out. Heading northerly to the valley of the Rosebud." Sketchily he told of how he'd first encountered Crazy Horse . . . about the Oglala seeing them heading for Cheyenne . . . now the Oglala war party led by Crazy Horse lurking upriver a short distance.

"They could have wiped us out," sputtered Gator as he suddenly realized Moss Hollabaugh wasn't dreaming all of this up. He scratched at his sideburns. "Any more grey hairs just pop out? Or just maybe every blade of hair I've got which isn't much has gone snowy white. Doggone it, Moss, those Oglala don't mess around."

"Reckon this evens things up between the Oglala and me, Gator. Headin' up to the Rosebud? Along with the rest of the Teton Lakota and the Cheyenne and a lot more plains Indians. Gonna be a bloody summer."

"Bloody down here, too, with all these holdups."

That brought Moss back to why he was riding shotgun for

the Deadwood to Cheyenne Stageline Company. Once he got to Deadwood the first order of business was a long talk with Jason Hassrick. With this in mind, he went over his meeting with Robert McKimmie, the notorious outlaw chieftain. Has the eyes of a killer, but somehow, Moss pondered, something seemed to be lacking in the man they called Little Reddy from Texas.

Meaning that just maybe Little Reddy isn't the real mind behind these holdups. Maybe someone in Deadwood? Moss didn't muse over this too long. Or maybe the man passing out inside information about gold shipments to these outlaws was over at Cheyenne.

"But at least," he murmured silently, "I've made that first contact. And in Deadwood there's sassy Miss Julia. Wonder if she missed me?" He leaned back to settle in comfortably, then closed his eyes. "Keep your eyes peeled, Gator."

Gator promptly snapped, "That's what they pay you to do, Hollabaugh." Then he let go with a chuckle. "Guess worry can kill a man same's a bullet. Yup, catnap, but once we hit Red Canyon them eyeballs better be peeled."

Eight

Of more interest to Claiborne Payne than the Laramies sawtoothing into the far purplish haze were the army encampments occupying land northwest of Cheyenne. The smaller post was Fort D.A. Russell, home of cavalry units that were engaged in activities against the Indian menace. Closer to Cheyenne lay Camp Carlin. Out of this vast quartermaster depot went supplies destined for most of the army's western forts.

"The army," reasoned Claiborne Payne, "wouldn't have located out here unless they'd foreseen a bright future for Cheyenne."

Cado Greer took his eyes from a wagon approaching by way of Cheyenne, the town a low scattering of buildings on a level stretch of high plains, and gazed at the sprawling army depot. Further northwesterly and angling toward the distant mountains was the ranch they'd left earlier in the day.

"Hard to believe that not too long ago we were cellmates," said Cado Greer. "Now you own that ranch and a hunk of that stageline. Speaking of which, Claiborne, maybe we should tell them outlaws to lay low for a spell."

"Can't," snapped Payne, "as moneywise I'm spread out too thin."

"All it takes is for someone in Deadwood to spill the

beans about us to old man Hassrick. Then we just might be doin' some sky dancing."

"You always did worry too much. That new bookkeeper, Risdale, saw what would happen if he crossed us. Same for Ace Taylor. Matter of fact, Cado, I was thinking of expanding things. Sam Bass could get more hardcases to ride for him. Maybe split up his gang then so's we can hit more than one place."

"Damn risky."

Claiborne Payne, as he ducked his head to shield his face from dust churned up by the passing wagon, laughed at the somberfaced Greer. The laugh had a hollow ring to it like a man trying to dodge the true nature of things. About a mile from Cheyenne now, he spurred his gelding into a lope and said to the other horsemen catching up, "Cado, we don't know how long they'll keep finding gold over in the hills. Let's face it, you've been getting your share of what's been stolen, an' knowin' you, salting it away. But I don't think it's enough for both of us . . . enough to live the highrollin' life on. And, dammit, Cado, I've got a lot of expenses."

"Yeah, stockin' that ranch took considerable."

"Cado, I want more than a ranch. There's talk of votin' in statehood out here. What with the railroad, no question but Cheyenne'll be made the new capital of Wyoming. Then money'll talk as to who gets voted in as governor."

"Lofty ambitions," muttered Greer around a speculative grin, "for a man with a checkered past. But you're right, once these Indians have been gotten rid of that railroad will fetch in a lot of settlers."

"If I was you, Cado, I'd start buying up what land I could in Cheyenne; as it won't be long before prices will skyrocket."

"Maybe, Mr. Payne, but dunno if land is my game. Always been a drifter. One dusty day I might make tracks out of here. But . . . all that gold being shipped out of Deadwood . . . keeps a man hanging in."

It was Claiborne Payne's original intention to spend a couple of weeks out at his ranch. He'd suggested a few changes to the carpenters putting up his new ranchhouse, got to know some of the cowboys, and when out looking over the spread of his land managed to track down and kill an elk near the base of Split Rock Peak. Mostly his going out there was to get away from his wife, as it was a living hell being married to someone you didn't love. Mandy had proved to be almost a carbon copy of her sister, the flighty Crissy Hassrick. Women with no bottoms, and who could spend on a day's shopping spree more'n a cowhand made in a month. His excuse for moving out of their red brick mansion to get a suite at the Inter Ocean Hotel was that it was closer to his work, though sometimes he would spend a night at home, enduring her tearful entreaties that she loved him.

Part of what had brought him heading in was that some of the gold taken by Sam Bass in a recent stagecoach holdup should be waiting in Cheyenne. But the shank of it was his need to see Pearl Logan again. Ever since their first tryst some two months ago it seemed he couldn't get her out of his thoughts. She was a statuesque strawberry blonde, one of the demimonde selling their favors over at the House of Mirrors. In his arms she was as explosive as a prairie fire, bringing out a passion he hadn't known in years. He didn't love Pearl, and perhaps he never would, but they couldn't seem to get enough of each other. That she was a whore only enhanced her loveliness in the eyes of Claiborne Payne, for whores had been all he'd known until Mandy Hassrick had appeared to change his life.

"But she's a classy bitch," he muttered in a private aside, as Pearl Logan liked nothing more than frequenting the fancy dress shops favored by the socialites of Cheyenne.

He found this amusing, as did a lot of other merchants and ranchers availing themselves of what was offered at the House of Mirrors and the other houses of prostitution.

Conducting the business affairs of the stageline had over the past months kept Payne out of the saddle, softened him up, and he could feel the sourness pricking away at his inner thighs. "Should have taken a buggy up there, Cado," he said sourly.

"Maybe," he laughed, "it ain't the horse but Pearl whose worn you to a frazzle. You gonna stop and see your wife?" He nodded at a sidestreet passing down a long row of elegant houses.

"She finds I'm back, Cado, all I'll be hearing is some more whining. I want you to head over to the stageline office and check out things."

"Yeah," Greer said, knowing that Payne was speaking of that stolen gold.

They were coming in on Yellowstone Road, which had merged into a wide street. Shipped in by the Union Pacific were the bricks and other material used to create a web of buildings more common to eastern cities. The Inter Ocean Hotel was no exception, three stories of brick, the name of the hotel scrawled in brick on the wide facade, above that, 1876, in smaller letters below all of this the name of the builder. Both of them took all of this in before Cado Greer kept jogging his horse down the street as the man he worked for swung in to dismount with a wearied sigh of relief. A hotel employee darted out to take charge of Payne's horse.

Inside the lobby, Claiborne Payne passed the portals of a door giving him a glimpse of the mahogany bar in the main barroom. He strode over a Brussels Carpet, past red velvet chairs and drapes to inquire at the counter if there were any messages.

"Glad to have you back, Mr. Payne," gushed the desk

clerk, as he passed over some folded sheafs of paper and a few letters.

As was his manner, Claiborne Payne turned a brusque shoulder to the clerk and found the main staircase. He knew without glancing back that right now hotel employees were scurrying upstairs to draw his bath, to leave some brandy and ice in the bathroom, trayfuls of tidbits in the main drawing room of his suite. Earlier on this hadn't been done, which resulted in some employees drawing their walking papers.

He strode into his suite and doffed his hat to toss it carelessly toward one of the overstuffed chairs. The hat hit an armrest and fell to the floor. But he could care less because crowding his bedroom closets were several western suits and a bunch of new hats and handmade boots. He hadn't bothered to pack any clothes when he'd moved in here. He figured as long as he hadn't Mandy would still think there was a hope of salvaging their marriage. The trick was in keeping her from running to her father, as once that happened, he figured Jason Hassrick might get someone else to run the Cheyenne end of the operation.

He peeled out of his leather coat on the way to his bedroom as two maids came in holding buckets of hot water. He closed the bedroom door as they went into the adjoining bathroom. Undressing, he took time to glance through the paperwork. First, the notes; he scowled as he tossed them into a wastebasket, for all of them were from his wife. Next he sorted through the letters, smiled at one that had been mailed out of Denver. And naked, he read its contents, and said idly, "Yup, Mr. Carrington, I just might invest some money in your meat packing plant."

Tucked in with the other three letters he brought into the bathroom was a yellow envelope. On a table dragged up to the white enamel bathtub were bottles of brandy and glasses and ice glittering in a container, wooden matches

104

and a box of imported Havana cigars. One window had been opened to let in a freshening breeze. Dropping the letters next to the box of cigars, he eased his skinny frame into the soapy water.

"Damn, that feels good." He stretched out best he could in the bathtub, and some of his trail aches started shortly to ease away. Soon he felt sweat begin popping out on his forehead, and most of his sour mood began dissipating. "Maybe I should have one of them maids come in an' give me a massage; about all they're good for," he chuckled.

He reached a languid hand for one of the brandy bottles, poured a glass about half full, and with the glass in hand settled back again as he set his mind on this uneasy relationship with the outlaw Sam Bass. Bass may take all the risks, but that didn't entitle the man to such a big share of the gold. Got to settle this more in my favor, he mused. With the brandy taking hold, he refilled the glass a couple more times. He brought flame to a cigar, and with a greedy glint narowing his eyes, urged himself, "Got to remember, Bass is reliable . . . but awful greedy hisself."

Now Claiborne Payne went over the full operation in his mind, of how his operatives in Deadwood had been relaying the news of gold shipments down to Sam Bass lurking further southwesterly in the Black Hills. News of any gold shipments were telegraphed from Deadwood to Payne's office here, and in a secret code. The only thing lacking was just how much gold was being shipped out on each stagecoach.

This is the damned Achilles' heel. The only one privy to how much gold is Hassrick . . . and he's about as tightlipped as they come. So Sam Bass could be skimming a lot off the top of those shipments, he complained. The key, he knew, was to bribe one of the local bankers as to the exact amount of gold contained in each shipment. But they're worse than Jason Hassrick when it comes to money. I ain't givin' up though.

Remembering the letters, he twisted his head to look at them. "What's this one?" he said aloud.

Sorting out the letters he scowled at a telegram showing that it had been sent from Deadwood. Quickly he tore the envelope open. Just as quickly he discovered that it had been sent by Ace Taylor. Above that he read, S.B. has pulled out. Stop. But have other interested party. Stop.

Claiborne Payne exploded out of the bathtub as blinding rage filled his eyes. He kicked at the nearby table and slammed it against a bathroom wall. "He's pulled out on me! That damned Sam Bass is gone!" Groaning in uncontained anger he punched out at the mirror in the wall cabinet, and as glass shattered, he screamed in rage, "Bass . . . you damned thievin' turncoat . . . gone . . . gone . . ."

For a moment his mind reeled with all the things he would do to Sam Bass if ever they encountered one another again. Slowly, the knuckles of his right hand stained with blood, and he let reason calm his terrible anger. He found he still held the telegram sent by Ace Taylor. Flicking a glance at it, the thought came that at least Ace hadn't cut out on him. And there was that new man over at Deadwood, Orrin Risdale. A simmering thought; what a sweet deal me and Sam Bass had going.

"That's over," he hissed between gritted teeth still clamped on a cigar. "Got to think . . . can't be over . . . not now, not with all that gold comin' out."

"What's Ace mean . . . got another party in mind? Got to be another gang of outlaws. Risdale, that's got to be the connection. Outlaws he worked with down along that Sidney run. But —" he crumbled up the telegram and backhanded it away — "too many loose ends."

He came out of the bathtub reaching for a towel. A calming reason drove his anger to the dark recesses of his mind. It came to Payne that perhaps it was meant to be this way. With Bass pulling out, he could send some of his men, the hardcases he'd hired on and even Cado Greer, to join up with this outlaw gang. Then the lion's share of whatever they stole would come to Claiborne Payne. Of course, he would have to see that Cado got a bigger cut. And here in Cheyenne, sooner or later, a banker or bank employee would succumb to the lure of gold.

You can trace banknotes but not gold ore. Which any bank clerk knows. Just got a hunch one'll show up before long to make some deal.

In the bedroom, he took the time to burn the telegram while smiling at a pair of red garters dangling from the headboard of his wide bed. Desire rose to chase away anything but thoughts of how he'd removed those garters from the graceful legs of Pearl Logan, to afterwards make love. Hurriedly he picked out a dark blue suit and matching Stetson and highheeled boots. And once he'd donned this rigging, along with picking out a couple of diamond rings encased in Black Hills leafy gold, he left the Inter Ocean to come upon dusk spreading cooling shadows along the busy street. If there were any thoughts of his wife they were buried in his lustful need to get over to the House of Mirrors. Left behind also was the worry of the stageline and what part he was playing in these stagecoach holdups.

"That Pearl doll; she'd better be waiting for me," he practically sang.

He always found it amusing when passing the Double Decker, another house of prostitution, that it shared the same block as the Presbyterian Church. The dark, stained glass windows of the church glared at the gaudy light pouring out of the brothel, the cribs and the barroom on the one floor. Striding past on the sidewalk, Claiborne Payne was tempted to go in for a quick drink, but he passed on as a bottle smashed through a windowpane to land in the middle of the street. The church seemed to draw back a few feet.

He left the competing buildings behind. Patting a pocket, he grimaced at finding he'd forgotten to pack along some cigars. But then eager expectancy unlined his face as he strode past a street lamp and came upon a large brick building, the lower windows framed by sandstone sills and lintels, and a few buggies tied out front. He headed on in.

The door had barely closed behind him than someone had called out, "Claiborne, my boy."

The room seemed larger than it was as it had floor to ceiling mirrors covering two walls, reflecting images of its occupants and the gaudy red furniture. A favorite hangout of local cattlemen, a few were in evidence, some holding glasses ambered with whiskey. He knew most of the merchants, had shared the favors of one or two of the courtesans spread about the large salon. Glancing about he saw to his dismay that Pearl Logan wasn't here. Masking his disappointment, he weaved over to Ed Bartelt, one of the ranchers, and as many out here, a bachelor.

"Still looking, Ed?"

"The Good Lord hates an impatient man. I hear your stageline got hit again, Claiborne — "

"Killed one of our drivers this time. Hard stopping these road agents."

"Here, maybe this whiskey will help."

"Muchas gracias." He stabbed a look at beaded curtains stirring, held there as a whore, one he'd never seen before, passed through ahead of her latest customer. "I expect you'd be holed up with Irene. That was her name?"

"Irene done cut out on me," the rancher bemoaned around a sad grimace. "Offered her this body and half my ranch."

108

"For a man tipping the scales at darn near three hundred pounds she passed up a helluva deal." They laughed together. Payne nodded his thanks for the drink and passed back through the beaded curtain in search of Pearl Logan.

"Ah, Mr. Payne, a pleasure seeing you again."

"Mrs. Watson." He tipped a finger to his hat. "I . . ."

At that moment an upstairs door opened and the woman he sought appeared on the encircling balcony. The silky black chemise under the feathery gown seemed to form an enticing halo around the curvaceous body of Pearl Logan, which brought him up the staircase. Coming to her, they drifted back into the recessed hallway passing to the rear of the upper floor. Savagely he wrapped his fingers in the mass of soft hair, brought his other hand to the small of her back as she stepped in close, their kiss full of lust and the need for one another.

"Come on," he said impatiently.

"Not just yet, lover boy."

"Pearl . . . it's been a . . ."

"Remember what you told me before, about needing the help of someone in the banking business. Got me a banker in there. Head teller at the Western Bank. While you were gone, Claiborne, we've been talking business . . . other than what you want now." She snuggled in close again, brought her lips around to nip at his earlobe. "He knows, my love, all about those gold shipments out of Deadwood. Well, you interested?"

"Yeah, yeah, you bet," he responded, her restraining hand holding him in place.

"Mr. Cecil Lambrowski is sleeping off a drunk in my room. So, do you want to hang around until he comes out of it?"

"A couple of buckets of water will take care of his beauty rest. What kind of deal did you strike with him?"

"That's between you and Mr. Lambrowski. But I get a cut out of this."

He grinned lewdly. "You'll get a cut and a lot more, Pearly baby."

As she hurried toward the back staircase, Payne entered Pearl's bedroom. Sprawled among the fluffy pillows and sheets was a short, beefy man wearing a rumpled suit. A red bulby nose centered a round face, the drunken snoring lifting the ends of the mustache. The coat lay open exposing a protruding belly and a shirt pocket crammed with pencils and a five cent cigar.

"Better than nothing," grumbled Claiborne Payne, as he reached for the cigar. He found matches in one of the coat pockets, took one out and scraped it into light across the man's stubbly cheek. "Better get him out back."

Puffing at the cigar, he slapped the drunken bank employee a couple of times, which caused one eyelid to rise, and Payne said, "Awright, Mr. Lambrowski, we're goin' for a walk. Come on now, wake up, dammit."

"Walk . . . yeah . . . who you . . ."

"The man who's gonna make you rich." He managed to get Lambrowski erect to stand on wobbly legs. Wrapping an arm around his waist, the other supporting the arm thrown about his shoulders, they moved into the hallway.

"In here," he said to Pearl Logan moving up the back staircase. He brought the drunken Lambrowski into an empty room.

The pail of water splashing across his upper body brought curses from Cecil Lambrowski, and a cry that he'd lost his spectacles.

"Cecil honey, this is the man I told you about."

"Uh," he mumbled, trying to swipe the water from his eyes, with the face of the man accosting him an unfocused blur. "Helluva way to treat a customer, Pearl. I've a good notion to—"

"Now, now, Cecil honey, I could just visit that pretty little wife of yours — "

"And she would, Mr. Lambrowski." He pulled up another chair and sat down. "This cigar tastes like horse droppings." He tossed it down to grind it out under the heel of his boot. "But when we make a deal you'll be smokin' Havanas."

Before leaving in the morning, Claiborne Payne enjoyed a hot bath at the House of Mirrors and the massage given him by Pearl Logan. He felt easier in mind as he turned a corner to head for the Inter Ocean Hotel. The advance he'd given Cecil Lambrowski after they'd struck a deal last night he considered an investment, a guarantee that the Western Bank's head teller wouldn't have a change of mind. And in Pearl Logan's bed there'd been moments when he had sorted out the gist of the telegram sent by Ace Taylor.

"Better this way," he smiled. Swerving across the sidewalk to enter the hotel lobby, his stomach's rumbling told him breakfast was the next order of business. He had a brisk nod for the smile of a hotel clerk as he began crossing toward the dining room, only to stop short when a woman rose from one of the lobby chairs.

"Mandy, I . . . I just got back . . ."

"Oh, Claiborne, we have to talk." The white bonnet held captive Mandy Payne's light brown hair. The cape thrown over her shoulders trailed down her back, and under that was a long-sleeved dress. She hurried to him.

There seemed to be a subtle shade of difference about her, he thought. She seemed more distracted than usual. Could something have happened to her father? But so far the pattern was the same, as he let her ramble on with protestations of how much she loved him, the doeish smile he found so repulsive, her reaching to clutch at his sleeve.

"I . . . I, Claiborne, please, I just can't go it alone . . ."

"Mandy, we've been all through this." He began walking her away from the inquisitive eyes of the hotel clerks and the few people idling in the lobby. "Come, I haven't had breakfast yet."

In the dining room they settled down at a window table. He gave their order to a waitress, whereupon he removed his Stetson and draped it over an empty chair, then he brushed back his thick head of hair, hating her presence, not revealing this in the patient smile.

"I just went on a hunting trip, Mandy. Look, as I told you before, perhaps we can work things out."

"Oh, honey, I miss you so." Fumbling around in her handbag, she found a lacey handkerchief and used it to dab at her eyes. "I got a letter from Julia."

"How is everybody?"

"Fine. Though daddy is worried about things . . . you know, these holdups . . ."

Their coffee arrived first, with his request for cream sending the waitress away. Mandy, dropping a cube of sugar in her cup, cleared her throat as a sudden smile sparkled her teary eyes. "Oh, honey, I can't keep it from you any longer. The doctor . . . I'm going to have a baby . . . our baby, Claiborne."

To his credit Claiborne Payne kept the angry retort from escaping his lips. Her statement had sent a wave of resentment flooding through his body, a feeling as though she had betrayed him. For he wanted the seductive Pearl, not this simpering daughter of Jason Hassrick's. Somehow he found himself reaching out for her hand across the white expanse of tablecloth, the hand of Mandy's grasping with a possessiveness that alarmed him. He spoke a few words of assurance, honeycoating them with the promise that he might move back into their house again.

"Your food, Mr. Payne."

"Ah, yes," he said, relieved for the intrusion.

"If it's a boy," gushed Mandy, "I want to name him after you, honey."

"Sure, why not," he said expansively, as Claiborne Payne suddenly discovered he'd lost his appetite.

"Julia's letter said she wanted us to come back . . . maybe stay longer this time."

"That would be nice."

"Really, I find journeying by stagecoach so exciting. Don't you, honey?"

"It has its moments, I suppose," he forced a smile to match hers.

That's it, he exulted inwardly, a way out of this damnable mess. There would be a return to Deadwood by way of stagecoach. But his wife would be traveling alone, and in the very near future, if he could arrange it. The rest of it sorted itself out in Payne's mind, that this must be handled by Cado Greer, for he trusted Cado. It would be Cado carrying a sealed message to this outlaw gang spoken of in Ace Taylor's unexpected telegram. What better way to test these outlaws than to do his bidding as detailed in that message Cado would bring to them.

"I was just thinking of Cado," he said to Mandy, "and here he is. You'll excuse me."

He shoved the chair away, and in rising touched her extended hand as he made his way around the cluster of tables. Lost in the reverie of the news brought by his wife, it was only when he passed out into the lobby to look at Cado that he saw the somber set to the man's face.

"That gold never showed up," Cado Greer said flat out.

"Yeah, as I just got word of Bass's pulling out of these parts." He told Cado about receiving the telegram. "When time permits we'll track Bass down, kill him. But it ain't all over, Cado. Ace has hooked up with others

113

who can handle what Sam Bass was doing."

"Bass was damned good."

"Any man holding a gun on someone else is good. What I want now, Cado, is for you to get some good horses together, and get our boys equipped as you'll be heading out."

Cado Greer grunted speculatively, "Eastward, I expect."

"Yup, to the Black Hills. Tonight we'll get together and go over it." He was about to narrate to Cado his making a deal with bank teller Lambrowski, chopped that notion off with the flicking of an eye. That would be his hole card, which made him feel a little better about the news dropped on him by his wife. "Okay, see you."

Claiborne Payne remained by the open doorway of the dining room, looking in at his wife. She was seated so that the morning sunlight lancing through the window brushed brightly against her profiled face. This shielded her anxious eyes from gazing his way.

"Has to be this way, Mandy," he murmured softly. "Once you get on one of your daddy's stagecoaches it'll be your last ride. But I'll see you get a proper burial."

And tugging at a coat lapel the husband of Mandy Payne strode smiling into the dining room.

Nine

It didn't take Orrin Risdale all that long to settle into the daily routine of filling out way bills or ledgers. From his desk in the bullpen office he could look out a window and see the expectant glitter in the eyes of those arriving on the stagecoaches. They'd left behind worldly possessions and families, came armed only with ready cash and a dream of striking it rich, everyone man jack of them stricken with gold fever. The first to fleece the would-be miners would be the merchants and hotels, and then the saloons and gaming joints, and a few would get mugged or killed even before they hit out for the gold fields.

Gazing about the office, he knew that before the week ended some of the clerks would up and quit. Just this morning three more had been taken on, as the stageline had more business than it could handle. One of the first items on his agenda had been to find out where the men riding the stagecoaches liked to hang out; a saloon on the main drag. His nightly sojourns there produced the usual small talk and worries amongst these men about the dangers of the trail. These men found out about gold shipments only after they reported for work. A special stagecoach would have horses hitched to it and would be generally kept in one of the barns until ready to go, surrounded by outriders which might include a couple of soldiers.

Only recently, and this was something passed on to Ace

Taylor, had the new Salamander safe been installed in the stagecoaches. Claiming to be robber-proof, these safes had been bolted to the frame of the Concord. Another precaution taken by Jason Hassrick had been his order that no passengers would be allowed on these coaches.

Fitted out in a dapper black suit, Orrin Risdale tugged at a shirt cuff as he took in the only woman working for the stageline company. As best he could he avoided Julia Hassrick; he could tell she resented his presence whenever there chanced to be eye contact between them. She also had little use for Clairborne Payne, which was brought out in a conversation he'd overheard between Julia and her father.

It doesn't help that she connects me to her brother-in-law, he lamented silently. Worry stirred in Risdale, the remembrance of that brazen murder committed by Claiborne Payne. Though he had no immediate plans to leave Deadwood, he had quietly sold his house to a local merchant and moved into one of the hotels. If he could, Orrin Risdale would have closed his Deadwood bank accounts and opened a new account over in Cheyenne. That would mean his having to board one of the Concords and risk running into Payne or maybe that Cado Greer. He didn't like being boxed in, but felt it was worth the risk as millions in gold bullion were being shipped out of here.

Working in Deadwood had kept alive in Orrin Risdale the constant dread of his running into Little Reddy and his outlaw gang. That was some setup they'd had going down in Nebraska. The worry of having to face up to these outlaws was temporarily thrust aside by Ace Taylor's sudden reappearance. The hardcase told him about the gang headed up by Sam Bass heading out of the Black Hills. Their spat of words in one of the bawdy houses went something like this.

"That Sam Bass was one cold hombre. But he's pulled out, dammit. Well, bookkeeper, you got any ideas?"

"Might have at that. Word has it that Robert McKimmie is still in the hills."

"McKimmie," snorted Ace Taylor. "Last thing we need is another bookkeeper."

"McKimmie is more commonly known as Little Reddy from Texas."

"A more brutal killer than Bass ever was," said the hardcase with a renewing of interest.

"Me an' Little Reddy were hooked up down on that Sydney run up here to the hills. He was good at it, holding up stagecoaches."

"Considering you was feedin' him inside information about gold shipments I wouldn't wonder none. Expect he'll throw in with us, bookkeeper?"

"He does I won't have to keep dodgin' my shadow. Yup, expect he will, Ace. Only problem is finding Little Reddy . . ."

"I'll tend to that. Got another chore you're to sink your teeth into — need a powderman."

One of the clerks calling out that a stagecoach had just arrived brought Orrin Risdale out of his reveries, which sent him up from the desk to study the wall clock. A quarter of an hour until quitting time. He waited until everyone's attention was on the stagecoach pulling up in the street, then he moved back to unpeg his hat and go out a side door. Curiosity brought him toward the front boardwalk, but he drew back upon spotting Moss Hollabaugh about to dismount from the Concord.

Hollabaugh, what does he know about me? Risdale questioned with some concern, as he retraced his steps to the back alley. Other than we both worked out of Sydney? Probably nothing to worry about, he decided.

Of greater concern at the moment to Orrin Risdale was finding a powderman. These new Salamander safes were nigh impossible to open by blasting away with six-guns or a rifle. The trick to getting at the gold stored inside was to use dynamite. Drifting into Deadwood had been a few hardrock miners, known more commonly as powdermen because of

117

their ability to handle not only dynamite but special caps containing fulminate of mercury. Sometimes these caps had a way of going off in a miner's hand, but handled right Orrin Risdale knew these Salamander safes could be blasted open without destroying their contents. After about a week of fruitless searching throughout Deadwood and in a couple of adjoining gold mining camps, he'd found his powderman.

"Only trouble is," he complained, "I've yet to approach this worthy." He'd acquired the name of a powderman from a local saloon owner at the cost of a hundred dollars. Learned further from a different source that the miner in question was an alcoholic, had for the past few weeks been frequenting Deadwood saloons. "Hope I locate Jesse Barfield before his kidneys give out . . . and probably be so shaky of hand he'll blow both himself and a safe to smithereens."

In the hours after midnight last night he'd finally traced the powderman down to Mrs. Finney's boarding house. Much to his dismay all he'd found was an empty room reeking of spilled whiskey. And as Orrin Risdale headed upstreet, there filtered to him now the scent of burning pine coming from chimneys. This alleviated somewhat a mixture of other odors knifing through the crowded streets of a town getting ready for another night of roistering and violence.

Along with getting from Mrs. Finney the fact the powderman had been lodging at her boarding house, Risdale also acquired her wrath over being shaken out of her bed at such a late hour. A couple of silver dollars did away with a lot of her cursing, and pried forth that Jesse Barfield liked to hang out at Shady Dick's Crystal Bar. Cutting down a side street, Risdale pushed aside a few misgivings as he approached a big wooden frame building and took in some hardeyed idlers taking command of a side wall. Their eyes said it all, that here was fair game, but a word from the bookkeeper kept them momentarily at bay.

"Gentlemen." Risdale pushed inside.

Orrin Risdale turned to his left and to a long plank bar cloaked in uncertain lamp light. The interior walls were unfinished, letting him see past upright studdings into a large back room where men sat playing cards and the pair of billiard tables were being used. Up front there were more tables and the crowded bar which Risdale wedged closer to. Spread throughout the saloon were girls of the line trying to sell their wares.

"Is Spike here?"

"Coburn, yeah. Spike, up front here."

One of the bartenders weaved around others of his craft setting out drinks.

"So, you're back."

"Have you located the subject of our conversation?"

"Barfield came in early this morning. So to keep him available for you, Mr. Risdale, a certain drink was administered. Nuthin' fancy; just a purgative. By now he should be comin' out of it." He came out from behind the bar, and Risdale followed past the bar and some empty kegs of beer. In a back hallway, the bartender pulled up by a closed door and swung around to gaze at Risdale. "Our deal was for fifty bucks. And another fifty for his bar tab."

"Another fifty?" he said resentfully.

"Somebody's gotta pay his bar tab."

"No matter," Risdale grimaced. "As you kept up your end of the bargain. I trust this is satisfactory."

"Don't know what you want with that drunken bum, Mr. Risdale, but it's been a pleasure." Shoving the door open, he headed back toward the bar.

Barely had Risdale opened the door than something clubbed into the panes above his head, and he ducked away. Across the room the powderman kicked a storage crate aside and spat out, "I'm gonna make donkey meat out of you."

Risdale slapped his coat aside and reached toward the shoulder holster. He held the J.C. Colt's .38 revolver out at arm's length, though he doubted it packed enough power to

119

slow down the enraged Jesse Barfield crouching at him. "Barfield . . . you are Jesse Barfield?"

"What the hell?" Confusion gave him pause.

"I've been looking for you, Jesse. Truth is we need a powderman . . ."

"Who in Hades is we?"

"Are you interested?"

"This better not be some kind of trick," he growled, as he straightened up to tower over Risdale. He had on soiled work clothes fitted over a beefy frame, had huge hands that were pitted and scarred as befitted a hardrock miner. It didn't appear as if he carried any kind of weapon as was common to men of this size. But what he packed was a nagging headache, and Risdale read an awful need to get at a bottle of whiskey.

Knowing the character of men like Jesse Barfield, the first thing was to win the man's trust, which caused Risdale to holster his J.C. Colt's. Brushing the opposite lapel aside, he unpocketed his leather wallet. "Mr. Barfield, we are seeking a man with your special abilities."

"A powderman, huh?"

"Here, a hundred dollars; enough to tide you over for a couple of days."

"What's to say I won't just take your money, stranger, and pull out of here?" he challenged.

"What I've given you is a mere pittance of what you can gain if you throw in with us."

"So far you haven't told me a damned thing."

"My name, at least for now, is none of your concern, Mr. Barfield. The work involved will take you out of Deadwood. And in a couple of days a man named —"

"I gather this be robbin' work, mister."

"Something of that nature, I can assure you."

"I don't come cheap. A hundred bucks; hereabouts a night on the town'll cost a man more'n this."

"We're speaking of gold bullion, Mr. Barfield."

"Figured you was," he snickered, and ran a hand up past his shaggy beard to rub it alongside his neck. "Guess any offer is better'n what I got now . . . which is plumb nothing."

"Expect a man named Ace Taylor to come by. I noticed your hands aren't all that steady."

"Your hands wouldn't be steady either you was poleaxed by a loaded drink," he growled angrily, which brought Orrin Risdale retreating toward the door. "Don't make it no longer than a couple of days, mister, as I've got expenses, too, dammit."

Out in the corridor, Risdale let the door bang close behind him. He cut toward a back door and eased into a murky alley, staying in the growing shadows until his eyes and senses grew accustomed to the greater darkness spreading over Deadwood. Then he went on to pause upon reaching the side wall stretching toward the front of the building, allowed a smile to show when he spotted those same men lurking up by the boardwalk. The twinkling of metal told him one of them held a knife or gun, and were waiting for his reappearance.

"Adios, gentlemen," he muttered in a quiet aside as he headed up the alley.

The routine of his working days never varied, first upon leaving the stageline office to find his rooms at the Grand Central Hotel. Refreshened by a hot bath and a change of clothes, he would have supper at any number of clubs before heading for the gaming halls. Later, if he found a woman that appealed to him, he would invite her up to his rooms. He shoved aside the fact that lately he'd been drinking too much, this caused by the double life he was leading.

Also he worried if the necessary players were being rounded up. And there's Little Reddy from Texas; somewhat unsteady of character. Just hope Ace Taylor talked Little Reddy into hooking up with us.

That this had been accomplished was revealed to Orrin Risdale when he entered the Grand Central Hotel and one of the desk clerks intercepted him by the staircase. "A Mr. Taylor is waiting in your rooms," was the whispered message. Upstairs, Ace Taylor related how a deal had been worked out with Little Reddy.

"I fired off a telegram to Cheyenne."

"Do you think that was wise?"

"Look, I don't want Payne or that Cado Greer thinking it was me takin' off with all that gold. As you've seen what Claiborne Payne can do when he gets upset. Little Reddy, he'll do just fine."

"I've found our powderman."

"You've got word on any gold shipments?"

"You remember, Ace, I must use discretion."

"That means you still don't know diddly."

"It means that a way must be found to move me a notch closer to Jason Hassrick. There is this other bookkeeper. If something happened to that worthy—"

"Why I'm here. Just give me his name."

"Sure, Ace," smiled Orrin Risdale, "and some of this imported brandy."

Ten

The voice of Gator Gruwell brought a lot more surging toward the stageline office.

"We've seen Crazy Horse!" he called out again while he was standing up on the Concord's front seat, waving one arm and the reins clasped in his other hand. "At least Moss here did! Go on, Moss, tell 'em wha'cha seen."

Moss Hollabaugh had just climbed down holding his rifle, and now he scowled up at Gruwell, undecided as to what to tell the people crowding in closer to press him against the Concord. Tugging at his hat brim, he got a look at Julia Hassrick just coming outside.

"Well, did you or didn't you see that murderin' Injun?" a miner said.

"There was more'n Crazy Horse we ran into," he finally said. He shoved forward to step onto the boardwalk, where he spun around to face the townspeople and the passengers they'd brought in gaping at him with disbelieving eyes.

"Just how many of them, Hollabaugh?"

"Actually we didn't get all that close," he said. "But it was Crazy Horse sure enough . . . and a lot more Teton Lakota . . . trailing northwesterly out of the hills."

"That's damned good news."

"I reckon it is," Moss said quietly, as he turned to smile

123

down at Julia Hassrick pushing closer. "Howdy, Julia, ma'am." He tried to put a certain elegance in his voice, but she wouldn't have none of that. She said curtly, "Is this the truth, Mr. Hollabaugh—"

"Ma 'am, I had occasion to set eyes upon Crazy Horse some years back."

"And where was that if I may be so bold as to ask?" she said skeptically.

"Down close to the Holy Road of the Oglala."

"Holy Road?"

"Perhaps," he said rudely, "you outta go to church more often." The last part of that sentence came back to her as Moss moved away. He went to where Gator Gruwell was waiting, near the stagecoach being unloaded by baggage handlers, and in stride they cut around the main building to make for the storage sheds.

Gruwell laughed. "Soon's I spouted off about us spotting them Oglala I thought one of our passengers was about to have a heart attack. First we see them outlaws hanging out at Six Mile . . . then it's Injuns we encounter."

"Lucky they knew we weren't carrying any gold."

"Which, them outlaws or them Oglala?"

"Both, I reckon. Gator, I'll see you later."

"Expect so, Moss. We won't be making another run for another couple of days at least."

"I expect so. That Julia, does she always spout off like that, or just to me?"

"Women," chuckled Gruwell, "I gave up on them some years ago; never could afford one or figure 'em out."

"Join the club," said Moss as he followed Gruwell into a front room built into one of the sheds. He crossed it to place his Henry in one of the rifle racks, and here a pot of coffee was heating on a woodburning stove. On a bare table lay a cribbage board and a used deck of cards. He threw Gruwell a silent nod before departing.

The upper walls of the canyon seemed even closer to Moss after the openness of the high plains. It was after five thirty now, but he held back from going in to see Jason Hassrick, the agreement between them was that Moss would slip up to Hassrick's large mansion after the stagecoach offices were closed. What he hadn't liked was Gruwell's calling attention to him. And it was a wonder that a reporter from one of the local newspapers hadn't been there, but Moss figured at least his luck was holding in that direction. As it had been on the incoming run when he'd struck that deal to throw in with Little Reddy from Texas.

On the way to his hotel Moss ignored the beckoning doors of saloons. The sun wouldn't set for another couple of hours. But even now miners were coming in on the winding trails, and here and there Moss could see tinhorn gamblers and other riffraff savoring to get at the gold dust these miners were packing. In a way the miners didn't care how much they threw away as tomorrow might see them finding that big mother lode.

Freighting outfits, such as a bunch of wagons just touching down into the canyon from the south, brought in most of the merchandise sold in Deadwood. The mule skinners in charge of those wagon trains were as foulmouthed as they came, but had to be to survive the long trips through mostly Indian country. Suits were becoming as common as the rigging of cowhands, and a man was naked if part of his attire didn't include a gun. Every so often a cavalry patrol would wend down main street. A message to the road agents hanging out here, Moss pondered.

"Hey, you big ugly galoot!"

That voice out of his recent past broke Moss's stride. He grinned at a man he'd shared a lot of dangers with on that long run up through Nebraska. Johnny Slaughter stood just inside holding one of the batwing doors open, and then Moss realized it was the saloon where others he worked with liked to hang out.

"Johnny . . . you old dog."

"Getting there but I ain't ready for a pine box just yet. Got me a girlfriend too."

"Asides what?" said Moss as he shook Slaughter's hand.

"Driving for the same outfit you are, Moss."

"I thought you wanted to chuck all of this and raise chickens."

"You ever see what chicken shit does to your boots," grimaced Johnny Slaughter as he drew Moss over to the bar.

Moss noticed that prominent among the other drivers were Shady Glover and one he knew only as Cacti Bill. Lounging at a table further back were Wacey Rydell and yard manager Pat Grady, his pleasant nod taking in both men. "So, tell me, Johnny, just why would a respectable stageline hire some renegade such as you?" A smile showed his appreciation for the glass of beer purchased by Slaughter.

" 'Cause I took a bath and shaved before I inquired about a drivin' job."

Wrinkling his nose, Moss said, "Smells like pickled pig's feet."

"My new girlfriend picked out this here vinegar cologne. She likes it good enough for me."

"Seriously, Johnny, up on those Concords we're just moving target practice for a rifleman."

"Yup, I suppose I could have struck out to the gold fields. But wadin' around in freezin' creek water ain't my game, I reckon. Somethin' you outta know." He touched Moss on the arm to bring them over to a window fronting just beyond the batwings, where Slaughter propped a boot on a convenient chair. "The name Ace Taylor mean anythin' to you?"

126

"Should it?"

"Man drops in here at times. Has that Colt's of his thonged too low to just be a drifting cowpuncher. Seems to be heeled as he springs for a lot of drinks. Paled skin gent like no matter how much he's outside just can't get a tan."

"Sorry," Moss shrugged, "just can't place him."

"What I'm gettin' at Moss is Taylor's awful curious about how we handle gold shipments. Maybe others are, too." He gazed out the window for a moment, the way a man would when he had more to say but didn't want to waste any words.

Moss had come to learn that Slaughter didn't waste much time over idle talk. When they'd ridden together on the Sydney run miles would slip past before Slaughter would point out some distant landscape, mostly to say that in between would be a place to watch out for an ambush.

A faint trace of blood lay where Slaughter had nicked himself shaving this morning, just to the right of his upper lip which was turned low to show his worry. And the grey eyes in his slat face showed that, squinted and glinting like a man about to speak his mind.

"Wouldn't be so concerned, Moss, if I hadn't seen this Ace Taylor hunkering over at the Gem Theater with that paper shuffler, Risdale."

"Yeah, Risdale . . . and now I do recollect setting eyes on Taylor before . . . pastyfaced like an albino."

"That's him."

"Look, Johnny, keep this to yourself."

"You know somethin' I don't?"

He wanted to tell Johnny Slaughter a lot more, but held back as he didn't want to draw a man he considered a friend in any deeper. He set his glass down on the window ledge. A smile poked through the two day stubble of beard. "How many runs have you made over to Cheyenne?"

"None as yet, Moss. But they're about done rigging up those new Concords; so's I expect to pull out sometime this week. But I reckon it can't be any different than what we had before."

"Longer."

"I heard about you running into those Sioux."

"They've pulled out Montana way."

"One less worry."

"Johnny, you keep your eyes peeled out there." His eyes quizzed thoughtfully. "Could be that new coach you'll be driving is rigged out to carry gold. Anyways, Mr. Slaughter, I've gotta run. You gonna hang around here?"

"Maybe as I've got my first paycheck in over a month."

A smile brought Moss away and out the door. His one fear at the moment was that either Risdale or the hardcase Ace Taylor had spotted Johnny Slaughter over at the Gem Theater, even though Johnny was a cautious sort. One thing for sure, when he dropped in on Jason Hassrick tonight he'd have a lot to narrate, and some of it about Orrin Risdale. Julia'll be there—a notion which brought a renewed spring to Moss's stride upstreet on the crowded boardwalk.

Once again Moss stood on a landing on the staircase spilling up from a mining camp gone mad with honkytonk music and lit up the length of the deep and narrow ravine known as Deadwood Gulch. Pine trees were stuck thick as porcupine quills into the rock walls, with more dark-cloaked pines wedged up around Whitewood Creek passing out of the ravine. The creek gave life to still more creeks; Deadwood, Fantail, Whitetail, Englewood, Yellow, Strawberry, Sheeptail, and others. Pitting the sandy bottoms of every creek were gold nuggets, and take that away and Moss knew nobody would have paid a plugged nickle to visit this place. Filtering upward as sort of a night companion was a nose-pricking stench caused by men whose only concern was of finding gold, and tonight, casting it into the clutches of the demimonde or gambler. A gun went off faint as a man farting downwind, one dog yelping set others to join in, and the moonlight simmering into the ravine skirting up from streets bathed in ankle-deep mud.

Moss held there as he was in no hurry. It was barely eight o'clock, the mansion of Hassrick's showing light on both floors. Wistfully he knew that it took money to own a place like that. It was a place meant to raise a family, and where a man could come home to the loving arms of his wife and children. He felt this was all behind him, that perhaps he'd gotten too settled into bachelorhood.

"Then why," he questioned audibly, "does she get under my skin . . . Julia?" Somehow he sensed that underneath all that aloofness there was a high-spirited filly waiting to be man-tamed. Before his entanglement with the army a couple of women had set marriage snares for him, but he'd adroitly sidestepped them, could barely recall their names now, only that one had been a pretty little brunette. But these or other women Moss had got to know hadn't been able to stir up feelings that he was experiencing about Julia Hassrick. Maybe she'd just stung his pride? Anyway, Moss chewed over as he started toward the house, there was the army still wanting him.

Since the last time he'd come up here, more work had been completed on a brick and wrought iron fence guarding the narrow fringe of front lawn, the fence cutting along the side of the house to hook up with a carriage shed. He found an open gate, passed into a square driveway, and had an anticipatory smile for the vague outline of someone standing just into the back doorway. At his approach the door was opened by a tall Negro wearing butler's attire.

"Mr. Hollabaugh, I presume." White teeth were bared in a face dark as a vein of coal, the eyes friendly and watchful and reflecting the barest touch of a coal-oil lamp hanging a short distance away.

Moss formed another smile for the butler, nodded politely as he removed his Stetson upon entering the back hallway to have the door closed gently behind him. At that moment a painful remembrance came of Wilbur Robeson just wanting to get home to his family, heroically the black man Robeson sacrificed all of that and his life for a white man. Just hope, he mused, I have the same courage to do likewise.

"Have you dined, Mr. Hollabaugh?"

"Grabbed a bite," he admitted, as the butler brought him deeper into the large house, with Moss hoping to get a glimpse of Julia. He could sense her presence, and that of the faint pricking of medicine when the butler stood aside to allow him passage into a room occupied by Jason Hassrick.

An ornately carved pool table occupied the other end of the room, the doors opening onto a walkway were closed, and alone at a table sat the owner of the Deadwood-Cheyenne Stageline Company. Sharing the table with a sumptuous spread of food were a few bottles of medicine and flickering candles. Hassrick sat at the far end of the table with pillows propped around him in the overstuffed chair. He gestured pensively at a chair, and Moss passed his hat to the butler before stepping over to sit down. He hesitated as a platter of meat was passed to him, and Moss said, "Guess I can't pass up some decent roast beef."

"A couple more of my coaches were hit; outbound to Cheyenne."

"Sorry to hear that, Mr. Hassrick."

"Heard about those Sioux pulling out of here which helps considerable."

"I reckon my past has caught up to me," spoke up Moss. He detailed the offer tendered to him by Little Reddy from Texas. "Some of your employees working up here have been tipping him off."

"Expected as much," Hassrick said bitterly.

"One of these scum could be that new bookkeeper—"

"That'd be Risdale?" Hassrick interjected.

"How do you want to work it?"

"First of all, this deal you worked out with these outlaws has them holding all the cards. You keeping on as shotgun." He poured brandy into Moss's glass as he studied the face of the younger man. "This gang of Little Reddy's is only one of several operating out there."

"But, as far as we know, the only gang being tipped off by some of your employees."

"Besides Risdale," he pondered, "who could it be? Trouble is, Moss, we hire someone; next week he quits to hit the gold fields."

"Risdale's a starting point." He ate slowly, wanting to string this out as there was half a chance that Julia might show up. The medicine smell wasn't so bad now that he'd had some more brandy. Which got him to scan Hassrick's face more closely, noticing also the slight tremoring of the hands. Aging had a lot to do with it and that bad leg, but mostly it had to be the strain caused by all these holdups. From Gator Gruwell he'd learned more had been winged than killed by these outlaws, that Jason Hassrick took it personal when this happened.

"Mr. Hassrick, you look like a man needing some time off."

"So my daughter tells me," he snapped. He set his glass down hard. "When I sink my teeth into something I just can't let go. The integrity of my stageline is at stake. To a lot of men out here honor, your word, has no meaning. But, dammit, its the bedrock

131

on which I built this . . . this stageline."

"Can't argue with that." He spun his glass around to create a wet pattern of spillage on the tablecloth, as the subject he was about to bring up might provoke some anger in Hassrock. Meaning that some people were damned touchy when it came to family. "What about your son-in-law?"

This brought Hassrock slumping back in his chair but still retaining a grip on his glass of brandy. With the other hand he reached up to brush back some unruly strands of greying hair; a scowl lined his forehead. He crunched his teeth together like a man finding something distasteful in his mouth. Then, to Moss's surprise, he let out a chuckling smile.

"Claiborne—asides being married to my daughter the man hasn't got too much goin' for him. Yup, he's taken on this Cado Greer."

"I've got Greer earmarked as a gunhand. And, Mr. Hassrick, your son-in-law has hired a few more of the same caliber."

"That so?"

"Can't be sure until I check it out . . . but hanging around Deadwood is a man I figure could be hooked up in this."

"Hooked up in what—"

"With your bookkeeper, Risdale."

"Makes sense, Moss. Why'd you drag Claiborne Payne into this as the man's working out of Cheyenne."

"Awful easy to send a telegram over there."

"Yes, awful easy. What you're trying to tell me, Hollabaugh, is that my son-in-law could be behind all of this." He leaned forward to pick up the bottle of brandy, the glint in his eyes that of a man ruling out nothing; the eyes gone hard, and despite the pain coming from his hip, filled with the awful enormity that perhaps Moss Hollabaugh could be right. "Should have done this before . . . as Julia suggested . . . check out Claiborne's bonafides. Too trusting, I reckon. Along with this notion that my son-in-law isn't all that smart."

"This is all speculation. Could be, I hope, I'm wrong about Claiborne Payne . . . for your daughter's sake."

"Mandy, yes, she'd take this hard. Trusting same as me. Should have been more like Julia. Well, what now, Mr. Hollabaugh? Hang around town for a few days, to keep tabs on Risdale."

"I don't want to disappoint Little Reddy from Texas by not sitting up there as shotgun."

"More than one can play at this game, Moss. Consider this as an opening gambit."

Once again she felt the exploring hand of her escort drift up the satiny expanse of her dress toward the deep well of her bosom. Only this time a word from Julia Hassrick brought the man's suggestive fingers away. Why had she let Crissy talk her into coming here? Everyone around Julia seemed to be enjoying the outrageous antics of a skinny man flitting about the stage as he strummed away at a banjo. She leaned in closer to Crissy clinging to the arm of her escort.

"Sis, I've had it."

"Why, Julia, the next act is a minstrel show."

"Just not my cup of tea." Julia's rising from her seat brought the man seated to her right scrambling up.

"It would be an honor to escort you home, Julia."

"Jack," she smiled sweetly, "I'd rather take my chances with the street muggers." Then she strode up the aisle and out of the Deadwood Theater.

She headed downstreet, glimpsing an occasional woman, but mostly it was miners prowling about on the

133

three blocks taken over by the marts of trade and pleasure. Three riders just touching onto the street brought a flicker of envy into her eyes, especially for the horseman in the middle. The woman wore fringed buckskins and a big-brimmed hat same's the others, rode as one accustomed to the saddle. What Julia wouldn't give at that moment to find out all the trails this trio of westerners had ridden. A feeling of restlessness quickened Julia's stride.

Even Deadwood is getting too tame, she admitted to herself.

Passing onto a sidestreet that would fetch her to the staircase wending up the canyon wall, she allowed a smile for a gambler doffing his hat. But her eyes were reliving the return this afternoon of Moss Hollabaugh. Rarely did her father allow any of the employees into his office, and it was yard manager Pat Grady that a man went to see for a job. Then on his way out Hollabaugh had dropped that snide remark off at her desk. Another overbearing cowhand, she'd thought at the time. Certainly not all that unhandsome, but just another hired hand. Then, why was it Moss Hollabaugh slipped occasionally into her thoughts? And this afternoon, her heart had seemed to skip a beat when she saw that Concord coming in.

"Come off it, girl," Julia murmured as she gathered up her long skirts and began moving up the rising walkway of wooden staircase, "you're too old to get moonstruck over a complete stranger."

As Julia Hassrick stepped onto one of the landings of the staircase still rising above her, something made her stop and glance back into the greater darkness below. There was something familiar about the man just starting up, and then he called up to her.

"That you, Miss Hassrick?"

"Sheriff, is something wrong?"

" 'Fraid it is," said Sheriff Seth Bullock as he labored up

to her. "Found one of your employees about a half hour hour ago, a miner found him. Man named Carl Landau. One of your office help, I believe—"

"Is he—"

"Yes, he's dead, Miss Hassrick."

She tried steeling herself, though the hand she brought to her lips trembled slightly. Landau, their chief bookkeeper, had decided to leave Iowa behind and accompany them here. She, as her father did, considered Landau a part of their family, a quiet man with a shy smile, and who'd never been married.

"His wallet and whatever money he carried was stolen. If you like, Miss Hassrick, I'll escort you the rest of the way home . . . break the news to your father . . ."

"No," she managed to say, "I'll do that. My father, he's been under the weather of late. Sheriff, thank you." Blindly she turned around and would have fallen if he hadn't held out a supporting arm. "Should watch where I'm going. Sheriff, please, we'll handle the funeral arrangements."

When Julia came off the staircase, it was to use the closer front entrance. In the wide foyer, and despite her efforts to ease in quietly, the butler materialized out of a side hallway. While a bare heartbeat later out of the study came a man she'd last seen this afternoon, and her father appeared a stride behind Moss Hollabaugh.

"Julia . . . where's Crissy, the others?"

She couldn't tear her questioning eyes away from Moss, which caused her father to say, "Ah, Mr. Hollabaugh is just leaving." He had a brisk nod for the butler, who stepped to open the front door.

"Obliged that you saw me," Moss said hesitantly. He took in a pearldrop of a tear touching Julia's lower eyelids; the concerned smile for her holding as he strode outside.

Even before the door closed Julia was moving over to

135

place a gentle arm around her father's wide shoulders. She managed to gulp down a choking fear of what she was about to say, brought her other hand up to clutch at his coat sleeve. "The others . . . they're still at the Deadwood Theater. I came home alone. On the way I ran into Sheriff Bullock . . . and he . . . he told me about Carl, about finding Carl out there."

"Finish it," he said with a twisting of his face muscles riding the lines around his eyes.

"Carl Landau was killed by a mugger. Oh, daddy, sweet, gentle Carl—all he had was us."

Somberly Jason Hassrick said, "Happens a lot out here. But . . . like you, honey, never expect it to happen to someone we love. Carl loved going home at night and get curled up with that Bible of his. Where, ah—"

"Sheriff Bullock has taken charge of the body."

"Yes, yes, there are some decent men out here after all. And, your sister, I'll wait up and break the news."

"That man, why was he here?"

"Company business. Nothing so important that it can't wait until later." Under ordinary circumstances that lame explanation would only serve to whet Julia's curiosity. Now he drew her toward the living room. "Carter, would you bring some brandy for us?"

An instinct of long intimacy told Julia Hassrick that her father was holding something back. And as for the man who'd just departed the house, it was clearly evident that this Mr. Hollabaugh was more than just another man riding shotgun for their stageline. Perhaps not tonight, or until Carl Landau had been laid to rest, would she demand the truth from her father. With this in mind she waited until her father had settled down on a sofa, and then she spoke.

"You know, Jason Hassrick, I'll find out the truth about this Mr. Hollabaugh."

"Do you really want the truth?"

"As long as you want me to take over running the stage-line I believe I'm entitled to that and more."

"The Pinkertons sent him here is about all I can say now, Julia. Only you and I know that."

"To do what? These robber bands hang out in the Black Hills, which is where this Hollabaugh should be, too."

"I've a feeling, honey, that Carl was killed for more than his wallet. Proving that is another thing."

"Which is where Hollabaugh comes in?"

"I'm hoping. I can tell you this. We believe that perhaps some of our employees are passing information about gold shipments to these outlaws."

"We've discussed this before."

"There were other things."

"You discussed with Hollabaugh?"

"Look, Julia, without proof you can't point the finger of guilt at anybody." He wanted to tell her that one of those under suspicion was her brother-in-law, Claiborne Payne. But doing so would only add fuel to her dislike of Payne, and more, cause hard feelings between Julia and Mandy.

"Yes, Carter, thank you for the brandy. Please, join us."

A sad smile lifted the butler's wide lips. "I considered Mr. Landau a friend. And I couldn't help overhearing some of what you said, sir. A pity everyone wasn't as trust-worthy as Mr. Landau was."

"Yes," agreed Julia. "Let's hope Mr. Hollabaugh can get to the bottom of this." Now that the shock of what had happened had gone away, she could think clearly again, knew that her father was trying to shield her from all of this. And Moss Hollabaugh—to her dismay his presence tonight had stirred up emotions that only came about when a woman cared for a man. But, another part of her said, this is ridiculous. "He's an impertinent . . ."

137

"What's that, honey?"

Through a blush coloring her cheeks Julia said, "Just thinking out loud." But when their eyes locked, Julia knew that her father had gained insight into her feelings, and the blush deepened. "Don't you, Jason Hassrick, read something into this. I, I . . . Carter, I'd like some more brandy."

Eleven

What struck him most of all about Jason Hassrick was this inner strength despite the man's being saddled with a crippling disease and these outlaw gangs playing havoc with his stageline. Moss was to learn the following morning of a further burden, revealing itself in a conversation going on at the next table at the DelRay Cafe.

"Landau was a bookkeeper over at that stageline."

"Was shot according to one of the undertakers."

His appetite waning, Moss left the rest of his steak and fried potatoes as he exited the cafe. A bitter musing; guess Orrin Risdale is making his move. Worrying him was just how Jason Hassrick would handle this. A lesser man would either call Risdale out or turn him over to the law. Having a friend gunned down cut to the bone. Then to have his murderer work for you, get paid a salary the same as men risking their lifes out on those Concords. All Moss could hope for now was that the owner of the Deadwood to Cheyenne Stageline Company didn't buckle under.

Among other things discussed last night was Hassrick letting Orrin Risdale be the stageline's liaison with the local banks. This was a duty performed up to now by Carl Landau. It boiled down to Deadwood banks combining their gold into one shipment, the time of departure known only by the stageline. This was like letting the fox into the chicken coop, in Moss's opinion. From here on Risdale would be shown the actual gold bullion being loaded into one of the new Salamander safes installed in the special Concords, and the Concord pulling out. What he wouldn't know about was a second Concord making that run.

The safe in it weighed down with rocks.

What Moss and Jason Hassrick still pondered over was just how Risdale or his confederates got word to the gang headed up by Little Reddy from Texas. He half-suspected the new telegraph line came into play, the outlaws having gained possession of a portable receiving sounder. Had to be, since the telegraph line pretty much followed the main stageline road to Cheyenne.

Lastly, and at Hassrick's suggestion, he'd vacate that high and perilous shotgun seat in favor of hanging around Deadwood. Moss hadn't argued as it just might give him an opportunity of setting eyes upon Julia again. For certain he'd see her when funeral services were conducted for the dead bookkeeper, Carl Landau. The thoughts of which turned his mind back to another scribe of ledgers. There'd be Risdale's confederates, the man spoken of by Johnny Slaughter, this pale-skinned hombre and that gang of road agents. But it seemed unlikely that a paper shuffler as he'd spoken of to Hassrick was pulling the strings of this robbing operation. Could it be that another telegram was being sent care of someone on Moss's list of suspects? And to Cheyenne?

Coming to a shadowed street corner still gripped by last night's chill, Moss looked northerly along the downsloping street at a stagecoach taking on passengers. It wasn't so distant that he couldn't make out shotgun Wacey Rydell jawing with a bystander. Handling the reins was Shady Glover. Coated baggage handlers were lashing down an accumulation of luggage. Only a handful of passengers were heading out so nobody would be forced to tether precariously on the back China seat. Common sense told Moss Hollabaugh to catch that stagecoach out of here. The sparkle of Julia's smile in his mind's eye brought a chiding smile of his own, and an observation shot out, "Hate to leave chores undone."

It took considerable willpower for Jason Hassrick to keep the accusing glimmer out of his eyes. It helped not to look directly at Orrin Risdale clustered with his other employees. Also coming in were Pat Grady and his yard crew and some of the men riding the coaches. Hassrick cleared his throat and said, "We've lost a good friend. None came better than Carl Landau. Burial services will be held tomorrow morning. We'll close at noon and all day tomorrow." He looked around for Julia, then remembered she was seeing about funeral arrangements. Then he stood there, just outside the door to his office, as some of his employees moved in closer to offer condolences, Risdale among them. No words were exchanged until he found Risdale edging in to mumble something, to have Jason Hassrick push back the rising moment of anger.

"Yes, Orrin, he was a good man. This means I'll have to lean more heavily on you now."

"Why, thank you, Mr. Hassrick."

Now he found himself standing along with Risdale, and he said gravely, "Strange thing is, that just the other day we were discussing giving you more responsibilities around here. Orrin, I want you to be my liaison with the banks. Come on in and I'll explain what's to be done."

Masking the elation he felt, Risdale followed behind the older man, limping as he eased behind his desk. As both men settled down, he pushed back his string tie dangling over the lapel of his suit coat. He knew that the stageline owner had a habit of building up to say something. This morning it took longer than usual, with Hassrick gritting his teeth together to squint down his eyes under the thick greying brows. Outside the office a clock chimed the hour, being ten now, the pecking sound assailing their ears coming from a newfangled invention called a typewriter. Then, for just a moment, he read something else into the gaze of Jason Hassrick other than a man sunken in grief. Cupping his hands together as if to pray, Orrin Risdale eased out a pious smile.

"Sometimes it is difficult to gather one's thoughts."

"It is," agreed Hassrick. "You also became acquainted with grief on that Sydney run."

"We lost a lot of good men."

"As we have up here. But, Orrin, this business doesn't allow us too many days off. Early tomorrow morning the banks will be bringing over any gold they want shipped out. That Concord, we're hoping, will pull out before sunup. But today I'll need you to drop over"—he pushed a sheet of paper across his desk—"to those banks you see listed here. Which Carl would have done. It'll take most of the afternoon . . . and I know I promised you the time off—"

"No, its quite all right, Mr. Hassrick. One has to earn his spurs." He sprang up, an eager smile gracing the smoothly shaved planes of his face. "And again, sir, my condolences."

"Yes, yes, of course. Ah, please close the door on your way out." And when the door was closed gently by Risdale, Jason Hassrick let out a disgusted exhaling of air. He reached down to pull open a desk drawer, out of which he lifted a glass and a bottle of corn whiskey. Usually a couple of fingers would do, but his anger was building and he about filled the glass. He picked it up and swung his chair to face a front window and crowded main street. For a brief instant he was gripped by anguish over what had

142

happened, then, gathering himself, he brought the glass to his lips to drain it.

"Damn you murdering son of a bitch Risdale . . . your day will come . . ." Hassrick pledged.

When Jason Hassrick's wife had passed away, Julia handled the burial arrangements. Julia was one of the few knowing her father's true character; underneath that gruff front he revealed to the world was a tender heart. Sometimes she wondered how he was able to handle all that was going on. She came to realize that a place such as Deadwood reshaped a man's thinking, sort of inured him, as it had done to her, to sudden violence.

An obeisant smile from a man bedecked in frock coat and a lacy shirt encouraged Julia to follow around an organ to yet another open casket on display. "We of the Black Hills Undertaking Company appreciate your business, Miss Hassrick. Isn't this a lovely casket . . ."

"Death is never lovely, Mr. Pierce. You mentioned he was shot twice—"

"In the shoulder."

"And again in the back. Which means Carl was trying to get away."

"I can only speculate on that. There were some bruises as though he put up a fight and his clothing was torn."

"This one will do, Mr. Pierce."

"Then we will have the burial services tomorrow morning. If you will care to look, Miss Hassrick, at our floral arrangements."

"That I'll let you handle," Julia said as she turned to leave. She went outside into the warmth of early afternoon, glad to get away from the clutches of the undertaker and that scent familiar to all funeral parlors.

Her first call this morning had been at the sheriff's office, where she'd talked Sheriff Bullock into taking her to the place where Carl Landau's body had been found. His deputies, Bullock had told Julia, had searched through the underbrush spilling away from the creek to higher ground, had found nothing to indicate that it had been anything but a mugging. And so he'd left, with Julia remaining by the creek.

What she hadn't told the sheriff was a deepening suspicion that this was premeditated murder. This very location told Julia that. Carl Landau would always take a pathway to the northwest after leaving work and head to his modest home wedged with others up along the canyon wall. Landau shunned the nightlife of Deadwood, was seen on the streets only when going to church or to buy groceries. So what had happened was as clear to Julia as the sun just coming out from behind a cloud. Upon leaving the stageline offices Landau had been waylaid and brought down to this lonely spot along the creek. Perhaps he had tried to get away, been shot first in the arm, with the killer coming after him through the thick underbrush.

"So, that's it," she murmured sadly.

Her father would, of course, say all of this was speculation. He would probably go on to say a woman's viewpoint carried little weight in matters of the law. Then, there was the man who'd been at their house last night, Moss Hollabaugh, the Pinkerton operative. Someone rude of manner, and just a little conceited, but a lot younger than someone as set in his ways as Jason Hassrick.

Wait a minute, Julia pondered. He also rides shotgun for us. He'll either hear me out or draw his walking papers.

Twelve

Above rimrock the sky was still coppered in blued tints. There was a wind, too, somewhat blustery but not able to stir up the dusty streets of Deadwood. While businesses handling hardware and groceries and such were shuttering up, every place that sold hard liquor was gearing up for the night trade. Over on Gold Street a new theater had placed ads in local newspapers saying it would open tonight; the enticement was free drinks and a massage parlor catering to sore-limbed miners. More tent saloons had sprung up in the spaces between buildings. Wild Bill Hickok, the notorious gunfighter, had accepted the decision by the city council not to hire him on as town marshal. Hickok could be found holding court at Number Ten Saloon.

Orrin Risdale had passed the saloon as he went about calling on several banks. The Miners & Mechanics Bank and the First National would be shipping out a hundred thousand in gold bars. With four other banks detailing their plans to ship an additional hundred thousand. On the way back to the stageline offices he found it necessary to detour into a saloon. He spilled more whiskey than he poured into a shot glass, filled as Risdale was with this startling news. Up until today he hadn't realized just how much gold was involved in these shipments.

"Two hundred thousand . . . one shipment alone'll set a man up for life. But all that money's gotta be split up too many ways."

What had caused his stomach to suck against his backbone was being actually allowed into the main vault over at the Miners & Mechanics Bank. Stacked in glittering enticement were those gold bars; a helluva lot more than was being shipped out. In the banks of Deadwood lay the mother lodes, an amassing of most of the gold brought in by the miners. He'd placed a caressing hand on some of those gold bars, and could feel a surge of envy to possess them course up his arm. It took considerable effort to pull his hand away and leave all of that gold behind.

"Here I am, out front so to speak," he muttered in a low and bitter aside. "Taking all the risks, for Ace Taylor an' Little Reddy's bunch . . . an' don't forget that Claiborne Payne. He ain't riskin' anything stuck over there in Cheyenne."

Supposing, Risdale mused, he told Jason Hassrick about his son-in-law's involvement in these stagecoach holdups. But that would leave Hassrick wondering where he had come up with this, and if it failed, well, Claiborne Payne wouldn't hesitate about using his knife. Part of a loaf is better than none, Orrin Risdale concluded, as he left to head back to the stageline offices.

Down in Deadwood Gulch night seemed to come quicker than out on the prairie. The slice of sky above Deadwood still held traces of daylight, and a few stars had poked out. The canyon walls threw back the raucous sounds of freespending miners. Earlier a mugger named Red Dake had picked out a couple of miners as easy marks. He'd picked them out upon their arrival shortly after noon, how carelessly they kept flashing leather pokes bulging with gold nuggets and where they took up lodging.

A couple of whores had tried to wrangle in on the deal over at Staley's Bigtime Bar, and almost had until the women had sought a bathroom, with Red Dake boldly going in, too. The butt of his revolver slamming into one whore's mouth brought the other one up clutching at her upraised petticoats, the scream freezing in her throat when he came at her.

"When you leave use the back door," came Red Dake's grim warning before he turned away and went back to the barroom.

Shortly thereafter, the whores seeming to have disappeared, the miners went on about the business of barhopping, with Dake trailing after. He knew the side streets intimately, what there was of them, and that at the rate the miners were pouring down the hard stuff he wouldn't have to wait too much longer. Then shortly after sundown he followed them down a side street, where they found the side door of still another saloon. When they settled down to play roulette, Red Dake also made himself comfortable across the street on a packing crate resting a short distance into the alley passing behind the Commerce Bank. From here he could see into the saloon.

Red Dake became aware of activity further along in the alley, a team of horses hitched to a covered wagon. Once in a while the back door of the bank would lurch open and men emerged, carrying boxes which they would place into the wagon. Another man was watching the horses, and at least three armed men stood guard.

Got to be gold bars they're shipping out, he pondered wistfully, and anyway, what could a lonely mugger do against all their weaponry. The sickening thud of the stock of a rifle slamming into the back of Red Dake's head drove that thought away and he tumbled off the packing crate.

"You might have caved his head in," one guard remarked.

"Might have," the other agreed.

"Wonder what he was doing out here?"

"Up to no good, I reckon."

"Yeah, nobody'll lose any sleep over that scum."

A soft whistle came from the man who'd clubbed the mugger, with one of those standing guard by the wagon waving in return. "Should be clear sailing from here over to the stageline offices."

They hurried over to climb into the wagon as did the other guards, with the other men coming out of the bank and locking the back door before going the opposite way. The wagon kept to the alley and then onto a side street well away from the place where Red Dake still lay unconscious. At the approach of the covered wagon, more men carrying rifles emerged from one of the Deadwood-Cheyenne Stageline barns, and with them, Jason Hassrick and his bookkeeper, Risdale.

"A simple operation, really," commented Hassrick as he limped aside, the wagon rolling through the open double doors. When it did, everyone went into the barn and the doors were closed again.

This was the third wagonload of gold that Orrin Risdale had witnessed arriving at the stageline barn. He took careful note of how the gold was being loaded in the new Salamander safe and other details about the interior of the special Concord. What disappointed him was of the gold being stored in special boxes. Which left in him a nagging doubt that any gold was actually being shipped. But what else could it be, there were so many guards, the air of secrecy about this whole operation, and now the other double doors opening and a six-span team of horses being walked in.

"To say the least, Mr. Hassrick," he said, "this is exciting."

"Just a job," responded Hassrick.

148

"I never realized so much was shipped out at one time."

"More than this at times," he said cagily, just to watch the reaction of Orrin Risdale. Shortly before the arrival of any gold wagons, he had drawn Risdale aside for a private word. Three men would ride inside with the Salamander safe, there'd be the driver and shotgun, and hooking up just outside of town would be a cavalry patrol from Fort Meade. He even ticked off the approximate times the special Concord would pull into the first few stage stations on the way to Cheyenne. This was all done with considerable effort by Jason Hassrick. But if this man, this damnable killer, was selling him out to the road agents, it could be no other way. Through his anger a sorrow worked its way into Hassrick's worried thoughts, for this could fail and some of his men could get hurt.

Within the span of a quarter of an hour the rest of the wagons bearing gold pulled into the barn. Once the gold had been transferred to the Concord, these wagons left, and so did Jason Hassrick with Risdale at his side. Coming out of the shadows was Hassrick's private buggy, and he forced a smile for his bookkeeper.

"Can I give you a lift?"

"No, it isn't that far to my hotel. But much obliged, Mr. Hassrick. And sir, you don't know how terribly sorry I feel about what happened to . . . to Mr. Landau. Well, good night, sir."

Another shadow stirred to bring the outline of a big-hatted man ghosting along the wall of a nearby barn. A cat, out in search of another tom or something to eat, spit at Moss Hollabaugh taking in the buggy pulling out onto Main Street. He had a different expression for Orrin Risdale scurrying away, and bitterly intoned, "Somewhere along the line he must have sold his mother dirt cheap.

149

Men died down in Nebraska 'cause of him."

Moss had for the last couple of days followed Orrin Risdale's nightly ramblings about Deadwood. The man would hit the gaming tables around eight o'clock, and it was generally stud poker in a high stakes game. Risdale liked to have a drink at his elbow and a woman hovering close at hand. Bookkeepers didn't make this kind of money, and so Moss reckoned it was blood money Orrin Risdale had gotten from his robbing partners down along the Nebraska stageline run. And it figured that Risdale was being paid off by Little Reddy from Texas. Night before last he'd followed the bookkeeper over to a boarding house, to have Moss learn about Risdale's taking on this powderman. But there'd been no sign of Risdale's other partner in this, the albino. As for Risdale, Moss knew he was on his way to his hotel.

At the appearance of armed guards, Moss ducked back into the lee of a doorway, and now the Concord rolled out of the barn. It was driven the short distance to another of Hassrick's barns, where the driver reined up. And here came the part that Hassrick hadn't bothered to tell his new bookkeeper. There was a brief flash of lantern light as the double doors creaked open, the light being doused as a second Concord came into view. The Salamander safe in this second Concord had been filled with rocks, the plan being for it to stick to the schedule of the other stagecoach. The Concord carrying the gold bullion would leave a half-hour later.

If everything went according to schedule, Moss pondered, the first Concord should strike onto that section of trail coming onto the Coney stage station some two hours after sunup. By this time Risdale or the albino would have gotten word to those outlaws.

"Well," said Moss as the Concord started moving his way, "let's hope it works out as planned." He knew the driver, a Kansan, sawing at the reins, then worry rimmed his eyes when he realized Johnny Slaughter was up there as shotgun. "Hope Johnny's first run out of here won't be his last."

Once the Concord had slipped away, Moss retraced his route along the building to hurry into an alley. From here his pace slowed. He took a side street to the main drag packed along its narrow limits with night denizens. Chasing after the bookkeeper these past few nights made him appreciate quieter places such as the High Plains. Out there it was generally a puma tracking down a mule deer in the stillness of a prairie night. Or a black bear defying gravity by trying for a honeycomb perched high in some pine tree. Here in Deadwood he could pick out, be it day or night, those preying on others. But the law arrested one of these night stalkers and three more came in. As for Moss Hollabaugh, one look into his eyes or the purposeful way he moved and a man intent on harm drifted elsewhere. Pausing under a porch jutting over the boardwalk, Moss took in the hotel across the street and light pouring out of the bookkeeper's room.

"Another hour until he leaves his hole. Time enough to grab something to eat."

Up in his hotel room all Orrin Risdale could think about was all of the gold he'd seen today, a fact that caused him to draw blood with the straight-edge razor. "Damn," he said into the mirror above the sink, and then around a grin, "To think a shipment goes out every day."

Bare from the waist up, only a few hairs covered the sunken parrot chest. The thin arms seemed to be whitewashed slats hooked to shoulder bones, one of them extending upward to have the long fingers of his bony hand curl around the hanging towel. He wiped the two patches

151

of blood and shaving cream from his face, held by the mirror as he gazed into his eyes throwing questions back at him.

One gang alone, he'd concluded, just couldn't cut the mustard. All Little Reddy had was about a half-dozen men. What was needed was more guns out there, at least twenty men. It meant splitting the gold up more, but the more you took the more there was to make a man rich. And that man would, of course, be Orrin Risdale.

"Ace Taylor," he muttered upon tossing the towel aside and turning to reach for a shirt, "is damned tight-lipped. So don't know how he'll react to what I've got in mind." The fear of Risdale's was of the albino deciding not to play along, of Ace Taylor's getting word to Cheyenne. On the other hand, Risdale knew the safe way was to bring Claiborne Payne in on this. But why? came a disdainful thought.

I'm the one in the driver's seat on this. But, easy now . . . first there's this Concord pulling out tonight. Should be easy pickings once Ace gets word down to Litle Reddy. But afterwards . . . I damn well want more than lunch money.

For this evening's night on the town the bookkeeper had picked out one of the tailormade suits that had been delivered earlier in the day, a vested banker's black with padded shoulders and a special coat pocket so's he could pack his Hammond Caliber .41 rimfire. The lifts in his black boots added to his self-assurance and gave a couple of inches to his stature, the hat a soft grey felt and more of an eastern style. A final touch was the blue handkerchief he placed in his lapel pocket. Although he'd armed himself with swanky clothes, a wary cunning in the bookkeeper came to life when he left his rooms, a sixth sense that scanned the immediate street outside the hotel before he pushed the lobby door open. Last night he'd picked up a warning vibration. Tonight his musings were more on getting word to Ace Taylor about that gold being stagecoached out instead of any thoughts of personal danger as he set out boldly along the street.

Not for one minute did the bookkeeper consider he was violating a trust. Working for Jason Hassrick was just a means to get at that gold. If anyone should have stirrings of guilt it should be Hassrick's son-in-law. The killing fangs of Claiborne Payne had struck once, so Risdale knew he had to tread carefully in what he said to Ace Taylor. He had a hunch that Taylor, though greedy, was no fool. Meaning Ace would think twice about cutting his ties to Cheyenne. Of equal consideration was the nagging possibility that Hassrick had fired off a telegram to the Cheyenne office about this latest gold shipment.

Somehow we've got to get Cheyenne out of this and get rid of Payne," he concluded.

The Melodeon, an unsavory saloon passing itself off as a theater, received through its front door a natty Orrin Risdale. Lingering upstreet under the double-decker porch in front of Liebmann's San Francisco Bazaar was Moss Hollabaugh. This was a departure from Risdale's nightly routine of dining at the Franklin Hotel.

Moss finished shaping a tailormade, and he studied the passersby when striking a match against a porch railing. It could be that the albino hung out at the Melodeon. One thing for certain was that Risdale hadn't gone over to the telegraph office. So this had to be a chore handled by Risdale's confederate. Flipping the wooden match away, Moss dragged on the cigarette, took in a bull team plodding downstreet under a banner the town council had strung across the street.

A conclusion reached by Moss was that the owner of the

Deadwood-Cheyenne Stageline Company could only do so much to stop these robberies. Paperwork tied Hassrick's hands as did the disease crippling his legs. And he'd have to renege on that promise given to the outlaw chieftain. So Moss had decided to forsake riding shotgun in favor of cutting a deal with the bookkeeper and the albino. Perhaps, as he suspected, the pair of them were hashing things over in the Melodeon.

Tugging at his hat, Moss strode on through cigarette smoke drifting past his eyes. At the Melodeon he held in the doorframe, then located the bar off to his left. A lot of eyes checked out the newcomer, the way the six-gun was thonged down, decided there was easier game to tackle. He didn't spot the bookkeeper, but Moss did manage a smile for a woman holding a tray as he wedged a boot up on the brass railing.

"Evening."

"Same to you, handsome."

"Want to earn another one of those?"

She dropped her gaze to the double eagle gold coin still twirling on the bar top. "Depends . . ."

"You buyin' her a drink too—"

To the bardog Moss said, "Yup." He kept his smile trained on the barmaid, not all that old but already hardened to this life. "I'm looking for an old friend . . . lean and a little shorter than me . . . paleskinned gent—"

"Another double eagle."

He picked another one onto the bar.

"Figure him for a gunfighter; calls himself Al Jennings."

"Then he's here?" His hand encircled her arm snaking toward the double eagles.

"Easy, mister, that hurts. Yeah, upstairs in one of the front rooms. You a lawman?"

"Never had that dubious honor." He released her arm.

"Jennings," she said anxiously, "he's mean as they come,

154

beat up one of the girls."

"Yeah, and thanks." Moss left a couple of silver dollars for the drinks being set down by the bartender as he turned and headed for the staircase. Going up he passed a whore coming down with a miner, tucking his shirttail into his grimy Levis.

The rooms, he found out, were spread along a balcony running toward the back wall and opposite. The bare wood floor creaked under his boots and the pine board walls were unpainted. He checked out one door for any sound inside the room, another, stayed by the third door as he heard the voice of Orrin Risdale echoing out. Quickly Moss yanked the door open to shoulder into the room. The men he sought were seated across from one another at a small table behind which a window let in starlight. Both the albino and Risdale sprang up, and Risdale pulled back the hand going for his shoulder gun when he recognized the intruder.

Moss said cuttingly to the albino, "Go ahead if you feel lucky." Before entering he'd brushed his coattail aside, and now he stood with his fingers brushing against his holstered six-gun, a smile on his lips.

"No, Ace, I know this man."

"You'd better, Risdale, or he's gonna be a dead one."

"Obliged, Mr. Risdale," he said calmly. "Yup, Ace, we both work at the same place."

"Hollabaugh, there, rides shotgun for the stageline. I . . . we worked together down in Nebraska."

"So?" Ace Taylor lowered onto the chair. "What is this, old home week—"

"I just want to be cut into this," Moss responded as he shuffled sideways to keep an eye on the albino and reached back to close the door.

"You'd better make that clear," Risdale said huffily.

Moss sickened inside at this protestation of innocence

155

by the bookkeeper. Men had died because of Risdale's treacheries. Staring at the man, and trying to mask his feelings, Moss realized that Risdale and the albino were past redemption. The eyes of both men held a hard, uncaring glaze, their faces expressing a shared cruelty as when a seal is pressed into wax.

"It'll be no clearer than this," Moss said goadingly. "About Little Reddy spilling the beans about you two."

As he'd hoped, and was ready for, Moss dipped his right hand to slap it gunward as the albino made his move. Ace Taylor spun up from the chair holding the .44 he'd snaked out of his holster, but the barrel was still levelling up when Moss's six-gun sounded, and the bookkeeper froze to his chair. A bullet sank into the folds of the albino's coat, about chest high, even so, the gun bucked in his hand. Then the hand holding the .44 revolver splayed out blood from a slug shattering his wristbone. Even when staggering backwards there was a hell-bent gleam in Ace Taylor's eyes. He tried reaching over with his left hand for his gun, blood staining the front of his shirt.

"Barroommm—"

Moss could hear his ears ringing from the walls of the small room throwing back the crackling of his gun, the slug punching into the albino and pitching him toward the closed window. He took glass and window frame on his plunge to the ground below. Thumbing back quickly the hammer on his weapon, Moss swung it to cover the bookkeeper.

"No . . . no . . . please," Risdale cried out, "I want no part of this."

"You're already part of it." Sidling to glance toward the door, Moss took in the heavy thud of footsteps coming up the staircase. Stepping over, he threw the bolt to lock the door, swung back and over to Orrin Risdale cringing to his feet. "I expect those are friends of Ace wondering about

156

his welfare. It's you and me now, bookkeeper. Part of a deal made by me and Little Reddy. Yup," he smiled at the confusion playing across Risdale's ashy face, "I'm gonna be your new partner up here."

"Certainly . . ." Frightened eyes took in the sounds penetrating into the room and of someone calling out Ace Taylor's name.

"You first."

"What?"

"Jump," explained Moss, as he shoved Risdale toward the window. "If the fall doesn't kill you Ace's friends will."

Then the door shook under the impact of those outside trying to break it down, and Risdale swung a leg over the windowsill and crouched there before a shove in the back from Moss helped him on his way. Moss scrambled out and simply let go, to land alongside the bookkeeper groaning in pain. For Moss there was a brief moment to get his wind back, a glance also for the albino staring back at him out of sightless eyes. Then he grabbed Risdale by the arm.

"Come on, let's vamoose before they start fanning lead down at us."

Together they came erect, and with Moss helping the limping Orrin Risdale behind the protective wall of the next building. "How's your leg?"

"It hurts . . . believe I just skinned it . . ."

"So, as I said, now you'll be dealing with me." Moving onto a side street, Moss headed in toward the darker maw of a canyon wall and the Dakota Saloon, the last building on the block.

"Where did you run into McKimmie?"

"Some days ago down at Six Mile stage station. We struck up a deal. Sorry about your pal, Ace, but he gave me no choice."

"Ace was the one getting word to McKimmie."

"I know all about that telegram scam. What about this

157

latest gold shipment, did Ace get word down there yet?"

"I . . . I don't know."

"Guess that leaves it up to us." He allowed Risdale passage into the saloon, the barroom occupied by a lonely bartender and about a handful of customers. Armed with a bottle of corn whiskey, Moss wedged down across from Risdale as he set the bottle down. He poured a drink for his table companion, allowing Risdale to down that shot glass and a couple more.

"I know that Little Reddy is only a hired gun. As was the albino. Same's you, Risdale, being just a glorified messenger boy."

The whiskey served to fetch back some of Orrin Risdale's cynicism, and as he reached for the bottle he said with just an edging of sarcasm, "I resent your implication—"

Moss's retort shot out harsh as the crackling of his Henry, "Your friend the albino made the mistake of pissing me off! He's dead . . . and you could be! We both work for the stageline, so what's to keep me from finding out what you know about gold being shipped out. You get my drift, bookkeeper, I really don't need you." A smile so cold it seemed to bring the touch of winter parted Moss's lips. Into his eyes came an even colder gaze. He let all of this sink into Risdale's frightened thoughts, let the silence build and the fear. Now came another cold volley of words.

"Was it you or the albino getting word over to Cheyenne?"

"You know . . . about that?"

"Just you and me, Risdale, and this bottle of whiskey." Now Moss filled his shot glass and Risdale's. "Unless you're holding out on me?" His eyes lifted suggestively.

"No, no, Hollabaugh, I swear, it's just Ace and me up here at Deadwood."

"What about Cheyenne way, is it just the honorable Claiborne Payne? Or others we've got to worry about—"

"Just Payne as far as I know," he scrambled out.

"Payne's smart," Moss said conspiratorially, "so he won't show you all of his hole cards. And he's really pulling the wool over Hassrick's eyes. Payne's hired on a bunch of hardcases."

"One I know of, a man named Greer . . . Cado Greer."

"He's the one who did the killing over at the Cricket Saloon?"

"No," exclaimed Risdale. "It was Payne! Just like that . . . in front . . . in front of everyone . . . used his knife." A trembling hand swept the bottle of whiskey up from the table. "He's worse than some animal . . . Payne."

"You realize what this means?" Moss demanded.

Risdale blinked in confusion.

"Simple, bookkeeper. You're expendable. Sooner or later Payne has to take you out. Since he can't have you going to the law about this."

"I didn't think about this," Risdale said hesitantly.

"The albino must have been sending coded telegrams to Payne. Men of Ace's breed get killed; a hazard of their craft. You'll simply take over for the albino, first by firing off a telegram or letter to Cheyenne. Once Payne learns about the albino's demise he'll have no choice but to give you a bigger share of the pot."

With these words there returned to the bookkeeper more of the old self-assurance, and less of a fear of Hollabaugh. "Yes," Risdale said eagerly, "as you say, Payne'll have to see things my way. You know, I'd just been discussing with Ace Taylor the need to revamp this operation. All this gold being shipped out. Until today I never realized just how much. Millions, Hollabaugh."

And Moss Hollabaugh had to look away from that lustful mask presented to him by the bookkeeper, had to choke away thoughts of how this man's lust for gold had resulted in men he knew going under.

"We'll need more than Little Reddy's bunch." Orrin Risdale glanced around before edging his chair closer to the table and continued in a lowered tone of voice, "Think what thirty or more men can do . . . say split them up into three gangs . . ."

"What about Cheyenne?"

"Payne? We can string him along. After all, we're taking all the risks. Why should he get a cut of this? Just send a couple of hired guns over there . . ."

Bold talk for a bookkeeper, Moss pondered. But out of this an idea had formed, though first he had to take control of the bookkeeper's wild ramblings. "I cotton to the idea of using more men out in the field. But simmer down, Risdale. As these walls have ears. First I'd worry about the present situation, that Concord pulling out of here earlier tonight."

"Yes, did Ace get word down to Little Reddy? The telegraph office is still open I'm hoping."

"Take care of that. And not a word to anyone about this. By the way, did that powderman leave yet? Yup, Risdale, I knew about that too. Among other things." He rose to stand looking down at the bookkeeper, his face set. "Remember, there's Payne over at Cheyenne . . . an' me here, Mr. Risdale."

Striding out of the saloon, Moss felt a prickling at his skin as if he'd come in contact with something unclean. But despite this, and the bitter anger he had for Orrin Risdale, out of the man's rambling had come the formings of a plan. It would mean making contact with the U.S. Army, and perhaps his being clapped into an army stockade.

But what else did he have have that would help to take out these road agents?

Moss wondered on his way back to his hotel if gunplay could have been avoided and decided it couldn't as the albino had been too primed up to hear him out. There should be some stirrings of regret over the killing instead of this drained-out feeling. Man, if you can call the albino that, deserved it, he mused.

The other one, Risdale, was just a lowlife. More so, since the bookkeeper had benefit of an education. Maybe he even attended Sunday services. As did a lot of hypocrites, just to keep in good standing with the community rather than because of respect for what the Good Book said. One thing for sure, Orrin Risdale was running scared. But his greed would keep him on at the stageline.

Interesting news, Moss felt, as to the character of Claiborne Payne. Killing a man in a crowded saloon was damned brazen, and by doing so, Payne had kept the bookkeeper in line. The only real evidence Moss felt he had against Payne was the bookkeeper's story of what had happened. That wouldn't be enough in a court of law, as a clever lawyer would tear Risdale to shreds. As Moss saw it, the way to get at Payne was through Risdale. And it just might work, because both men wanted to get at those gold shipments.

But to turn against one's family as Claiborne Payne has done. He left that bitter refrain on the boardwalk as Moss went into the lobby of his hotel. The lobby was empty, the wall clock showing it was almost eleven, and until now he hadn't realized how tired he was. Leaning over the counter, he lifted the one key out of the pigeonhole cabinet. His hotel wasn't as pretentious as the Grand Central up another block, but he could afford the rates. Upstairs, Moss paused by the door to his room, checked behind him, with Moss realizing he was still edgy over what had happened. Unlocking the door, he eased into his room, to right away

161

pick up the lingering aroma of perfume. His eyes swiveled to the creaking of bed springs.

"About time you got here."

The light that came in from the hallway and the two windows peeking down at main street revealed to Moss a woman pushing up from where she'd been sitting on his bed, and when she spoke again he knew with a flickering of surprise it was Julia Hassrick.

"Well, Miss Hassrick, I don't know what to say. Other than you could have lit that lamp." Which Moss did, and turned to Julia with a half-smile, which her accusing eyes chased away.

"This isn't what you think, Hollabaugh."

"And what is that?" The smile returned.

"Let's call a truce," she said. "Well, you could close the door."

"Okay, lady, as you command." Closing the door, he stood by it as Julia sank onto a chair by one of the windows. He went over and sat down on the other chair on the other side of a small table centered between the windows. The curtains were pulled, and he let his attention drift to the action on the street below. Her presence, he realized, had to be because she'd found out he was working for the Pinkertons. At least Moss hoped she considered him something more than a man able to handle a rifle.

"I have every reason to believe Carl Landau was murdered."

"My feelings," he affirmed. "I saw you and the sheriff heading out to the creek. I checked it out earlier, and dropped in to see the undertaker. Julia, if I may call you that—"

"Moss . . . doesn't have much of a ring to it. But, if you insist you may call me Julia." Suddenly her laughter rang out in the room, forced perhaps, but knifing through the web of tension between them. "I'm sorry, I . . . let's just

162

say Moss will do."

"My folks thought so. Julia, wouldn't it be better if you leave this to your father and me."

"Because I'm a woman?" she snapped.

"Because I don't want to see you get hurt."

That accusing look went out of her eyes as she considered Moss's words. "You must forgive me if I'm being overly protective of my father. As for you, Hollabaugh, I'll accept what you just told me." Now straight out she added, "I believe you know who murdered Carl."

And now Moss realized he had to tell Julia Hassrick that he'd also committed murder, that by doing so she would be drawn into the danger of what was to come. Perhaps he should just tell her to leave, and early tomorrow morning before the funeral, get together with Jason Hassrick. Indecision playing across his face, Moss studied the face of the woman in his room. Perhaps it was the way lamplight played across her face or highlighted the hair flowing over her shoulders, or again just her presence, but the urge to take Julia in his arms was strong. What didn't help was that her eyes never left his, until he broke them away.

"Julia, I . . . I was involved in a shootout, earlier tonight. I gunned down the man who murdered Carl Landau." He shifted on the chair, trying to sort out what to say next.

"He deserved it, whoever he was." Reaching out, she touched his hand. "Please, Moss, I could leave. I know you must have a lot on your mind. But, why? Carl was no threat to anyone?"

"Got to level with you, Julia. There's a lot going on here. What I'll need is a few days to learn more. You can understand that?"

"Is my father in any danger?"

"That's hard to say, Julia. You could be now. Me, it's

163

my job." He wanted to detail her brother-in-law's involvement in this, and more, to take her in his arms. They rose together, standing close, with Moss ever so conscious of the heady scent of her perfume and the way her eyes gazed up into his. More than an unspoken truce had sprung up between them. Then, to his disbelief, she took the single step that brought them together.

Moss Hollabaugh found Julia's lips seeking his gently, like a woman still uncertain about a lot of things. Before he could bring up an arm to encircle her shoulders, Julia Hassrick drew away and toward the door. She reached the door and turned around with a swirling of skirts. She said, "Are you coming to the funeral?"

Her words brought back her reasons for coming here, and Moss replied, "Yes, I certainly will." He crossed to the door and opened it. "Afterwards, Julia, I'll be heading out for a few days."

"One thing before I go, Moss. My father didn't say it in so many words, but could some of our employees be involved in this?"

"That could be. We ship out a lot of gold; a tempting target for a lot of people around here, Julia. You know, we sent out more'n one Concord earlier tonight. One's a decoy. We're hoping things work out as we planned. Julia, I could walk you home."

Framing an assured smile, she said, "I'll see you tomorrow, Hollabaugh." And then she was gone.

And without Julia in it, the room seemed a much lonelier place. What had happened between them, Moss was still puzzling over as he began undressing. Later, in bed, he brought back to the forefront of his thoughts his long talk with the bookkeeper.

Should go to the local law, Moss debated silently, about all of this. But just who can you trust in Deadwood? Which means I've got to own up to my past. That means having a powwow with the army.

And if that didn't work out, and the U.S. Army announced in Deadwood newspapers that it had captured a wanted man, meaning former army scout Moss Hollabaugh, any chances he might have had with a woman such as Julia would evaporate.

Julia, you're some woman alright. Beyond you though, are some who got gunned down all because of scum such as that bookkeeper and the albino and others . . .

Somewhere in the crowded confines of a gold town baying at the moon gunfire crackled, a familiar sound to Moss Hollabaugh, and the suggestive laughter of a whore picking its way through the open windows.

Never thought when I left Oregon life would get so infernal complicated. What did Johnny Slaughter once say, yup, to roll with the punches, or that don't work, to get yourself a good dentist. An' keep your eyes peeled out there, Johnny boy.

The added worry of Slaughter riding that high Concord seat on his way to Cheyenne brought Moss worming onto his side to cast an eye at the clock on the chair by his bed.

Goin' on one; enough worry for one day.

Which brought his mind again on Julia, and soon he fell asleep.

Thirteen

Little Reddy from Texas figured he'd been witness to every human depravity in a criminal career of long standing. He'd murdered out of hand, seen others do the same, knifework or guns, seen the handiwork of the Pawnee and Comanche, in white men being scalped or their skin peeled away from chin to pelvic bone. Last night two whores had gone at it over him, with Pawnee Liz coming to his bed after she'd about decapitated the other woman, a redhaired hussy. If anything, it had made Pawnee Liz appreciate him more.

Then Cado Greer and other hardcases had pulled into the Six Mile stage station around midday. They'd forgone the stageline buildings to head right over to Cuny's place, just to the east. It was Greer who came in alone to seek out Little Reddy.

"Ace Taylor told me you'd be dropping over." Little Reddy didn't bother taking his boots down from the other chair at the table, so that big and slow-moving Cado Greer had to drag one over; neither of them were at the handshaking stage as yet.

"Mind if I slake my thirst?"

The Texan slid the bottle over with his left hand.

Greer picked it up as he sat down, and before drinking, he took from an inner coat pocket the letter given to him by Claiborne Payne. The envelope had been folded twice, and was torn and soiled with dirt, and he'd read what Payne had written to the Texan, which he announced in a scorning voice. "Could have told me to tell you that, about taking out his wife." The bottle was at the halfway mark when he brought it to his lips, and it was empty as he burped and heaved it into a dark corner.

Nodding, Little Reddy took the time to unfold the envelope and pull out the single sheet of paper. What he read brought a grin. "Just was ruminating about human depravity. Payne's right up there with the Apache, I reckon. Five hundred if I gun his missus down. Can't care too much for her."

"He likes the whores," snorted Greer.

"Who don't."

"Bardog," growled Cado Greer, "get your ass over here with another bottle . . . an' we want some chow, too." It took some doing to get Greer worked up, but the long ride over from Cheyenne had given him ample time to decide that he didn't like taking orders from Little Reddy, as had been his agreement with Payne. To take orders from a man half his size was bad enough, and now to sit here gazing at that mocking smile on a man he could easily hammer into sawdust was getting him at the ragged edge of doing something reckless.

The bartender was about as big as Greer, but soft through the middle. He came over with a bottle filled with barrel whiskey cut by adding water, and for taste, molasses. He had a fleshy face and hard flinty-black eyes which threw the newcomer a challenge as he set the bottle down. He answered to the name of Garth, and claimed to have worked on Mississippi steamboats as a bouncer. Though he had overlooked the rowdy behavior of the outlaws, more than one cowhand or miner had felt the sting of his fists. A hideout weapon he preferred using was a blackjack which he carried in a back pocket. He said to Little Reddy, "You know this hellion?"

Before the Texan could answer, Cado Greer's arm swept up in a backhanded blow that caught the barkeep right under the chin. Garth seemed to rise up with the force of the blow before plunging over backwards, and he landed heavily. Greer labored to his feet, and snarled his rage as he brought the toe of his boot slamming into the barkeep's upper chest. Neither Little Reddy or the other outlaws clustered nearby nor the other bartender came forward as Greer kept kicking away, a final kick of his boot into the head of Garth knocking him out.

"You busted him up bad," the Texan said to Cado Greer reclaiming his chair. "But Garth had too high an opinion of his fighting abilities."

"That was no fight," Greer muttered.

"Look, Cado, just what the hell is eatin' at your craw, if you don't mind my askin'?"

"Forget it."

"Nope, as we'll be workin' together." He looked around at the outlaws riding with him. "They take orders from me. I expect your men will follow what you have to say. What I'm saying, Cado, is that we can ramrod this together, swap opinions of what to do."

Cado Greer's eyes showed he was considering what the Texan had just said, though his face was still flushed with anger. He forced a grin after a while, that went away when he said, "Ace Taylor is our man over at Deadwood. And there's another; some bookkeeper, Risdale."

"You can count on Risdale as we parded down in Nebraska. Had a sweet thing goin' until that stageline went under."

"We bought it out. Got it operatin' again."

They ignored the other bartender and two men coming over to carry away the man still laying unconscious close to their table. Little Reddy was detailing just how they'd been keeping in touch with the albino, Ace Taylor. That earlier in the week the albino had brought down a man with the talents necessary toward dynamiting open the new safes carried in Concords owned by the Deadwood-Cheyenne Stageline Company.

"Until these new safes have been installed in those Concords they haven't been shipping out any gold. But there's a heap of gold up there, Cado, which I aim to get."

"I didn't care for that deal we had worked out with Sam Bass and his bunch. But," Greer spread his large hands apart, "Bass cut out of here. Which leaves you and me, Little Reddy."

A nod from the Texan brought Dunc Blackburn and the deck of cards he was holding over to the table. Little Reddy announced for the benefit of everyone there, "This is Cado Greer . . . who'll be joining up with us. Bevans, why don't you and Wall go out and get acquainted with the others. Tell 'em the drinks are on Little Reddy from Texas. As for you, Mr. Greer, I hope you're feeling better."

"A mite. So?"

"There's this letter from Payne. And the matter of that five hundred dollars he'll give to the man gunning down his missus. An easy five hundred for someone like you or me. What say we cut, the one of us drawing high card to do the job on Payne's wife?"

What the Texan said caught Cado Greer by surprise. He wasn't out here to make war on women, though he should have expected something like this from Claiborne Payne. It was like Payne to have others do his dirty work. But taking out a woman, even a whore, hit against the grain as far as Greer was concerned. Further, Mandy Payne didn't know what was going on, since her love for her husband had blinded her to Claiborne's robbing ways and his lust for other women. He'd come to look forward to the few invitations to dine with the Paynes as Mandy always made him feel at home. Dammit, she's too good a woman for it to come down to this.

Greer let his thoughts ramble on as he gazed back at the Texan's challenging eyes. Vaguely he could hear the others crowding in like timber wolves getting the scent of blood. He rasped phlegm and any uncertainties of how he felt into his mouth and chucked a yellowy stream at the floor. Doing as Payne wanted, he felt, was courting bad luck. Nor did you have a woman ride along when a job was to be pulled.

Impatiently Little Reddy shuffled the deck of cards.

"Okay, high card."

He let Little Reddy cut first, scowled at the sudden grin lidding the Texan's cloudy-grey eyes. Greer simply reached over and tipped over a few cards, the bottom card proving to be the eight of hearts. "Damn . . ."

"Guess you've just got yourself an easy five hundred," shrugged the Texan as he showed Cado Greer his bottom card, the three of spades. "Yo, here come your boys, Cado." He waved a friendly hand at five hardcases following William Bevans into the barroom. "Yup, Cado, we should play hell with any stagecoach now."

Cado Greer shoved away from the table, walking outside toward his horse tethered with others by a watering trough. Rippling through him were afterthoughts of unease. At first it hadn't made sense Claiborne Payne wanting to get rid of his wife. Mandy Payne fitted in with all those other Cheyenne socialites, would be of considerable help if Payne threw his hat into the political ring. Last night it came to him, just a casual remark of Payne's, but something that had exposed the stark truth to his motives. Mandy Payne was expecting. Sure, that had to be it. Killing his wife was Payne's way of removing any entanglements to the past.

The next person on Payne's hit list has gotta be me, he deduced.

To hell with all his conning talk of me managing that new ranch of his, or at the stageline. Cado Greer, jamming his hat down lower to screen out the afternoon sunlight, came in by his horse nickering a greeting. He stared at the stage station buildings and what he could see of the road spilling down from the north.

Something'll have to be worked out with Little Reddy from Texas, without tippin' my hand to Payne. You forgot, Claiborne old pal, I know how your dirty little mind works, he chuckled.

Now that he'd strung it out in his mind, Cado Greer felt some of his anger dissipating. He could handle Little Reddy, as he'd judged the Texan to be out for the gold and nothing else. As for Mandy Payne, word would be brought to them of her heading to Deadwood on a Concord, same way as they'd been informed of any gold shipments from that Black Hills mining camp, by illegal use of the new telegraph setup. He had to give Claiborne Payne credit for putting this operation together, meaning that as long as something worked properly don't mess with it.

As for your wife, Claiborne, what you got in mind for Mandy could happen to you, old pard, Greer ruminated.

Briscoe Larkin figured he had the loneliest job in the Black Hills. While he was stuck out in this old line camp cabin, everyone he rode with on the outlaw trail took daily rides over to Cuny's hog ranch to avail themselves of the drinks and whores. Scarcely a year ago Larkin, a thin, easygoing Midwesterner, had left an Iowa farm town and his job as a telegraph operator behind in search of bigger things. His expectations and dreams had gone bust in the Black Hills mining camps. Younger than James Wall, another member of the gang they called the "Kid," Briscoe Larkin in order to survive had lucked out in Custer. He landed a much needed job as a telegraph operator, but it was here that Ace Taylor came into the picture. Together with the albino and some stolen telegraphic equipment, Larkin headed down here to start a new life as an outlaw.

First off, Larkin strung some wire to the main telegraph line, a distance of about a half mile. Afterwards all he had to do was rig up the stolen receiving sounder at the cabin. He found out there were a lot of telegraphic messages flashing from the Black Hills to Cheyenne on an around the clock basis. Coded messages from Ace Taylor came over the line around sundown.

Alone, as he'd been ever since everyone had cut out around mid-morning, Larkin had tried his hand at whittling to pass the time. Another diversion had been his taking the field glass and going to a hillock overlooking the main road. A few lonely horsemen came passing by into the Black Hills, and freight wagons, and then a stagecoach laden down with would-be miners. All this time, Larkin worried about not hearing from the albino since Sunday, four days ago. Little Reddy had likewise expressed his concern just this morning, but it hadn't kept the Texan from riding over to Cuny's and seeing Pawnee Liz.

"That woman's a morsel," Briscoe Larkin said as he bent an ear to the dots and dashes clicking over the telegraph rig on the table. "Let's see . . . Fred Jonas has arrived in Deadwood . . . will wire back later . . ."

Frowning to show his concern, he rose and began building a fire in the stove as lowering shadows were beginning to touch the inner walls. Knowing the others, they'd stay at Cuny's. With the fire going, he took a hike through the other rooms in search of anything to drink, and came up with some whiskey in a bottle. It wasn't until night had really settled in, and he was about to fall asleep at the table,

172

that the sounder began clicking out a message passing down the line. Halfheartedly he cocked an ear.

The first part of the message passed by his sleep-filled thoughts, and then the following clicking of words stifled the yawn.

. . . arriving Hat Creek station sometime this evening. Stop. Ace Taylor.

"Almost missed it," he blurted out. "But . . . it ain't like Ace Taylor to spell it out so plain?" The notion that perhaps the albino had run afoul of the law held Larkin to his chair, or even that the message meant Taylor was heading out this way. Unlike Taylor not to use our code, he pondered.

Fetching him out of the cabin was Briscoe Larkin's fear of the Texan. If there was a gold shipment going through tonight, and he didn't carry word to Little Reddy, it would be curtains for him. Out at the corral, he eyed with some uncertainties the dun-colored bronc. The bronc stirred when he ducked in between the poles, trying to shape a wide loop with his lasso. The horse could sense Larkin's fear as Larkin pursed his lips to whistle it in. But it held there, and evaded the first awkward tossing of the lasso. Then, when Larkin was reeling in the lasso, the bronc charged in only to avoid capture and find the far side of the corral.

"You measly hunk of dog meat," he yelled, "I don't get word to Little Reddy . . . both of us are in deep trouble."

Easing to the snubbing post in the center of the corral, he flung out his lasso to have it settle around the bronc's neck. This time, it merely stood there as Larkin worked his way along the length of rope until at last he'd curled his hand around the halter. After that it was merely a matter of throwing on a saddle and heading uproad toward Cuny's hog ranch, with the bronc bucking a little to work out some kinks in its backbone.

* * *

In the light of a full moon hanging southeasterly, the rider out front swung his bronc toward willow trees. He went loping through, the scattering of following outlaws crouched low over saddle horns to evade the stinging lash of branches. Opening up to them was a dry wash turned muddy by a recent rainfall. One or two horses slipped in the uncertain footing, with curses from their riders urging them after Little Reddy from Texas. Going along for the first time was Briscoe Larkin and powderman Jesse Barfield, his face twisted up with the uncertainties of their sudden departure.

Hanging back with the men he'd brought over from Cheyenne was Cado Greer. There really hadn't been any time to talk this over with the Texan, as the sudden arrival of Larkin at Cuny's place with the news of a gold shipment sent everyone scattering for their horses. All Greer knew was of their heading by this devious route to a place just this side of the Alkali Springs stage station. Man could lame a horse, he groused, as we should have stuck to the main trail.

Greer thought about working his way up to palaver with Little Reddy, but scowled the notion away. For right now he was nursing the beginnings of a hangover, and it didn't help his disposition either being jarred about in the saddle. Another thing, it went against his cautious nature just taking off like this.

"A pretty moon."

"Shut up, Philby," Cado Greer shot back. What he wanted to do was slow down so's he could relieve himself. How long had they been riding? At least an hour, through a darkscape of hill piled upon hill and along passages where moonlight didn't penetrate.

Bouncing in the saddle to Greer's right, outlaw Gab

Philby asked dryly, "Wonder why he brought her along—"

"What are you mumbling about now?"

"Oh, you didn't know, Cado? Up there, riding alongside Little Reddy, that whore of his . . . Pawnee Liz—"

"Why, that stupid . . ." Cado Greer's teeth snapped together. The anger of before was a mere prelude to what erupted now; his eyes piercing the darkness in search of the woman. His anger brought him sawing back on the reins so hard the bronc broke stride and began humping its shoulders up, and with a vicious stab of Greer's spurred boot bringing it into a canter. Bad luck, that's all this would cause, bring a curse down upon all of them. Underbrush slapping against his legs, he tore past slower riders to reach out for the reins of Little Reddy's horse.

"What the—" Little Reddy spluttered.

"This is all wrong, McKimmie, dammit," Greer said raspingly, as both of their horses wheeled up to begin milling about in a half-circle. Greer brought his horse around to face Little Reddy's drawn six-gun. "Go ahead, tell everyone we're out here. Is this some kind of lark or what . . . you bringin' her along . . ."

Leathering his six-gun, the Texan said quickly, "Don't fret none about her as Pawnee Liz can damn well handle a gun, better'n some I know."

Cado Greer's jawbones bunched up, but he didn't say anything, but kept staring hard at the Texan as he sorted out how he felt. The woman wanted to say something, though to her credit she read the mood of Greer. Maybe it was thoughts of the gold which kept her from flaring back at Cado Greer, anyway, Pawnee Liz tucked her hat lower as she pulled her horse away to leave the pair of them to sort this out. Greer didn't seem to know she had drifted her horse away, blinded as he was by all of this. Then he dragged in night air like a man making up his mind, and calmly he said to Little Reddy, "Just feel her being along is

175

bad luck. An' just didn't think we'd be headin' out so soon. Okay, can't be that much further . . ."

Little Reddy grinned, and then he nodded to a sheltered place screened by cottonwoods and brush fringing below, to have both of them spur over and dismount. As they squatted down, the others rode in closer, slowly, to slide out of their saddles. Overhead, the moon was sending down enough light to show clearly a map Little Reddy was scratching in the sandy ground with a broken piece of branch. He made quiet conversation as he did this, letting Cado Greer know he carried no resentment over what Greer had done.

"Should have sounded you out about her first, I guess," said Little Reddy.

"Me, I'm feeling all that booze I poured down. So what do we have?"

One of the things Johnny Slaughter found out was of the stageline running its Concords around the clock. This cut in half the time it took to get out of the gold fields to Cheyenne. On a moonlit night such as this, keeping to the road wasn't all that hazardous. But when bad weather struck, which it often did into the Black Hills, both the men riding the stagecoaches and the horses were hard pressed to keep on the move. A comforting fact to Slaughter was a stagecoach inbound toward Deadwood, one they'd passed less than an hour ago and loaded down with passengers. The driver of the other stagecoach had slowed down some to say that he hadn't spotted any riders lurking along the road.

Strung out ahead of the Concord were the remnants of an escort column of cavalrymen sent out from Fort Meade. Back about a half-mile lay the stage station at Alkali Springs, but the mind of Johnny Slaughter was set further back along the line to just outside of Deadwood. Here the officer in charge of the army patrol had divided his men, which hadn't made any sense to Slaughter. He stabbed a thoughtful glance at driver Alex Hardy.

"Just how much gold are we carrying?"

"Enough, I reckon, to warrant having an escort."

"Another coach must be pulling out later tonight."

"I expect that's why some of them bluebellies stayed behind. You try your hand at panning for gold, Slaughter?"

"Been considering it."

"Here," he held out a plug of chewing tobacco, "it'll ease your worries. Wish it were darker, though."

Staring back at the cantering column of mounted cavalry and the Concord were rocky tors bristling with pines, then higher up cathedral spires barren of trees, these rock formations a barrier through which the road narrowed to gain passage out onto the plains of territorial Wyoming. Sometimes these rocky guardians would pull back and the stagecoach road would pass through a summery meadow thick with grass and flowers. They'd change horses at the next stop, Harding Ranch, though the stage station still lay at least ten miles uptrail.

"Gets to you after a while, these rocks."

"They do, Johnny. Especially at night. Up ahead, trail's barely wide enough for a man on a horse much less what I'm driving." Worriedly he took in their escort of cavalrymen loping their horses around a downsloping bend in the road, the rock spirals to either side closing in tight. "Good place for an ambush."

Hunkered high in the rocks were the ambushers, lining up their rifle sights on the men in blue uniforms and the Concord picking up a little speed to close the distance on the gravelly road. Just a little more, urged Little Reddy from Texas, in a silent and joyous refrain. Hiding lower on the sheer hills were Cado Greer and his men, more or less blocking the road, and back with their horses were the powderman and Briscoe Larkin.

"An escort," he muttered to Kid Wall, "means Ace Taylor was right. That coach ain't bouncin' any too much; so it must be packin' a lot of gold."

"That Cado Greer has sure enough got a mean mouth."

Sighting in on the Concord, Little Reddy said, "Man's big enough to say what he thinks. Though Greer's mouth could get him in a heap of trouble."

The night air was as still as it got in these hills, the clip-clopping of hooves piercing into the rocks, and the heads of the escorting soldiers bobbing either way as their anxious eyes searched for any movement. As yet their rifles were still in saddle sheaths, the iron wheels of the Concord making grating sounds as it came over bigger rocks embedded in the road. And now the death-dealing guns of the road agents opened up.

Johnny Slaughter was among the first to be hit, a slug from Little Reddy's rifle ripping into his upper body. He tried rising from the seat, died as another slug punched into his head, and he toppled from the seat to land alongside the Concord being pulled up by Alex Hardy. It seemed to Hardy that from every angle rifles were spouting out flame. Inside the coach the pair of armed guards were firing back; one of them yelled out at the driver, "For God's sake, Hardy, get us out of here!"

About half of the cavalrymen had been hit, three of them being spilled out of their saddles and their horses shying away. They were calling out to one another in the confusion of the moment, dismounting, trying for their rifles, a couple managing to ride their horses under some screening trees, but even here they drew rifle fire.

"Where's the bugler . . . sound retreat . . . where's that damned bugler . . ."

"Back with the others, Sarge!"

178

"I'm hit?"

"Me . . . I'm dead . . . Sarge?" And the cavalry private was, too, sagging to the ground with the tragic knowledge that the bullet that struck him had caused a mortal wound. Moments later, his own dead pronouncement filling his eyes with dread, the private went limp.

Some of the horses were hit, their neighs of fear and agony mingling with the shouts of the cavalrymen and the terrible roaring of the guns going on and on. But in fact it was only a matter of minutes before the ambushers were pushing up cautiously from the rocks to begin picking their way down to the killing ground below. The Concord was no longer on the road, it had followed the driverless horses to become ensnarled in pine trees. Inside the coach one of the guards was still alive, though blood trickled down his face from where a bullet had nicked against his skull. Filled with the horror of what had happened, he managed to open a door and tumble to the ground. From there he scrambled to his feet, and screened by the trees, broke away. He found a rocky cairn and spilled himself into it, the fear of it all rimming his eyes with tears.

"What about those hosses?"

"Prime stock," commented another outlaw. "I could sure use that grey."

"You could if you could catch it," grinned the man to his left, and moved in cautiously to view the dead soldiers.

It was down on the road that Cado Greer eased over to the Texan, saying, "You're right about dead men not tellin' any tales."

"Now there's the gold, Cado. I agree with you, too, about not sending any of it on to Cheyenne."

"What the hell can Payne do? About time I cut loose from him. A man paying someone else to kill his own wife . . . damn Payne anyway . . ." He ignored the Texan's woman sidling up, a glance southward revealing their

179

horses being walked in as Greer ambled toward the Concord, and then Little Reddy caught up with him.

"How's it look?" Little Reddy called out to one of the hardcases standing by an open coach door.

"The driver and this one are dead. What about the horses?"

"They're not much good except to pull a wagon. But go ahead, pick any you want. Look at that strongbox, Cado." He swung grinning eyes to Greer standing to one side of the open door, let his gaze swing to powderman Jesse Barfield ducking in under low pine branches. Barfield had packed along a gunny sack which was slung over one shoulder, and stepping past Greer, he looked in at the Salamander safe, and then at the Texan, McKimmie.

Barfield said casually, "Just another hunk of iron, I reckon. If you don't want gristle and blood spattering up things, you'd better get that body out of there." Without further comment the powderman lowered his sack to the ground, out of which he removed a stick of dynamite.

"I'll lend a hand," said Greer, as he stepped forward. Reaching in, he wedged his large hands under the dead man's armpits and pulled him out to where Little Reddy could wrap an arm around the lower body. They carried the body over to lower it just beyond a Douglas fir, with both men stiffening at the nearby barking of a handgun. Then through the trees they could see the man who'd fired the gun standing over a dead horse. "Too bad about that."

Little Reddy merely nodded as he looked up to survey a patch of night sky poking through a gap in the trees. "Nice night to pull a job like this."

"Don't bother you none we killed all those men."

"Cado, they weren't just going to hand us that gold. And nope, as I've seen what those bluebellies did down in Texas."

Over by the Concord, Jesse Barfield looked at the fuse

he'd just cut shorter before putting his knife away. This was a spitter, cut shorter than the fuse he'd placed into the stick of dynamite, now set in place in the lock on the safe. In his mouth there was a lighted stub of cigar, and now Barfield turned to find the Texan. "Call out to your men that it's fire in the hole time."

"Okay," said Little Reddy, "but let me check out how you've got that dynamite rigged first." He ambled over and looked inside the coach. "Think one stick'll do it?"

"More'n that an' there won't be much left of this stagecoach much less that strongbox."

Through a growing smile Little Reddy clapped the powderman on the shoulder, and spinning away, he yelled out, "Take cover, boys!" Then he sought shelter among the trees.

Barfield remained there to give everyone a chance to find shelter, checking the empty traces of the coach as he did so. Along with the horses being taken away, the driver's body had been lifted down off the front seat. As a powderman, he knew that once a fuse was lit it was too late to correct an oversight. Then, he used his cigar to light the split fuse, and from there touched it to the fuse wedged into the stick of dynamite. Quickly he broke at a trot for shelter, to crouch in close to Cado Greer and the Texan. Barely had he settled in then an eruption of bright flame and sound brought their heads down, and then pieces of stagecoach littered the trees around them.

Laughing, Little Reddy exclaimed, "Guess one stick was enough. Come on, let's get at that gold."

Eagerly all three of them and the rest of the road agents broke in toward the Concord. Most of the framework of the coach, Little Reddy saw, had been blasted away, but though the lid of the strongbox had been blown open it was still intact in the reinforced underbelly. The outer metal covering of the strongbox was powderburned and still hot to the touch, as the Texan found out when he jerked his hand back.

"Damn, someone get me a stick or somethin'."

Dunc Blackburn shouldered in and used his rifle to lift open the strongbox lid. He stood there as others crowded in for a greedy glimpse of what they'd just killed for, their eyes not registering it at first, then disbelief and shocked anger twisted their faces into ugly masks.

"Rocks!"

"Just some damned rocks!"

"Yeah, that damned albino sold us out," came Pawnee Liz's high-pitched voice.

Cado Greer wheeled away from the clustering of outlaws around the stagecoach. He strode away, gripped by anger and the treachery of it all, but mostly that if he stayed there it would be to have it out with the Texan.

"That woman comin' along brought a curse down on us. Little Reddy should have known better," he complained. He came out from under the trees to pass along the road to where one of the hardcases was guarding their horses. Strewed about were the dead soldiers and some horses.

Damned fools died for nothing. But next time it ain't gonna be me riding with that foolhardy Texan.

Fourteen

Moss Hollabaugh went over to the stageline offices, going in the back way to find Jason Hassrick alone in his office. Hassrick was sitting behind his big desk spooning sugar into his coffee cup. He told Moss no word had come back about either stagecoach, so for a while they swapped encouraging words that maybe both had gotten through.

"Julia told me some of what happened last night."

"It couldn't be helped," said Moss.

"Killing someone is never easy," agreed Hassrick. "So far my doubledealing bookkeeper hasn't shown up. Do you think Risdale was taking orders from the man you killed . . . could be lying, as that's his strong suit." There was a bitter, wearying sound to Hassrick's words.

"I figure Risdale's in over his head. Right about now he's looking in all four directions. Looking out for me and Cheyenne."

"Yes, dammit," said Jason Hassrick. He clattered his cup off the saucer, spilling coffee onto his desk, then abruptly, he set the cup down. "To think that my daughter is married to such a monster. Last night, when Julia told me about how Claiborne had killed that man, I was stunned. I refused to believe it. That perhaps Risdale was simply telling another lie. That—"

"Easy, Mr. Hassrick."

"Yes, it doesn't help my spouting off like this." He settled back in his chair, with his eyes throwing Moss a silent question.

Picking up on it, Moss said, "There is a possibility that Risdale could head out. Besides Cado Greer, one of Payne's hired hands, Risdale is the only witness to that killing done by Mr. Payne. Just to make sure, I'll try to find Risdale. You'll be okay?"

"Guess," he smiled, "I'm more worried about what's happening out on the trail."

Moss turned in that direction when the office door opened, and in came Julia Hassrick to announce, "A coach just arrived from Cheyenne. Shady Glover said he passed both outbound coaches, that he hadn't seen any road agents."

Moss said, "Whereabouts, Julia, while still in the hills?"

"I expect he'd have sighted them," said Hassrick, "someplace between Red Canyon and Cheyenne River crossing. Still, that would put both outbound Concords in hilly country. At least this time Fort Meade sent out some cavalry."

"Well, father," she said, "cheer up. I hate to see you so gloomy."

"I shall try, my dear."

"Oh, I forgot to tell you, I received a letter from Mandy. And guess what"—a sudden smile brightened her eyes—"you're going to be a grandfather."

"That . . . is good news."

"And Mandy's coming here."

Moss studied the way the owner of the Deadwood-Cheyenne Stageline Company reacted to the news that he would soon be a grandfather. Behind that gruff smile for Julia, Moss had caught a glint of something else. Perhaps it had been a feeling of revulsion by Jason Hassrick that his daughter was carrying a baby sired by Claiborne Payne. There was also the parting words of Hassrick to Julia that by rights she should have been the first daughter to present him with a grandchild. A grin came to Moss at how Julia had fled her father's office.

The sun was camped directly over Deadwood, not seeming to move, spearing light into seamy nooks and crannies. Only the lack of wind kept a malodorous scent from sweeping into the buildings. It was a stench that Moss couldn't get used to, as he also had little use for all the riffraff just stirring out of their nightly havens. He'd tried Orrin Risdale's hotel. He'd been to a few of Risdale's haunts. He was hungry, but Moss could forsake a noon meal as it just could be that the bookkeeper was on the run like a rabbit barely a leg ahead of some coyotes.

Moss vacated the boardwalk and fell in with the crush of traffic. Up in the next block a freight wagon had broken down, the right back wheel crunched in under the wagon. From there Moss took in the telegraph office, which brought to mind the telegram sent by Orrin Risdale. Moss's idea behind sending the telegram was to smoke Little Reddy's gang into the open. Risdale claimed there was only Little Reddy and maybe five more road agents.

Those outlaws will come a cropper trying to go against that cavalry patrol. Sure hope Johnny Slaughter isn't hurt, too, he contemplated.

He continued his search for the bookkeeper until mid-afternoon, at which time Moss went into the Bodega Bar. In him was a restlessness that only came about when he was out on the trail riding shotgun. Hungry, but unsettled by this feeling that something was wrong, he passed the side table and the free lunch and found a spot at the bar.

"Hollabaugh, haven't seen you since Tuesday."

"The usual, Jake."

Along with the stein of beer the bartender slid a newspaper before Moss, to jab a finger at the bold headline proclaiming the demise of Custer and his Seventh Cavalry at the Little Big Horn. "A massacre what it was."

Right away all Moss could set his mind on was the strange man of the Oglala, Crazy Horse. According to the newspaper every Indian tribe from the Oklahoma Strip and clear up to Canada had come against the United States Army in the form of Colonel George Armstrong Custer. Fresh ink smudging his hand, Moss set the paper aside. He knew it was bound to happen, as this was a vision of Crazy Horse's. Engrossed as Moss had been in his search for the missing Orrin Risdale, now he cocked his ears to what others were saying around him. The greatest shank of it was there'd be a war against them red devils. The news had put a halt to any gambling activity in the Bodaga, though a miner was trying to coax the operator into getting the roulette wheel going, Custer's demise or no.

Moss's beckoning finger brought the barkeeper over. "Jake, you know about everyone working over at the stageline. I'm looking for a bookkeeper, Risdale."

"I know that dude. S'matter of fact, Risdale left about . . . oh, ten, twenty minutes ago. Where I don't know?"

"Good enough," said Moss as he paid for his half-finished drink and headed for the door.

At least, he mused with a feeling of relief, Risdale is still hanging in. One of the reasons for his not going in to work was that the bookkeeper did not want to face Jason Hassrick. Perhaps, too, Risdale was still shaken up over the killing of Ace Taylor. Risdale's the kind of man liking to keep his hands from getting dirty. And speaking of dirt, he could be heading back to his hotel for a change of clothes, as Moss had the hunch Risdale had spent most of last night and today in saloons.

Indecision held Moss just outside the saloon. While the ingrained habit of checking out the activity on the street brought him glancing southward. He wasn't certain at first, but stayed there watching a pair of horsemen at about where Deadwood and Whitewood creeks enjoined.

They loped in over the plank bridge to downslope onto main street, one of them a big man and on a big, rangy bronc, but still his spurred boots hung awful low to the ground. The other rider was smaller and leaned-out and struck in Moss no memory chords. But no question but that the big man was Cado Greer. They went on by without noticing Moss rooted under the Bodaga's shading porch.

As yet Moss hadn't tied in Greer's being here with that gold shipment, the only thing of concern to him that Cado Greer was here to see bookkeeper Orrin Risdale. The burly hardcase Greer was Claiborne Payne's shadow, which could mean that Payne was in town. Heading after the pair of riders on the boardwalk, Moss considered the possibilities of Risdale sending another telegram over to Cheyenne. A man as shady as the bookkeeper could be working both sides of the street. By informing Claiborne Payne of how the albino had been killed, Risdale was hoping the same for me, pondered Moss. But that gunfight had taken place last night, with Cheyenne better than a two day ride from here. Or, could it be that Cado Greer had called it quits with Payne?

Part of Moss's questions were answered when Greer and the other hardcase swung onto a side street where the bookkeeper's hotel was located. Cutting across the street, Moss kept pressing down Main Street at a faster clip. Two blocks later he veered onto the side street, to hold up. For the hardcases had just swung down from their horses before the Merchant's Hotel. As he tied his reins to the hitching rail, Greer must have told his companion to wait by the horses, as big, plodding Cado Greer then pushed around some idlers and entered the hotel. Now it was the other hardcase passing up the lobby door to cut into an alley.

"It must have been the albino telling them about Risdale moving in here." Tugging at the brim of his hat, Moss strode on.

On this windless and hot day a lot of windows in the hotel had been opened, and a pair of windows on the second floor looked into the bookkeeper's room, Moss's view of the hotel from across the street. Crossing over, he eased in between the horses. After untying the reins from the hitching rail, he turned them away and barked as he waved his arms, "Awright, get! Go on now!"

With both of the horses breaking away and toward main street, Moss swung back to snap a glance up at the second floor windows as there passed through them the frightened cry of a man. Moss broke toward the open lobby door. At a fast trot he passed through the lobby to bolt up the staircase. Palming his six-gun, he stepped through the doorframe and one of the large rooms occupied by Orrin Risdale. A splattering of blood on the wall above the liquor cabinet spelled it out for Moss, as did broken bottles and glasses littering the carpeted floor. A man as big as Greer would have used his fists, which meant the bookkeeper was still alive. Spinning away, he hurried into the hallway, registering that the back staircase was to his right.

Down on the first floor, through the screen door, he glimpsed Cado Greer packing the bookkeeper over one shoulder. Underbrush stirring told Moss the other outlaw was ahead of Greer and breaking trail down to Whitewood Creek. Without hesitating Moss shouldered the screen door aside and took off after them.

The brush and scrub trees lining both sides of the creek were a barrier in which Moss soon became confused about which way they'd gone. Stung by lashing branches, and with burrs clinging to his Levi's, he simply kept pressing in deeper until suddenly the creek was there, a ribbon of shallow and muddy water and not all that wide, with the canyon wall just a few rods away. First he checked the southern reaches of the creek, heard the vague buzzing of a passing honeybee as he turned to head the other way, the muddy bank sucking at his boots and the thick underbrush screening the sight and sounds of Deadwood.

Further to the north, Cado Greer shrugged the unconscious bookkeeper from his shoulder into the cold creek waters. Risdale came up gasping for air and blinking his eyes into the awareness of where he was, some place between the canyon walls. The big hand of his assailant reached down to grab the front of his coat.

"Rocks . . . just some damned rocks!" Greer shouted as with one hand he lifted Risdale up.

The effects of the first and only blow which had slammed Orrin Risdale into the wall in his room had broken his nose and given him a slight concussion. At the moment he was incapable of framing any protestations to Greer's anger. He hung there held upright by the hardcase's powerful arm, to have a sob burst out of his throat when a backhanded blow struck just above his eyes, the force of it spilling both of them back into the creek.

Still retaining his grip on the bookkeeper's coat, Cado Greer struggled to his knees and shouted, "Taylor? What happened to Ace? You scummy . . ."

"You hit him that hard again, Cado, an' you'll snap his neckbone." The outlaw caught movement downcreek, and in one motion he whirled that way while clawing for his holstered sidearm. His six-gun was clearing leather when Moss's own gun spat out flame. One moment the outlaw was fixing to add another notch to his gun, the next instant he tumbled dead to the ground.

"Leave him be, Greer!" warned Moss Hollabaugh, as he stepped past the dead body of the other hardcase.

Hesitating, Cado Greer finally gave the bookkeeper a shove that sent him sprawling over to land hard on the bank, with Risdale's legs still in the water. Suddenly he was going for his Colt, like a man totally out of control. Greer took a slug in the midriff, and despite this, managed to trigger his own gun to score a hit. Then under the impact of two more bullets jerking into his chest, his knees buckled and he slumped down. Still clinging to life and still dangerous, he tried raising the barrel of his Colt's. And then surprisingly, Cado Greer smiled a bitter smile and weakly tossed the weapon away. He focused on Moss hunched over a bare ten yards away.

"Bad luck . . . bringing his woman along . . ."

"Did Payne send you here to kill the bookkeeper?"

"Not here." He coughed as one hand seemed to drift off on its own volition to try and stem the blood seeping from the stomach wound, but he didn't drop his gaze. He kept staring at Hollabaugh, a more urgent glimmer in his eyes now for Cado Greer knew he was dying.

"Rocks . . . all we found on that stagecoach. Damned Risdale . . . sold us out. Must tell you about Payne." Greer fell over onto his side like an oak being chopped down.

Moss, clutching at where a slug had grazed his left arm, shoved his gun into the holster and came in closer to crouch down. "What about Payne?"

"Wants . . . wants his wife killed . . ."

The shock of what he'd just heard squinting his eyes, Moss reached out a worried hand as the outlaw's eyes closed, and he said quickly, "You sure?"

Determined to tell what he knew, Cado Greer struggled to stay alive, the hatred for Claiborne Payne fueling him. He opened his eyes, "Sending Mandy . . . here on stagecoach. Letter, there's . . . a letter . . . Little Reddy has it. Will pay five . . . five . . . hun . . ." Shuddering, Cado Greer went limp.

And Moss murmured sadly, "All because of this damnable gold." Then he stiffened at the sudden barking of a gun, a slug from it pounding into the ground near his boots.

"Now you know about me!" said Orrin Risdale, crouched a few yards away and about to break away into the underbrush. His hair was plastered to his skull and the

190

creek waters had washed the blood away, though his face was swelled from where he'd been struck by Greer. His clothes were dripping water and clung to his small frame. If Moss read him right, the bookkeeper meant to leave no witnesses behind.

Desperately Moss threw himself toward the underbrush. He rolled over as Risdale's small handgun sounded. Without seeming to aim, Moss triggered his six-gun. Just the one slug was needed, the slug ripping into the bookkeeper's eye socket. Reflexively Moss triggered his weapon again, the hammer came down on an empty chamber. He lay there for a while, taking in the bodies sprawled around him, dragging grateful air into his lungs for coming out of this alive. Then in rehashing all that Cado Greer had said, all Moss could think about was Johnny Slaughter heading out of Deadwood as shotgun on that stagecoach. And then it hit him, and bitter anger hardened Moss's face for he knew another friend was dead.

"Came from up this way!"

"Yup, you're right, sheriff!" someone else shouted. "Up north more!"

Moss got painfully to his feet. Still clutching at his arm, he sought the underbrush. Wanted as he was by the army, Moss knew that his version of what had just happened wouldn't carry too much weight with the local law. He came in under some scrubby willow trees to hold there as brush stirred around him. Shortly the searchers had worked themselves past him toward the creek, which allowed Moss free passage out and back toward the Merchant's Hotel.

Boldly he used the back door of the hotel to gain access to the stairs and the bookkeeper's room. Closing the outer door, he found the bathroom, where he peeled out of his shirt. The bullet had cut along the outer portion of his forearm to leave a painful welt. He cleansed and bandaged the wound, put on his shirt as he went in search of any records Risdale might have been keeping which would tie him in to Claiborne Payne.

Only now did it occur to Moss that everything was breaking in Payne's favor. Killing Cado Greer had been a matter of survival. In musing it over he just might have been able to talk the bookkeeper into giving up. But hammered as he'd been by Greer, Risdale had figured there was no other way out. Now both witnesses to Claiborne Payne's committing cold-blooded murder were dead. And all Moss came across were a few scattered papers and some bank books showing that Orrin Risdale had salted away a little over five thousand dollars.

He left the same way he'd entered the hotel, by the back door. Coming onto main street, his intention at the moment was to beeline over to the stageline and break the news of the killings to Jason Hassrick. Meanwhile the sun had slipped behind the canyon wall to darken the streets. But it would be at least another hour before flame would lift from coal oil lamps. It was about now that he began noticing those coming his way on the boardwalk, all of them gesticulating their excitement. They stepped out into the street to gaze beyond Moss, and like a lot of others he stopped to turn around. Rolling in past the first few business places was a Deadwood Cheyenne stagecoach, a lonely soldier handling the reins. The coach was trailed by the remnants of the cavalry patrol sent out from Fort Meade. Tied to the saddles of their horses were the soldiers gunned down by Little Reddy's bunch of killers.

Moss got this choked up feeling in his throat, because he knew that inside the coach would be Johnny Slaughter's body. Around him there was little movement or talking as the townfolk viewed this funeral procession. Across the street an opened window suddenly dropped shut, the noise making a few horses wheel about and stamp their shod hoofs, but firm hands on the reins held the horses in the passing column.

192

The boardwalk being blocked forced Moss to step out into the street as he continued on toward the stageline offices. Further on he could make out people he knew, Julia among them, pouring outside. The stagecoach drew up, and yard manager Pat Grady conferred with the driver. Then it went on to slip behind the office building, the cavalrymen holding out in the street.

The last to come out of the building was Jason Hassrick limping on his cane, and immediately his eyes sought out the officer commanding the patrol. Swinging down, Lieutenant Cassidy handed his reins to a sergeant. "Sir," he said to Hassrick, "they were all wiped out . . . those going out with that decoy coach. But the other coach got through. It was as if . . ." His voice broke.

"A terrible thing to happen," Jason Hassrick said quietly. "A terrible tragedy."

"They were waiting just on the other side of Alkali Springs. I figured at least two dozen . . . maybe more."

Moss, who'd come in to stand just behind Julia Hassrick, wondered if the bookkeeper had been lying about Little Reddy's gang only numbering around seven or eight hardcases. But what was it that Cado Greer had been shouting out, something about them finding only rocks? Which had to mean that Greer had brought more than one gunhand with him from Cheyenne. So together with Little Reddy's bunch they had gone after that stagecoach.

He reached out to touch Julia's shoulder, to have her gaze back at him, and Moss said softly, "We need to talk."

The urgency in his voice brought Julia to work her way through the press and go behind Moss into the building. As he removed his hat and by force of habit ran his fingers around the inner hatband, she took in the slight bulge under his left shirt sleeve, the sleeve stained slightly by blood. "You've been hurt?"

"It could have been worse. Some of the men who are responsible for all of this butchery are dead. Do

193

you remember Cado Greer?"

"Why, I believe he works for Claiborne—"

"What's this about Claiborne?"

They glanced over at Jason Hassrick stepping through the doorway. Behind him came the lieutenant, who hadn't bothered to wipe the trail dust from his worn uniform. He had just a trace of grey in his dark brown hair, the lined face that of a man in his mid-thirties. In Moss's opinion Lieutenant Cassidy was certainly no West Pointer, he was more probably a mustanger.

"I was just telling Julia about having to use my gun, Mr. Hassrick. Killed two men—Risdale and one of Payne's hired guns, Cado Greer. Lieutenant, Greer was involved in what happened to your men. Oh, guess I overlooked shooting a third man, one who came in with Greer. Guess seeing that stagecoach roll in unsettled me some."

Hassrick limped over and settled down on the edge of a desk, and acidly he said, "Risdale deserved what he got, Hollabaugh. But it's my fault . . . what happened out on the trail . . ."

Lieutenant Cassidy said, "Infested as these hills are with outlaws nobody is safe out there."

"There's something else," broke in Moss. "Something Cado Greer told me before he died. It could be that your daughter is on her way over here from Cheyenne."

"Mandy?" exclaimed Julia. "Why, yes, she wrote us about that."

"The way Greer told it your son-in-law wants her killed."

His face going ashen, Jason Hassrick blurted out, "Why, that coldhearted son of a bitch . . ."

"Moss, I . . . are you sure?"

"From all that's happened it's gotta be gospel the dying words of Cado Greer. He spoke of Payne sending a letter, which Greer passed on to that outlaw, Little Reddy from Texas."

"Moss, what can we do?"

"Reckon the only way, Julia, is for me to saddle up a fast horse and head out on the stageline trail. Payne offered five hundred dollars to the man gunning down his wife. Little Reddy's got a mean temper, doesn't care who he kills. Right now after finding rocks in that safe of yours, Mr. Hassrick, all he knows is he's been double crossed . . . wants to strike back. An', too, right about now five hundred looms as a lot of money."

"I'll go with you."

"Can't risk you getting hurt, too, Julia."

"Moss is right," said Hassrick. "Still, Moss, you can't head out there alone."

"Mind if I go along?" said Lieutenant Cassidy.

"Obliged if you did," replied Moss.

"Good, then I'll go muster my men."

"One thing, Lieutenant, there's something you should know . . ."

Moss put on his Stetson as he glanced into Jason Hassrick's inquiring eyes, and then Hassrick cut in with, "I believe I know what that is. Perhaps some things are best left unsaid, Moss?"

"Some things, I reckon. But jawing about it now is just more time lost. We'd best see to our horses . . . an' once we're trailbound, Lieutenant Cassidy, I reckon I'll confess some past misdeeds."

Fifteen

Under a sky sprinkled with stars they pulled into the Red Canyon stage station. They'd come in at a gallop, their horses lathered up and about spent, the unexpected presence of shadowy riders causing those in the stage station to douse the lights.

"Bugler," said Lieutenant Cassidy, "sound off before they open up on us."

As the staccato notes of a bugle brushed past his ears, Moss Hollabaugh broke away from the others. He could discern in the dark recesses of an open doorway someone pointing a rifle at him, and he called out, "Mort, this is Hollabaugh."

"Sure enough it is. Awright, turn on those lamps." The station manager stepped toward Moss swinging down from his horse. "Trouble, I expect—"

"Trouble is all I've seen lately. We'll need fresh horses."

"Can oblige that. A terrible tragedy what happened today. Can't believe everyone got wiped out."

"More of the same'll happen if we don't get there in time," said Moss, walking his horse toward the corrals. "Give me a rundown on the stages leaving Cheyenne earlier today."

"One should be through here in about an hour," pondered the station manager. "Next one won't come through

196

until tomorrow morning sometime. That help you any?"

"It will have to do. Mort, while we're switching to fresh hosses, maybe you could rustle up something to eat."

Within fifteen minutes they were trailbound again. What moonlight there was out of a quarter moon didn't help any too much in picking out twists or chuckholes in the main road. They'd columned out in pairs, heading southerly at a gallop, sharing a fear of not getting to that stagecoach in time. Earlier, as he'd ridden alongside Lieutenant Cassidy, Moss had revealed his once being an army scout.

"So . . . that's it," Moss said, "I just couldn't see them murdering that Teton Lakota."

"Was me I'd do the same. As for your running into Crazy Horse, not too many white men have done that and lived to tell of it."

"I don't believe Crazy Horse got killed up there at the Little Big Horn. At least I've got this feeling he's still alive."

"Well, Custer sure isn't. Funny, I was supposed to get transferred to the Seventh Cavalry; paperwork got snarled up some place. Mr. Hollabaugh . . ."

"Yup, Lieutenant."

"You were a civilian when you scouted for the army. A good army lawyer would say all you did was break your contract. We could just leave this between us."

Moss's thoughts leaped at the idea, but the realization came in the next sobering intake of breath that his account with the army had to be squared. Besides, there was Julia Hassrick, the fact her father knew all about him. And of equal importance was his determination to rid himself of a lot of old luggage he'd been packing around too many years.

Lieutenant Cassidy's warning voice brought Moss out of his reveries, to become aware of the sound of an approach-

197

ing vehicle. Two miles ahead lay the Cheyenne River crossing; he spurred after the lieutenant seeking the openness alongside the road. They made out a stagecoach, skylining before sweeping at a cantering pace into the deeper blackness below. Ahead of them for some distance the road lay straight and open, and when the stagecoach appeared again, the bugle sounded a warning. Lieutenant Cassidy yelled, "Yo the coach — we're cavalry out of Fort Meade!"

Once the Concord had been allowed to roll in between the watching horsemen, the driver said, "Didn't know the army let its soldier boys out after dark. Hollabaugh, that you?"

Waving a casual hand, Moss said, "See anybody along the way?"

"A lonesome run this traveling at night. Nope, not a soul."

"Are there any women aboard?"

"Packed with would-be miners is all . . . an' some riffraff. The usual scattering, Hollabaugh." Then he was working the reins to bring his horses into motion and throwing back dust at the riders lining both sides of the road.

Moss said quietly, "The next coach left Cheyenne about three hours after this one pulled out."

"What if Hassrick's daughter isn't on that coach?"

"Can't take the chance she isn't."

The worry of what Claiborne Payne intended for his wife kept Julia Hassrick hanging on at the stageline offices. It was almost eleven, and sharing her concern were the regular night shift of a few clerks and the yard hands. The crew was bolstered by the presence of Pat Grady, who'd just come in to confer with Jason Hassrick.

"Coffee, Julia?"

She waved the clerk away and turned back to look out a front window. Earlier she had gone with her father to view the bodies being removed from the stagecoach. It was all she could do to hold back the tears, and her fears that the same thing could happen to Mandy. And to Moss Hollabaugh out there someplace. She was discovering he was a man of considerable character, but still somewhat of a mystery, though Moss's parting words revealed a past connection to the army. Now crossing the street was a messenger she recognized as working for the telegraph company. Enroute from Cheyenne there were operators stationed at Fort Laramie, Hat Creek, and Red Canyon Station, so it was possible this could be a message from Moss Hollabaugh. She hurried over to intercept the messenger just opening the front door.

Hurriedly Julia opened the envelope as one of the clerks flipped the messenger a quarter. A momentary flickering of disappointment danced in Julia's eyes, but then she forced a smile and said, "At least that gold shipment arrived safely in Cheyenne."

"Glad to hear that."

Nodding, she moved back to her desk. Perhaps, she deliberated, it wouldn't occur to Hollabaugh to avail himself of the telegraph line. And a lot of times the operators along the line closed down for the night. But to stay here and not know about Mandy was becoming unbearable. On the verge of sitting down, Julia checked the wall clock; going on eleven o'clock. Earlier she'd tried talking her father into going home, the past few days had been a wearying load for both of them. Why stay here waiting for word that might not come until tomorrow sometime?

"Enough of this," she said flat out, and stepped around her desk. Entering Jason Hassrick's office, she took note of the bottle of whiskey being passed around, and more carefully of how tired her father looked.

"You here to join us?"

"Why not," she retorted, and watched as Pat Grady reached for a glass to pour whiskey into it, which he handed to Julia.

"Cheers," said Jason Hassrick with a forced joviality.

Julia held out the telegram and said, "At least that gold shipment reached Cheyenne. But why are we hanging around here. Mr. Grady, I want you to ready one of our Concords."

"Just what do you have in mind?"

"Look at us, hanging around here with our worries when Mandy is heading into danger."

"Perhaps she hasn't left Cheyenne," questioned Jason Hassrick. "Then again . . ."

"Yes, then again she's on her way here."

Yard manager Pat Grady took in the nod of approval from the man he worked for. He said to Julia, "Okay, I'll tend to it. For driver I can get Shady Glover . . . but . . ."

"Riding shotgun? Myself and three or four more."

"Julia, dammit, I'm not staying behind." He dropped his hands upon the armrests of his chair and began pushing to his feet.

"It'll be an awful rough ride," she said quickly, and then let it drop, for once Jason Hassrick got that look of fire burning in his eyes arguing would be a waste of time. As Grady hurried out of the room, she added questioningly, "Along the way, Father dear, I want you to spill the beans about Hollabaugh."

Her last words held him behind his desk for a moment. He took in the glimmer of concern in his daughter's eyes, and his sudden smile brought a blush to her face. "I'll be damned . . . a man's finally got to you. Reckon you're entitled."

200

The more miles Moss Hollabaugh and these cavalrymen covered, the more it seemed like old times. Other than this, Moss knew Lieutenant Cassidy and his men were getting saddle weary. Back at the last stage station, McGinnis Ranch, there had been another change of horses.

It was darker now, as the moon had scudded below the western skyline. Except for the one stagecoach heading for Deadwood, they had the road to themselves. And at the pace they were keeping up, Moss knew that vague black strip further out on the plains, just east of the Black Hills, were trees lining Cottonwood Creek. Out here, too, there was less chance of them running into nightriders.

"How much further to Cuny's hog ranch?"

"The next place beyond Cottonwood."

"What you got in mind, lo'tenant?"

"That Texan could be shacked out at Cuny's."

"Yeah, with that woman of his, Pawnee Liz. Past midnight now."

"Little Reddy and the scum he rides with like to yowl all night."

Straightening some in the saddle to get the kinks out of his back, Moss said, "It'll be more'n Little Reddy's bunch staying there. Those coming over from Cheyenne with Cado Greer. They might have left."

In a grimmer tone of voice the lieutenant said, "Could be, but whoever's still there had better speak up about where they've gone."

From here on they lapsed into silence upon passing the Cottonwood Creek stage station cloaked in darkness. Some time later the order came to rest their horses, and to head out again at a ground-eating canter. Anxiously they keened their ears ahead half-expecting to hear the reports of gunfire. But over the thudding of hooves all they heard were the mournful baying of coyotes.

When Moss signalled they were nearly at Six Mile stage

201

station, the cavalcade slowed to permit Lieutenant Cassidy time to issue a few orders. "Cuny's place is further away from the main road; got a windmill out back of it. And it still might be open. Sergeant Piersal, take half of the men and head further along the road past the station buildings. Then cut in behind Cuny's. Me and Hollabaugh and the rest will ease in the front way."

"An', sir, if they make a break for it?"

"I'll make it plain, sergeant, I don't want any getting away. We'll hold here for five minutes."

Uncorking his canteen, Moss drank just enough to sate his thirst, and then he said, "Doubt if I'd take any prisoners either after what happened, lo'tenant. But I'd appreciate keepin' at least one or two alive. Cause if we kill all of them there'll be nothing to tie Mr. Payne into this."

"I hear you, Moss. Can do." The lieutenant removed a glove, and rubbed some specks of trail dust away from his eye. "Payne is about as heartless as they come. But do you really believe the dying confession of another outlaw?"

"Greer's I do. You hear that?"

"Sounds to me like a banjo. Means Cuny's is open. And it's time to go in." Twisting in the saddle, Lieutenant Cassidy looked back at the remaining soldiers. "Less than a quarter mile to the stage station. From there on we'll go single file and easy. Then spread out when we're coming onto Cuny's."

"Sir, some whores are staying there, at Cuny's. They could get caught in the line of fire."

"They could, which just might play against us."

Moss had taken the lead, out about fifty yards, and now at a walk he brought his horse off the main road and drew his six-gun. To his left lay the main stage station building, and scattered to either side were sheds and barns and a few horses stirring in the corrals. He held up by the last building, a shed with a crumbling roof, as under him the bronc

202

whickered a greeting to three horses tied out in front of Cuny's. He fixed his gaze on the light pouring out of the windows of the hog ranch as the lieutenant pulled alongside.

"Memory serves me right there's some corrals on the other side, sort of down in a hollow. If those outlaws night here that's where you'll find their hosses. Those three out front; could belong to cowhands in for a good time or more of Little Reddy's ilk."

"Seems peaceful enough except for that banjo wheezing away. The gent playing it sure needs some lessons."

"Any of your soldier boys quick on the draw?"

He smiled at Moss. "Meaning they'll be going in with us. Randall, Carradine, fall in with us. The rest of you spread out . . . maybe around those trees . . . and that rockpile there."

First one shooting star drew Moss's gaze to the southeasterly sky, then barely had this one vanished than another blazed a milkish trail on the same course. He spun the cylinder on his handgun, to holster it as a nudge from his spurs brought the bronc stepping ahead. They rode up to dismount in the deeper black pressing along the side wall of the saloon. Moss, turning to Cassidy, said softly, "The last time I came through here I made a deal with Little Reddy. Got this notion that if I go in first he won't be so prone to go for his gun."

Trailed by the others, Moss passed along the wall to turn the corner and saunter past the horses tied out front. Through a front window he could glimpse people milling about, and then he was ambling inside like a cowhand seeking a drink and some companionship. Smoke hung in a dirty pallor under the low ceiling in the barroom, brushing against Moss's Stetson as he stepped to the bar. About the only change in Cuny's, he noticed, was the decided absence of Little Reddy from Texas. A bartender came over to make a halfhearted swipe at beer spillage on the worn planking, and to say he remembered Moss from working for the stageline.

"Still do," he responded, over the uneven plunking of the banjo and of those in here satisfying themselves that the newcomer wasn't a starpacker. "Expected an acquaintance of mine to be here. That Texan—"

"He ain't here but I am!"

The next thing Moss felt was something hard jabbing into his back, causing him to grimace. Then came a dry crackling, an all too familiar sound of someone drawing back the hammer of a gun. Before him the barkeep had sidled away, to leave Moss the only one standing at the bar. Slowly he lifted his hands and began easing around, thinking the man holding that gun on him was one of Little Reddy's men.

"Been a long time, damn you, Hollabaugh," snarled Spade DeLong, the once-upon-a-time Big Horner. "I was here before . . . when you was talkin' to Little Reddy. But this time it's different. Hold it there; that's right. Now elevate them hands a heap higher."

"Yup, it has been a spell," Moss said calmly, his voice hard and reaching out to everyone there. "This scum and some others were after one lonely Oglala."

"He's an Injun lover!" exulted DeLong. He stood with his legs spread apart in a pose of defiance, his eyes glowing red embers told Moss he was carrying a load of rotgut and beer. DeLong hadn't worked up the nerve as yet to reach out and get rid of Moss's holstered gun. Nervous saliva trickled out of the corner of his mouth, twisting into hate. "First, damn you, I'm gonna bust one of your kneecaps . . . then . . ."

"Tell everyone here I'm wanted by the army?"

"Yeah, damn right you is, Hollabaugh. This time I aim to collect for all the misery you caused me."

Nodding toward the open front door, Moss said, "Guess this is your lucky night, hombre, as here come some soldier boys."

Crabbing sideways, but keeping one eye on Moss, he glared at an officer and a couple of enlisted men pushing inside. Then it was Moss lashing out to knock the six-gun away. He grabbed DeLong with both hands and spun the man in to the bar so hard that DeLong went to his knees, only to have Moss lift him up.

"There's two ways we can do this; the easy way, or if you don't tell me what I want to hear, it'll be me rearranging your face. Where's Little Reddy and his bunch?"

"Officer," yelped DeLong, "ain't you gonna do something?"

"Sure," said Lieutenant Cassidy, who promptly unleathered his sidearm. "Everyone, go about your business. Or if any of you feel lucky, go for it."

"What is this?"

"This," said Moss to Spade DeLong, "is you telling me what we want to know. Where's Little Reddy?"

"He . . . he left . . . sometime after dusking—"

"Left don't tell me diddly, dammit!"

"Headed south then . . . on the stageline road."

"You hear that, lo'tenant."

"Yo—which means some more hard riding."

"You, DeLong, I ever see you again it'll only be one of us walking away. I expect to be back. So I was you I'd seek a healthier place." Moss felt a terrible urge to use his fists, and also a sense of revulsion. Also, he feared that perhaps they wouldn't stop Little Reddy in time. Shoving DeLong away, he strode toward the door trailed by the others stepping backwards with weapons still drawn.

Claiming their horses, they hooked up with the others, knowing for certain there'd be a gun battle.

"Either way, lo'tenant, after this is over I'm heading for Cheyenne."

"Don't blame you none, Moss. They called Custer the Son of the Morning Star. This Payne's got to have been sired by the Devil!"

Sixteen

Once again Little Reddy from Texas had gone back on his word. His vow that he'd hold in camp until Cado Greer got back from Deadwood was broken when that message was sent over the telegraph line about Claiborne Payne's wife stagecoaching out of Cheyenne. But it had taken considerable argument to get his men out of Cuny's. For everyone, including the hardcases Greer had brought along from Cheyenne, was still worked up over what happened the other night; not so much over the killings but about coming out emptyhanded. And this time Little Reddy had ordered Pawnee Liz to remain behind.

Hunched in the saddle girthed around the belly of his dun-colored bronc, Little Reddy rode at the head of his pack of ambushers. They were just jogging along, some of them owly drunk and passing bottles around. Some seemed to be growing hostile, and Little Reddy knew this was because his leadership was being questioned. The quick-tempered Texan ruled by fear, if anyone really got out of line it would be their draw against his.

Coming up to jog alongside, Dunc Blackburn muttered, "Lightening up."

"Coming onto dawn."

"What's so special about holding up this particular stagecoach?"

"That's right, Dunc, you wasn't told. Aboard that coach should be the wife of the man Greer works for."

"Payne's wife? So?"

The Texan flashed a rare smile. "Payne put a bounty on her head. A measly five hundred. But I figure alive she's worth a helluva lot more."

"You mean hold her for ransom?"

"You can include blackmail in that. Got me this letter of Payne's . . . details the whole damned thing."

Blackburn's puzzled scowl squinted his eyes. "You don't kill her, Payne'll probably get someone else to do it."

"Probably. But I've been considering Payne is son-in-law to the man owning the stageline, Hassrick over at Deadwood. Just supposin' Hassrick was to see a copy of Payne's letter?"

"I'm beginning to get your drift, Little Reddy. Payne will pay a helluva lot to get that letter back."

"And his father-in-law will fork over a lot of cash if he wants to see his daughter again."

"A deal like this don't come along too often. Up yonder, could be Eagle's Nest."

The place Little Reddy picked out to wait for the oncoming stagecoach was just west of the road where stubbly pine trees quilled a rise of land. Crumbly red rocks formed a ledge down from which they had a field of fire. As his men gathered around in the chilly breaking of a new day, the Texan said, "Listen up. That stagecoach is due most any time. All I want is a woman supposed to be on it. After that you can divvy up any money you take from the passengers."

"What if there's gunplay?"

"There won't be any once we take out the shotgun. I want the driver alive . . . so's he can carry a message back to Deadwood. Is there any argument about that?"

"I still say we should'a waited for Greer to get back."

Little Reddy looked at the hardcase. He shrugged and said matter-of-factly, "Nobody's keeping you here. But you decide to stay you shut the hell up and follow orders." His stare backed the hardcases's eyes away, and now Little Reddy gestured southwesterly at the road. "They'll hit that low spot, have to walk their horses up from there to about opposite where we are. I'll take out the shotgun. Okay, let's take care of our horses."

Payne was as edgy as he'd been in a long time. A man alone now that Cado Greer and the other hardcases had pulled out. Just like that the telegrams had stopped coming from Deadwood, and it wouldn't surprise him any if Ace Taylor had left the hills.

Cado's been gone, what, going on two weeks now? While that gold was shipped out two days ago. So by now he should have gotten word to me.

Claiborne Payne's worried thoughts pounded like a sledgehammer at an anvil. Some of it lingered from last night when he'd brought Mandy over to the stageline offices. Even then she'd clung to him, not wanting to leave him behind. The Concord finally pulled out none too soon, that embroidered scarf of Mandy's fluttering good-bye though he'd already set his footsteps in the direction of the House of Mirrors.

Even the amorous charms of Pearl Logan couldn't still the hammering of his worries; the albino pulling out, Cado Greer pulling a double cross, maybe that book-keeper over in Deadwood, that Orrin Risdale, going to the law or cutting a deal with his father-in-law. What about that letter he had sent along with Cado? A major error in judgment. Little Reddy might not throw the letter away but use it later in an attempt to get more'n the five hundred dollars. The Texan was expendable, but for now he was needed. As was Cado Greer as long as gold was being shipped out of the Black Hills.

Despite their long association he always felt uncomfortable in the presence of Cado Greer. He envied Greer his blustery ways, the way the man could handle a gun and men. Payne felt overshadowed, inadequate somehow. Which was the chief reason he'd never fully trusted Greer or anyone else for that matter. Even now he had detached himself from Mandy, consigned her to the grave. There she was, stagecoaching toward Deadwood, while he lingered back here.

"Damn!"

"What's wrong, honey?" inquired the scantily clad woman stretched out with him in the feather bed.

That "damn" pushing back the darkness in Pearl Logan's bedroom was one of the last words spoken to her by Payne as he threw the coverlet aside and rose. The other words were "see you later" as Claiborne Payne got dressed to leave the House of Mirrors and stride down the dark street toward his hotel some blocks away. Lingering here in Cheyenne, he'd decided, was all wrong. He must head over there and check things out.

"Cado, and that Texan, could be pulling some kind of scam."

Low-hanging clouds had moved in to blot out the stars and fetch in a chill from the northwest. Except for one man up on the ledge and the two across the stagecoach road, the outlaws were hunkered around a campfire. Their horses were tethered closer to the base of the hillock thrusting up between them and the road. The collecting mist was worrisome to all of them.

Like the others, Little Reddy had donned his coat. He sat hunched over on a flat rock, further away from the fire, his down-turned eyes taking in the patches of fog deepening in the trees and low places, the clouds holding back dawn's light. Waiting was part of it. And though possessed of a violent temper, the Texan had learned to bide his time. For those losing their patience never lasted too long out here. Another precaution he always took was to have stowed in his saddlebags some coffee and a hunk of beef jerky, and a pot to make coffee in. Some of his men hadn't even packed along tin cups. Those who had wouldn't let anyone else use their cup much less anything else they owned. What he had, mused Little Reddy, was a pack of vultures, and if the opportunity ever presented itself, they'd sure as hell turn on him. Keeping their allegiance meant he had to do most of their thinking, present them with targets of opportunity, such as this stagecoach.

Hate these cold mornings, came Little Reddy's silent lament.

Across the road in a thick stand of scrub trees the voice of outlaw William Bevans was another bitter lament. "I tell you, Kid, Greer pulled out for good."

James "The Kid" Wall had doffed his hat. Now he was reshaping the brim, white showing above the crease in his forehead, and the thinning hairline, although Kid Wall was the youngest of the outlaw bunch. He had a long face, a small mouth, odd-shaped ears tucked in tight to his skull. And being somewhat youthful, a devil-may-care kind of attitude which had oftentimes got him into trouble.

"Nope, I figure he didn't," said Kid Wall. "This woman Little Reddy told you about, maybe she's a looker."

"All I know is the man killing her gets half a thousand dollars; peanuts when you think what we can get from one gold shipment. Damn, Kid, finding all them rocks—"

"Me, I hate this waiting." Kid Wall turned to look at what he could make out of the road ribboning away into shifting layers of mist and the formless clouds above. A tree or rock formation would appear, then be distorted away, and now he exclaimed questioningly, "Thought I saw something movin' this way?"

"Could be it?" Bevans came up to stand alongside the other outlaw, working the lever on his Henry. Then he snaked the rifle to firing position as a covey of sharp-tailed grouse broke from cover, their beating wings making a whirring noise as they barely cleared the trees, Bevans' horse whickered as it reared up. Now other sounds broke the misty silence, the echoing voice of the driver urging his horses over a shielded rise in the road, the rattling of link chains and creaking of wheels, and Bevans whistling through pursed lips as he waved at the lone outlaw keeping watch up on the ledge across the road. Finally there was an answering wave, which brought Bevans and Kid Wall striding toward their horses.

Climbing into their saddles, they reined out from under the trees while keeping a wary eye on the stagecoach; it followed the downsloping road and dropped out of sight. With the arrival of Little Reddy and most of the others, William Bevans spurred forward. "Should be clearing that last rise any minute now."

Little Reddy said, "Split up and take cover on both sides of the road. I'll take out the shotgun . . . an' the driver in case he wants in on it." The Texan held in the middle of the road as his men scattered out to regain concealment. Then he brought the bandanna up to cover the lower portion of his face. The next moment the stagecoach was lifting out of the clearing mist, being pulled at a walk by the six-span team of horses, scarcely fifty yards away.

Spotting the lone horseman blocking his passage, the driver started to saw back on the reins. The man riding shotgun was bringing up his rifle when a slug from Little Reddy's pierced into his chest. As the driver threw up his

212

arms, other masked men swept in to surround the stage-coach; Little Reddy booted his rifle.

"We're not carrying any gold."

"I expect not," smiled Little Reddy. "Dunc, get those passengers outside." About to swing down out of the saddle, he heard one of his men cry out that horsemen were coming in from the north, then a gun barked. Wheeling his bronc around, he saw to his dismay cavalrymen answering the gunfire of his men milling their horses about in confusion. Behind the incoming riders sunlight suddenly came to poke through a rift in the parting clouds, blinding Little Reddy from Texas trying to use his six-gun. The man he fired at, someone clad in western garb, kept on coming hunched low over the saddle horn.

It was Moss Hollabaugh, with a trooper just behind and Lieutenant Cassidy opposite, slowing out of a gallop. Moss yelled as he triggered his handgun, "Give it up, Little Reddy!"

In the turmoil of what was happening, his men going down around him, and his own fear prickling at his temples, Little Reddy swung his frightened bronc around to try and get around behind the stagecoach. He could use the woman as a shield. Twisting in the saddle, his snaring eyes located Hollabaugh, and he fired wildly. It was the last time he used his six-gun as both Moss Hollabaugh and the lieutenant fired together, both scoring hits. Mortally wounded, the Texan still managed to hang in the saddle, finding he could no longer hold onto his weapon. Desperately he tried bringing his horse to the open stagecoach door and to the woman and other passengers cowering inside.

"Five hundred . . . to the man . . ."

Reining up sharply, Lieutenant Cassidy took careful aim with his service revolver. It bucked in his hand, and he grimaced through his anger when the slug fragmented into

Little Reddy's head. The sight of the Texan spilling out of the saddle persuaded those of his men still alive to try and break away. Only one of the outlaws got away; the others went down and the rest threw down their weapons.

Moss looked up at the driver. "What about him?"

"Plugged dead center, Hollabaugh. You sure saved our bacon."

Dismounting, Moss went over to tell the passengers the firefight was over, and he stood aside as they clambered out to take a look at the bodies strewn up and down the road. To Mandy Payne he said, "Ma'am, are you all right?"

"I am now. How awful."

He held out his canteen. "Here, a sip of water might help." Tying his reins to the door, Moss turned to walk over to the Texan's body. He swung Little Reddy over onto his back, and then Moss began a search of the man's pocket. It was an off-chance his finding that letter of Claiborne Payne's. The trouser pockets produced some small coins and a pocket knife, but in an inner coat pocket he found a worn black leather wallet. Folded in with about a hundred dollars in paper money was what proved to be the letter written by Payne. He was reading it when Lieutenant Cassidy came over.

"We've got five prisoners, Moss. We'll be taking them back to Fort Meade to stand trial."

"They deserve whatever they get."

"Look, Moss, I don't think the army is all that interested in having you stand trial. What you did here will go a long way toward having them drop any charges."

"Just the same, I'd sleep a lot better if things were cleared up. This letter, lo'tenant, is going to help send the man behind all of these robberies to jail." He handed the letter to Cassidy, adding, "Gonna have a few words with Payne's wife."

He came up to Mandy Payne milling about with the other passengers under a clearing sky. The mist was lifting rapidly, with vaporous white tufts of mist dancing back into low places, barely discernible under trees. The sun just clearing the Black Hills was drying out the dew-sparkling prairie grass. A dark blue cloak was draped over her shoulders, and her light brown hair was pinned up under the veiled hat, and she wore suede gloves. There was a look of vulnerability to her.

"Aren't you Hollabaugh? One of our shotguns?"

"I was, Mrs. Payne. Are you okay?"

"Now I am. My doctor back at Cheyenne . . . well, Mr. Hollabaugh, we're expecting our first child. Which is why Claiborne insisted I go to Deadwood."

"I see." Moss returned her uncertain smile. Now he realized he just couldn't come out and tell Mandy Payne about the letter. That could wait until later, until after her husband was arrested. "Mrs. Payne, when you get to Deadwood will you be so kind as to say hello to Julia for me. Now if you'll excuse me."

He strode back to Lieutenant Cassidy and reclaimed the letter. "Guess you won't be needing me here."

"Take care when you get to Cheyenne, Mr. Hollabaugh. Good army scouts are hard to find."

"Obliged for that." There was a quick handshake, and then Moss vaulted into the saddle.

Once the stagecoach and the activity around it were lost to view, he set his mind squarely on Claiborne Payne. He knew with a grim certainty there'd be gunplay. But this time there'd be no Cado Greer or any hardcases around, just the two of them. A litany of names came whispering to him out of the loneliness of the stagecoach road cutting southwesterly. Wilbur Robeson . . . Johnny Slaughter . . . others taken out by these road agents . . .

Bloody summer—been that and more, he observed.

The beginnings of the stageline road out of Cheyenne passed through open prairie. Through here the men manning the stagecoaches weren't as alert as they'd be further uptrail. Also departing from Cheyenne were horsemen and an assortment of vehicles and supply wagons.

Around the middle of the morning the stagecoach reached the stage station at Hutton Ranch, where Claiborne Payne got out with the other passengers. He moved to stand aloof from everyone, and even though this waystop was under his charge, he took no interest in how it was run. His concern as he touched flame to a cigar was for further along the trail to Deadwood.

"Little Reddy should have gotten to her by now. Only worry then is if he's still hanging onto that letter."

"What a marvelous day."

He turned irritated eyes to one of the passengers coming over, an Englishman from London, whose pompous voice went on, "A truly marvelous day, eh, Mr. Payne?"

"Yes, I suppose it is."

"But dear me, sir, I haven't seen any of your American Indians —"

"You probably won't," Payne said flatly as he moved toward the stagecoach.

Eagerly the Englishman kept pace, as he said, "Surely we shall encounter some road agents. We have those in England, you know."

"The only difference is that out here they shoot to kill."

"Oh, dear me."

Once the journey resumed, Claiborne Payne turned a cold shoulder to those wedged inside the coach. He sat by an open window, gazing out with disinterested eyes. His intentions were to hold to the stagecoach only until they reached the Six Mile stage station. If, when he got there, the deed was done, he must act the role of sorrowing husband, this for the benefit of those running the stage station.

But why hadn't he heard from Ace Taylor over at Deadwood?"

The strident voice of the man driving the stagecoach interrupted Claiborne Payne's private thoughts. "Could be trouble ahead. You sure you seen some riders?"

The man riding shotgun replied, "Saw something. Just past that bend in the road ahead where the ground drops away . . . but could be a coyote, too."

Across the aisle the Englishman's face paled, and he said weakly, "Heavens, I trust they won't cause any trouble."

"Better check your weapons," a burly miner rasped to everyone.

The sudden increase of speed of the stagecoach going from a slow lope to the faster pace of a gallop dislodged some of the passengers from their seats. Shoving the Englishman away, Claiborne Payne swept up his gun as bullets began plunking against the coach. Dust churned up by the front wheels formed a blinding curtain, though this didn't keep some of the passengers from firing back. Up front, the man riding shotgun kept peppering away at the muzzle flashes of men firing from a hillock a short distance away. Then the stagecoach was out of rifle range, the driver chortling, "Just two of them bastards. An' damned poor shots."

"Driver, we've got a wounded man!"

"Guess they could hit somethin' at that." He drew back on the reins, shouting, "Whoa, now. Whoa . . ."

The leaden slug that had penetrated into Claiborne Payne's midriff had at the time brought a look of disbelief onto his face. This wasn't supposed to be happening; only to his wife, Mandy. Now the pain was spreading and the blood and a darkening numbness. He brought up a hand stained with his blood to grasp a supporting arm.

"This isn't right. Not now . . . the gold . . . so much gold . . ."

"Easy, man."

". . . so much gold . . ." The words rattled out of Claiborne Payne's throat as he died.

Seventeen

There would be other stagecoach holdups and more people getting killed. But at least the bloody Little Reddy gang was finished. And so was Moss Hollabaugh, once he'd learned of Claiborne Payne being gunned down enroute to Deadwood. The letter Moss had sent to the owner of the Deadwood-Cheyenne Stageline told of his quitting, and it was in the form of a farewell note to Julia Hassrick.

Shortly after this, Moss had headed into southeastern Wyoming to take a southern route through the Black Hills and to wind up at Fort Meade. Lieutenant Cassidy broke the trail for Moss, meaning that he had told the post commander the role Moss had played in taking out that bunch of road agents.

"That about sums it up, Colonel Miller."

"Quite a story, Mr. Hollabaugh. You did save that Oglala. In a way Crazy Horse kept his braves from taking your scalp. Now there is a tactician. On numerous occasions he outflanked and outfought our cavalry. Then came the battle of the Rosebud."

"Now the great chief of the Teton Lakota is on the run. Guess he'll never see his Holy Road again."

"As for now, Mr. Hollabaugh, I'll forward this report on

219

you to army headquarters. Lieutenant Cassidy, consider your prisoner under house arrest."

In the weeks to come house arrest for Moss Hollabaugh meant his being confined to the vast grounds of Fort Meade, nestling along the eastern fringes of the Black Hills. About every night he shared reminisces with either Lieutenant Cassidy or other officers who were veterans of the Indian Wars. It would have been a simple matter, as some of his friends suggested, to simply ride out. But he remained there, a man firm in his desire to see this through.

As for Claiborne Payne's letter, it was still in Moss's possession. It would serve no honorable purpose, he realized, to expose its contents to Payne's wife. He reckoned Mandy Payne still loved and grieved for the man she'd married. Let it remain as it had been written in the newspapers, that Payne was just another victim of these road agents. And let's hope, too, if she gives birth to a son, he's brought up right, Moss prayed. Rummaging through his saddlebags, he soon found the letter, which moments later was just a mass of flame in the fireplace.

This could have been an omen, because the next morning he was summoned to the post commandant's office. In quiet prose Colonel Miller stated that all charges against the former army scout had been dropped.

"Sir, it was your recommendation that brought this about."

"Going back to when this happened, Moss, it was all brought about because of gold."

"You can add greed to that. But, anyway, it feels good not to have to be looking over my shoulder. Looked for Lieutenant Cassidy at his quarters, but he was off someplace."

"My orders of a sort sent Cassidy up to Deadwood."

"Deadwood. That place has been on my mind lately. Well, Colonel, if you ever get out to Oregon . . ." Their handshake was warm, lingering, and then Moss was out of the room and heading down a corridor.

Out on a walkway fringing along the parade grounds, he stopped for a moment to check out the sky now that he'd be riding out of here. Fluffy white clouds, a slight breeze, bespoke of a good day for riding. Through the open main gates he studied the road passing northerly and into the hills and on to Deadwood. He still had some pay coming, and he recalled Jason Hassrick's statement that he would open a bank account under Moss's name.

Rubbing a pondering hand along the side of his neck, Moss murmured, "Reckon that money can gather interest. And there's Julia . . . about as headstrong as they come. I expect someday she'll get over being a manhater and settle down with someone she can control. Nope, you'd best strike out for Oregon, or . . ." A rueful shake of his head brought Moss striding across the parade grounds toward the stable buildings.

Sometime later he brought his saddled horse over to his quarters to pack his gear; then he was tying in his saddlebags behind his saddle. Astride the bronc, he loped it to the beckoning gates, only to pull up abruptly. "There's Cassidy and Julia?"

She sighted in on Moss at the same time, and reined her gelding, as did a smiling Lieutenant Cassidy. She wore cowboy gear, and as she closed in, Moss could tell from the set look to Julia's face that more was going to be discussed here than a simple goodbye. Cantankerous, argumentative . . . these and other descriptive words came to Moss, folding his hands before him and slackening the reins.

"Out exercising your hoss, Miss Hassrick."

"Nope, Hollabaugh, I'm here to see the released prisoner."

Frowning, he looked beyond her at the lieutenant. "You

221

knew the army was going to drop those charges—"

"Knew last week, Moss. But it was the colonel's idea. Ordered me to drift over to Deadwood."

"Another boldfaced lie I reckon." Moss uttered this to Lieutenant Cassidy reining away. Now, alone with Julia Hassrick, he lapsed into silence as they took the measure of one another.

Julia said accusingly, "You were leaving? But for where, Mr. Hollabaugh?"

"Man's got to make a living. Got tired of riding shotgun for your stageline or any other. Guess I had my mind set on Oregon."

"Do you love me?"

"Uh?" For a second his mouth hung open. "Huh . . . I . . ."

"Well, Mr. Hollabaugh?"

"That's a two-way street."

"I'm willing to cross over to your side of it."

"What's that supposed to mean?"

"That I'm going where you're going, come hell or high water, Mr. Hollabaugh."

He grinned. "Still haven't told me you love me, Miss Hassrick."

"Do I have to?" She reined in closer, with just a misting of a tear in her eye.

"Nope, as I guess you don't at that." As he leaned in, they kissed. Then it was Moss breaking away. "You know, your pa will have a hard time running that stageline. That is, if we head for Oregon."

"We could lend him a hand. Nothing permanent you understand."

"Yup, as Deadwood is a lot closer. To a preacher, that is."

"Just won myself a double eagle. Bet Mandy you'd pop the question."

He took out after Julia spurring toward the main gates. "Woman, there are things we've got to square away."

"Such as?"

"It's a long ride from here to Deadwood. So for starters . . ."